LORD OF THE NILE

"Fans of Egyptian lore and facts will find O'Banyon's historical right up their alley. She sprinkles political intrigue and love throughout the pages of this enjoyable book."

HAWK'S PURSUIT

"O'Banyon's third book in her Hawk series is possibly the best yet, with a regular little spitfire heroine, great verbal sparring and some very emotional scenes."

THE MOON AND THE STARS

"Fast-paced and filled with adventure, this is a great read . . . O'Banyon has created some wonderful characters, an interesting plot and an entertaining book."

HEART OF TEXAS

"O'Banyon excels at bringing the grit and harsh beauty of the West and its brave pioneers to life . . . *Heart of Texas* gets at the heart of the West and its readers."

RIDE THE WIND

"Ms. O'Banyon's story is well written with well-developed characters."

TYKOTA'S WOMAN

"Constance O'Banyon delivers a gripping and emotionally charged tale of love, honor and betrayal."

TEXAS PROUD

"*Texas Proud* is another good read from Ms. O'Banyon."

A New Man

Glancing over at Wolf Runner, Cheyenne would not have known him for the same man she'd met in Santa Fe. Gone was the veneer of civilization he had adopted in town. He seemed as one with this harsh, rugged land. His dark hair flowed loosely about his shoulders. He walked with the grace of a predatory cat and Cheyenne could see by the tilt of his chin that it was his pride that gave him an edge of arrogance.

When they remounted their horses, a feeling of kinship swelled her heart. Something inside touched that part of her that was Indian—her spirit cried out to Wolf Runner's. But would his answer?

Other *Leisure* books by Constance O'Banyon:

WIND WARRIOR
ENCHANTRESS
COMANCHE MOON RISING
DESERT PRINCE
DAUGHTER OF EGYPT
SWORD OF ROME
LORD OF THE NILE
HAWK'S PURSUIT
HAWK'S PLEDGE
THE MOON AND THE STARS
HEART OF TEXAS
MOON RACER
THE AGREEMENT (SECRET FIRES)
RIDE THE WIND
SOMETHING BORROWED, SOMETHING BLUE
   (Anthology)
TYKOTA'S WOMAN
FIVE GOLD RINGS (Anthology)
SAN ANTONIO ROSE
TEXAS PROUD
CELEBRATIONS (Anthology)

CONSTANCE O'BANYON

Wolf Runner

LEISURE BOOKS NEW YORK CITY

A LEISURE BOOK®

August 2010

Published by

Dorchester Publishing Co., Inc.
200 Madison Avenue
New York, NY 10016

ISBN 10: 0-8439-6439-1
ISBN 13: 978-0-8439-6439-4
E-ISBN: 978-1-4285-0858-3

Visit us online at www.dorchesterpub.com.

This is for you my lovely daughter, Pamela Monck.
So often do we walk the same path.
Many times you have been the teacher and I the student
and I am the better for it.

Wolf Runner

Entreat me not to leave thee, or to return from following after thee: for whither thou goest, I will go; and where thou lodgest, I will lodge; thy people shall be my people, and thy God my God.

—*Ruth 1:16*

Chapter One

The sun hit the gathering clouds, turning them bloodred, as if nature was warning of the impending battle.

The two young Blackfoot warriors were alert, their weapons near at hand. They heard every sound, waiting, watching, their dark eyes piercing into the stillness, past the boulders where they had taken a stand. Though it was early morning, already it was sweltering, and as the day advanced, the heat would only become more oppressive.

Wolf Runner, the taller of the two, was hit by a sudden gust of wind that sent blistering heat against his skin and fanned his long black hair. He did not move, or blink, although granules of sand irritated his eyes. His attention was riveted on the path below.

Waiting.

As the hours passed and the wind stilled, sweat popped out on Wolf Runner's forehead and ran into his eyes, but his concentration was unwavering, his anger uncompromising. When he saw a wrong, he would not yield until he saw it righted. Today he would avenge the brutal rape of four innocent Blackfoot maidens, and the death of three of them. He would crush, without mercy, the renegade Cheyenne warriors who were guilty of the atrocities.

The tribal council had met as soon as word had

reached them that several Cheyenne warriors wearing war paint had entered Blackfoot land and had broken their laws. Wolf Runner and Firethorn had been sent forth to stop the marauders and to avenge the women they had killed.

Suddenly there was a sound of distant riders approaching. Wolf Runner turned to his companion. "There are five of them."

Firethorn nodded in agreement.

Although they both had rifles in their saddle holsters, they had decided to use bow and arrow, since the arrow was silent and might not alert their enemies that they were under attack until it was too late for them to retreat to safety.

Wolf Runner reached for his bow and armed it with a flint-tipped arrow. Pulling the bowstring taught, he became even more alert and took aim.

Waiting.

Firethorn crouched down beside Wolf Runner, his dark gaze skimming across the sky where a flock of crows had suddenly taken flight. "They draw near."

Wolf Runner nodded grimly.

"Can we be certain the riders are those we are seeking?" Firethorn asked, positioning his arrow.

"Who else would it be?" Wolf Runner watched the clouds pass over the sun, casting the day into shadow. "This is the way they will leave on the way back to their village." The clouds had moved away from the sun and Wolf Runner squinted in the glare. "I want the leader. High Woman, who they left for dead, told how brutally he had treated the others before he killed them. She told me the other four would have let the women go, but he insisted they die."

Crouching behind a wide boulder, Wolf Runner's

gaze slid over the craggy slope as he prepared to en-
gage the enemy in battle. There was nothing in his
heart but coldly controlled rage against the Cheyenne
war party. His eyes were clear, his hand was steady.

"They approach the narrow trail and will soon be
in sight," Firethorn stated with assurance. "Let us
hope their leader is among them so we can have our
revenge this day."

The heat in Wolf Runner's eyes intensified. In the
past few years the Cheyenne had often crossed into
Blackfoot territory because game thrived in abun-
dance throughout the Powder River Valley. Until now,
the Blackfoot had allowed the Cheyenne to hunt in
their territory, seeing no harm in them. After all, the
elders had agreed, there was enough game for all, and
their Cheyenne brothers were suffering.

But that had changed when the renegades wearing war paint violated their women.

Tightening his hand on the bow, Wolf Runner
waited. "I mark the leader for death," he said quietly.
"If he is among this raiding party, let it be my arrow
that pierces his heart."

Firethorn knew how the women's deaths had disturbed Wolf Runner. "It will be as you say."

"Although we do not know his name, we will know
who he is when we see him. He wears two yellow feathers in his hair and rides a black-and-white pinto."

The sound of thundering hooves grew louder and
Wolf Runner tensed. "They are almost below us. We
should allow them to reach the bend at the bottom
of the hill before we strike."

Firethorn nodded, pulling an arrow from his quiver.
"I will go for the last warrior and any others who try
to escape. You take the lead rider."

They did not have long to wait before four Cheyenne warriors rode into sight. Wolf Runner quickly glanced behind them to see if another approached. Then he carefully scanned each warrior, but none wore yellow feathers and rode a black-and-white pinto. "Where is he?"

"Probably rode away like a coward," Firethorn answered.

Wolf Runner could not claim victory if the leader was not among the warriors in his sight. "Why would he do that? He could not know we are waiting for him."

"He would expect it."

The first Cheyenne was just below—he searched the cliffs and cautiously waved the others forward.

"They are young," Firethorn observed. "Too young to have war paint on their faces."

"Pity they will not live to reach manhood," Wolf Runner commented in a cold rage. He rose up quietly and sent his arrow flying true, striking the enemy who rode in the lead of the war party. He swiftly fired a second arrow before the first warrior hit the ground. And Firethorn took out the one who rode in back of the others.

Wolf Runner bound down the hill with Firethorn at his side. "Let us not slay this one. I want to speak to him. He might have information about the one we seek."

By now the remaining Cheyenne warrior broke into action. He was armed with a rifle, and fired at Firethorn. Seeing where he was aiming, Wolf Runner leaped in front of his friend, and the bullet hit him instead.

At first there was no pain, just a burning sensation. But Wolf Runner did not let that slow him down.

He jumped off a boulder, flung himself at the rider, and knocked him off his horse, taking them both to the ground.

The Cheyenne's rifle flew out of his hand and he stretched out his arm, reaching for it, but he was not quick enough. Wolf Runner pulled an arrow from his quiver and placed the tip at the warrior's throat, trying to see the man's features past the black war paint that streaked his face. "Move and you are dead."

Firethorn saw the blood spreading down Wolf Runner's chest. "I will take care of this last one. You are wounded."

Fighting against a growing weakness and the dizziness that threatened to take him down, Wolf Runner snarled, "I want some answers from him." His gaze settled on the young warrior. "Why do you sneak onto our land like thieves and harm our women?"

"I have heard of you," the Cheyenne warrior said, staring into Wolf Runner's brown, green-flecked eyes. "You are the son of Wind Warrior and the white woman." A smile curled his lips as he glanced at the gaping wound that bled freely. "Even if I die, I have already drawn blood from the one we came to kill. It could be that I have already dealt you a mortal wound."

Firethorn bent down beside them, his arrow pointed at the Cheyenne's heart. "Why would you want to kill Wolf Runner? Answer me."

Fighting to remain conscious, Wolf Runner pricked the man's skin with the tip of his arrow, watching blood seep down the Cheyenne's throat. "I am going to give you a choice." He licked his dry lips and shook his head, trying to clear it. "You can live or you can die slowly and in pain. It is for you to decide."

The warrior took a deep breath. "What are your terms?"

"I would know the name of the warrior who led your raiding party on our women. Tell me and live, so you can take a message to him that I will be coming after him, and there is nowhere he can hide that I cannot find him."

The Cheyenne saw truth in the eyes of the Blackfoot warrior. "I see no shame in not wanting to die, so I will tell you—his name is Night Fighter—he is nephew of our chief, Bold Eagle."

The world seemed to swirl around Wolf Runner and he fought back the blackness that threatened to engulf him. "Why does he want me dead? I do not even know him."

"But he knows of you. He knows you have lived in the white man's world. He knows you speak with equal authority to the Indian, the white man, and the wolf. He knows your family has great power, and he wants to walk as you walk."

Wolf Runner looked stunned. "Why?"

"Night Fighter believes if he kills you and eats your heart, he will become a great and powerful warrior, as you are, in the white and Indian world."

Firethorn looked at the Cheyenne in disgust. "This man talks nonsense. Kill him now."

"No," Wolf Runner said. "He believes what he is saying, and I gave my word he would live."

Wolf Runner felt pain like a fire in his chest and it took all his strength to hold the darkness at bay. "Get on your horse and go," he said, standing with effort. He would not allow his enemy to see his weakness. He swayed on his feet as the Cheyenne reached for his rifle. "No. Leave that."

He watched the warrior scamper to his feet and mount his horse. Then Wolf Runner closed his eyes. "He has gone and will not see me fall."

Wolf Runner slumped forward into darkness and would have hit the ground if Firethorn had not caught him.

But for the somber drumbeat that filtered through the Blackfoot village all was quiet as everyone waited, watched, hoped that Wolf Runner would survive his deep wound.

Wolf Runner's father sat near the lodge opening, his head bent in sorrow, while the young warrior's mother held Wolf Runner's hand, speaking softly to him.

"Live, my son. Your life has only begun—there is still much left for you to do. Live for those of us who love you."

Chanting had begun outside the lodge and Rain Song spoke fiercely to her husband. "Make them stop the death chant. My son will live!"

"Rain Song, his wound is deep," Wind Warrior reminded her sadly.

"Our son is strong—he will not die!"

"Even the strongest can succumb to a wound such as the one Wolf Runner has."

Rain Song knew her husband sometimes saw into the future, although he would deny it if asked. She looked at him in agony. "Have you seen his death?"

Wind Warrior knelt beside her. "I have seen nothing like that. What I saw was the damage done by the bullet I removed."

She turned her head into his chest and felt his arms go around her. "Why did the council have to choose Wolf Runner to face the Cheyenne?"

His hands slid up and down her back comfortingly. "Because he is the best of the young warriors."

"I know, but—"

"Silence, my wife," he said gently. "Do not let his

spirit hear your lamenting words. If you are to stay at his side, sing to him. Let him hear a joyful song."

Rain Song gathered her strength and wiped the tears from her eyes. It took her two tries before she could get the words out. She sang loud, and put her heart into the words she had sung to her son when he was but a child.

After singing for over an hour, she finally saw Wolf Runner's eyelids flicker, but she kept singing as if her words could keep him from slipping away from her. Her song wound its way through the village and everyone paused in their grief to listen. Rain Song was singing for her son, and the beauty of her voice touched them all.

It was toward morning when Wolf Runner opened his eyes, licked his dry lips, and looked into the teary eyes of his mother. Somehow he managed to smile.

"I . . . heard you calling me back . . . my mother."

Rain Song gently touched his forehead—it was cooler. She met her husband's gaze and smiled.

"Our son will live," Wind Warrior said.

Her gaze searched his. "I have been thinking."

"I know you have."

"When our son is well enough, I want him to return to Washington to live with Uncle Matt and Aunt Cora." Her voice rose in a panic. "He needs to leave here."

Wind Warrior pulled his wife into his arms. "I think it is you who needs to feel Wolf Runner is safe. You must let him go so he can find his own path. He is a Blackfoot warrior. Without fear or hesitation he did what was asked of him."

"And he almost died."

"But he did not."

Rain Song glanced up at Wind Warrior, her eyes

sad. "My head tells me you are right, but my heart is not convinced."

Touching his cheek to hers, he said, "Rain Song, our son was not happy while he was in Washington."

She stiffened. "He told you this?"

"He did not have to. I saw it in his eyes when he returned."

She was quiet for a moment as she absorbed what he said. "When he is well, you must take him to the mountains, where he can heal in mind and spirit."

Wind Warrior looked at her tenderly. "And they say I am the wise one."

Chapter Two

Wolf Runner ran down the trail, leaving his family's private encampment in the heart of the mountains.

He and his father had spent the summer months together while Wolf Runner's wound healed. In early autumn, when Wind Warrior had satisfied himself that his son was strong enough to be on his own, he had returned to the Blackfoot village.

Spending a solitary winter in the mountains had restored Wolf Runner's health and cleared his mind of any doubts about his future. Unmindful of the heavy snowfall or the chilling winds, he had hunted, meditated, and freed himself of the veneer of civilization he had acquired during his year's sojourn in the white man's world.

Wolf Runner did not slow his pace as he leaped over a huge tree that had fallen down onto the pathway during a recent landslide, an occurrence that happened often on this particular trail. He was young, healthy, and reveling in his restored strength. When he reached the lower part of the mountain, the trail leveled out for a time and he was soon joined by four silver-white wolves that stayed close to his heels.

If anyone had been watching they might have thought the young warrior was being pursued by the pack, when in actuality they were matching his steps.

The alpha wolf, Satanta, was the grandson of Chinook, a wolf that had belonged to Wind Warrior's mother. Sadly Chinook had died ten winters past, but all the silver-white wolves in the pack had descended from that noble animal.

These wolves were Wolf Runner's constant companions and had remained with him throughout the winter season—now they were accompanying him back to the village.

Wolf Runner paused at the bottom of the mountain to look about him, awed, as he always was, by the splendor of the wilderness. The rustling of the wind through the pine trees seemed to have a music all its own. If it had been his choice to make he would not leave the mountains; but duty called and he must return to the Blackfoot village. He had promised himself that he would find and punish Night Fighter, and that was foremost in his mind.

There were signs of spring when he reached the base of the mountain; trees were budding, and fresh green grass had managed to push its way through the snow.

Pausing to catch his breath, he removed his pack and set it on the ground beside him. He reached for his water skin and poured water onto an indentation in a large round stone and watched as his wolves thirstily lapped it up. Only when they had drunk their fill did he tilt the water skin and take a deep drink, thinking that nothing was sweeter than water from a mountain stream.

Wolf Runner watched the antics of his wolves, laughing as they frolicked and played. He preferred their company to that of most humans. Hoisting his pack onto his shoulders he placed his hand on Satanta's shaggy head. The wolf pushed against his leg and stared right into his eyes.

"Let us go home," he said, starting off in a run, and the wolves loped along beside him.

Among the thick branches of a pine tree Wolf Runner spotted a puma crouching in the shadows, but at the sight of the wolf pack, the huge cat quickly disappeared up a cliff.

When he broke out of the wooded area, Wolf Runner came to an abrupt halt. Firethorn was seated near a campfire waiting for him while two horses grazed in the nearby meadow.

Firethorn bore a striking resemblance to his father, Chief Broken Lance. His eyes were keen and dark, and he was good-natured and found it easy to laugh. He was sometimes called the jokester of the tribe because of the pranks he liked to pull on his friends. Although Firethorn was a mere two years older than Wolf Runner, he was in actuality Wolf Runner's uncle. Wolf Runner's mother had been a white captive, adopted by Firethorn's mother and father as their own beloved daughter. Firethorn, like the rest of the tribe, looked upon his adopted older sister with great love and admiration. Rain Song had helped bring Firethorn into the world, when she and his mother had been caught in a valley with a deadly prairie fire raging around them. Since that time, she had loved and cared for Firethorn like a second mother.

Wolf Runner and Firethorn were the best of friends. Wolf Runner trusted no one to protect his back as he trusted Firethorn.

"Why are you here?" Wolf Runner asked, fearing something might be wrong at the village. "Is everything all right—is my family well?"

Firethorn doused the campfire with water and watched steam rise in the air before he answered.

"Your family was well when I left the village seven days ago. I have been camped here for five days waiting for you to come down from the mountain."

Wolf Runner tied his pack to the back of his horse and mounted. "There has to be a reason you are here." He smiled. "Otherwise you would not have left Spring Maiden, fearing some other brave would claim her for his woman."

Absently Firethorn eyed the four wolves that restlessly circled Wolf Runner's horse. "I have no fear she will turn to another," he boasted, grinning. "She thinks only of me." Firethorn turned his solemn gaze on his friend. "Your father wants you."

Wolf Runner studied his friend's face for a moment. "Do you know why?"

"I cannot reply to that. He did not tell me."

Just ahead lay the path that led deep into the heart of Blackfoot country. "Then let us ride," Wolf Runner said, nudging his horse in the flanks and turning in the direction of home.

It was late the next afternoon when Wolf Runner allowed his gaze to skim toward the Powder River, which snaked its way across the high plains for as far as the eye could see. Their home was sometimes beside the Milk River, but for now the encampment lay along the Powder River.

Wolf Runner caught sight of a pronghorn antelope bending its sleek neck to drink; although the river was more than a mile wide, the depth merely reached as high as a man's waist at its deepest point.

A short time later, they reached the village. A joyous uproar rippled through the children who had gathered around Wolf Runner's horse, laughing and shouting, "The wolves have returned!" The animals liked to roll and play with children, for they had been born in the village and knew little of the ways of wild wolves that roamed the land.

Wolf Runner dismounted, while Firethorn led his horse away. As he glanced about the village, Wolf Runner saw that nothing had changed; thirty-seven tipis were situated beside the river, which was full to its banks from the spring runoff of the nearby mountains.

Sensing someone behind him, he turned to see his younger brother, Little Hawk, studying him closely.

"At last you return, my brother," Little Hawk said, smiling in welcome. "Our mother has watched for you the last few days."

With a soft-spoken command from Wolf Runner, all four wolves fell back, sitting on their haunches. Placing his hand on his brother's shoulder he looked him over carefully. The boy was eleven summers and favored their father in appearance, while Wolf Runner favored their mother with lighter skin and green flecks in his brown eyes.

"I see you have grown, little brother. It will not be long before you will demand a tipi of your own."

"Had you stayed away longer, I would have taken yours," the young boy stated, smiling. "I am glad you are home."

Wolf Runner walked with his brother toward their father's tipi. "Let us not keep my mother waiting."

Those who welcomed Wolf Runner home quickly surrounded him. His grandfather, Broken Lance, who was chief of the tribe, looked his grandson over carefully, while his grandmother, Tall Woman, extended her hand to him. His mother's adopted parents were as near to his heart as any blood grandparents could be.

"Welcome home, Grandson," Broken Lance said with feeling. "You have been missed."

Wolf Runner clasped his grandfather's arms, all the while smiling at Tall Woman. "It is good to look upon your face once more, my grandmother. I am glad you are both in health."

His father came out of his tipi, and it was easy to see the pride in Wind Warrior's gaze as it settled on his eldest son. "Your homecoming has been anticipated by all, but none so dedicated as your mother."

"Father," Wolf Runner said, dipping his head to honor the man he respected above all others. But his eyes moved over the crowd, looking for the one person he wanted most to see. When he did not see her, he turned to his father with a questioning glance.

"Your mother and sister are gathering reeds along the creek bed. I am certain they will have heard of your return by now." He smiled and nodded toward the path that led to the woods. "They come."

Although she wore a buckskin gown and her blond hair was braided with beads, no one would take the woman who approached for a full-blood Blackfoot. It was she who had taught him that a man can walk two paths and be proud of who he is in both worlds.

His mother.

Wolf Runner had the urge to hurry to her, to take her in his arms and pour out all he had learned in the months he had been in the mountains. But he did what was expected of him. He folded his arms across his broad chest and waited for her to reach him. He smiled inwardly when she did what he could not— she ran to him.

Rain Song broke many of the Blackfoot tribal customs, and no one questioned her right to do so, for she was beloved of the tribe, even if they did not always understand her ways. She went into Wolf Runner's arms and lovingly gazed into his face.

"My son, my heart is gladdened at your return. I can see that you are fully recovered."

Before Wolf Runner could speak, his young sister tugged on his buckskin leggings, and his eyes widened when he saw how tall she had grown since last he had seen her. "Little princess," he said affectionately, lifting White Feather in his arms. "You are already a beauty like our mother, and you have her green eyes. Will I have to keep all the young warriors away from you when you are old enough for courting?"

"None will be as handsome as you—so I will not have them," she said loyally.

Her answer made Wolf Runner laugh. "Oh, I think you will when the right one comes along."

White Feather grinned and said in all seriousness, "No one except our father is as brave and strong as you."

Wind Warrior looked at his only daughter, his eyes soft with love for the precocious child. "You can visit with your brother later, White Feather. Tend to the reeds you have gathered and we will call you when we have finished speaking."

Wolf Runner set the child on her feet and followed his father and mother into their tipi, where he sank down on a buffalo robe, sensing they both had something they wanted to speak to him about.

His mother spoke first. "When you were young you traveled with me twice to the ranch I inherited from my mother and father. Mesa del Fuego now belongs to you, as my eldest son."

He said nothing but looked astonished.

"Someone," his mother continued, "wants to buy

the ranch. It is now for you to decide if you want to keep it, or sell it, and to do that, you must go to Santa Fe right away."

Wolf Runner looked to his father, hoping he would understand the pledge he had made to find the renegade Cheyenne. But help would not come from that direction—his father refused to meet his gaze.

In truth Wind Warrior knew what his son was feeling—Wolf Runner was a warrior of great commitment. But Wind Warrior also knew his wife needed to see her son safe. He had held her in his arms at night when she had awakened after having nightmares about their son's death. She must have peace.

"I do not wish to hurt you, my mother, but the ranch should go to my brother, who has always loved it. As for me, I am done with the white man's world. And even if I was not, I feel honor bound to complete the task set to me by the council. I will find and destroy the Cheyenne warrior who killed our women."

His father touched his shoulder. "Others have already taken up that duty. Although Night Fighter is elusive, they will soon find him. Your mother has signed the proper papers and Mesa del Fuego now legally belongs to you. That makes it your responsibility to decide what is to be done about the ranch."

Not liking the thought that others would take up his fight, Wolf Runner turned to his mother. "That would mean I would be gone for months. You have no connection to the ranch. Your parents died when you were but a baby and you have no memory of them. Until you came to our village you lived at Fort Benton with Aunt Cora and Uncle Matt. Why does this place suddenly mean so much to you?"

Rain Song blinked to keep from crying. She could not tell him that his near death haunted her and she wanted to send him away until Night Fighter was found. She could not keep all danger from him, but she could, and would, keep this one away. "What is important to me is that you go to the ranch."

Wolf Runner dreaded the thought of making the trip to Santa Fe, in New Mexico Territory, but he could not deny his mother. "When do you want me to leave?"

"You will not be going alone," Wind Warrior told his son. "Cullen Worthington will be arriving in three days to accompany you."

Cullen was a friend of the family and visited them often. He had been a cavalry officer when his wife had been taken by the same Indian who had captured Rain Song. Sadly, Cullen's wife did not live to reach the Blackfoot village. When Cullen resigned his commission, Rain Song had offered him the job of foreman of Mesa del Fuego, and he had agreed to take it.

Wolf Runner looked at his mother questioningly. "I will go and I will see this thing done."

Rain Song placed her hand on her son's. "Thank you. Remember when you get there, if it is your wish to sell the ranch, do so without hesitation. Cullen will help you with all the details." She paused. "I have another matter I would ask you to look into while you are in Santa Fe. There is a woman called Ivy Gatlin who lives there. Although I do not remember her, Aunt Cora told me she was kind to me when my parents died."

"What am I to do?" Wolf Runner asked, astonished because he had never heard of the woman.

"Cullen says Ivy wanted me to know that she is very ill and worried about her granddaughter. That is all I know."

"You want me to visit her?"

Rain Song looked troubled. "More than that, I want you to see if she needs anything. If she does, take care of it for me."

Wolf Runner nodded. "I will."

Sighing, Rain Song absently patted her son's hand. "That will ease my mind."

Standing, Wolf Runner looked troubled. "I had thought I was done with the white man's world. But I go now to make ready for the journey." He glanced down at his wolf, Satanta, who had ambled in and dropped down beside him. "He will go with me. And I will take my own horse because he has no fear of Satanta."

Wind Warrior frowned. "Consider this—when you board the train, Satanta will have to ride in the cattle car in a cage."

Wolf Runner stared into the animal's eyes. "Satanta will endure it for a short time. I will take him out of the cage every chance I get and allow him to run free."

Rain Song laughed. "You cannot do that. The people in Santa Fe would panic."

"Nonetheless, he goes with me. I will not have him grieve as he did when I was in Washington City."

Wind Warrior watched his son turn to leave and he stood, accompanying him outside. "There is something that troubles me, my son, but I cannot quite grasp the meaning. So I will say these words to you as they came to me, and perhaps you will know what they mean later on."

Pausing in midstep, Wolf Runner looked at his father, waiting to hear what concerned him.

"I say this to you—" Wind Warrior frowned before he continued, and it seemed to his son that he was looking inward. "I see a hard decision for you, and I do not believe it has anything to do with the selling of the ranch. What seems right to you at the time may be wrong in the end. I feel you will suffer if you do not listen to what your heart tells you."

Puzzled, Wolf Runner nodded, wanting to set his father's mind at ease. "Your words are always wise. I shall remember them when I reach Santa Fe."

"Whatever it is will be important in your life." Wind Warrior looked into Wolf Runner's eyes. "I do not know why this message came to me, but heed it." Then he pressed his hand on Wolf Runner's shoulder. "Go now and make your preparations." He watched his son walk away with Satanta trailing behind him. There was a feeling of heaviness in his heart.

He did not know how or why, but Wolf Runner would find his destiny in Santa Fe.

Chapter Three

Wolf Runner walked beside the swollen river, thinking he would miss summer in Blackfoot land. Hearing footsteps behind him, he turned to stare piercingly at Blue Dawn.

"Would you have left without telling me good-bye?" she asked, hurt apparent in her tone.

Blue Dawn had come of age two years back, and Wolf Runner had watched with interest as other warriors showered her with attention. He had often wondered why she had not accepted one of them as her husband. She was pretty and sweet-tempered, most of the time—but she did like to have her own way and pouted when she did not get it. Her huge brown eyes sparkled with life. She was small, coming only to his shoulder, and he felt protective toward her. They had been friends since childhood, and he wanted to see her happily settled with a man who would care for her.

"I would not have left without speaking to you first," he told her.

She raised her head so she could see his face. "You have just now returned, and now you will be gone again. How long will you be away this time?"

"This I cannot say. But I will not stay one day longer than it takes to complete my task." He frowned when she moved closer to him. "You should not be here alone with me."

"Little you care what I do." Blue Dawn stomped her foot. "Why is that, Wolf Runner?"

He laughed because her statement was so outrageous. "Sometimes I do not know how to answer you. Tell me, when I come home, will I find you have finally chosen one of the many warriors who look upon you with favor?"

He was surprised when he saw tears well in her eyes.

"I want none of them!"

"You only say that because you do not want to leave your mother's tipi. One day you will change your mind," he cajoled, answering her as he would his little sister.

Anger took hold of her. "You always do this to me. Do not think you know how I feel."

He arched his brow at her. "I would never presume to know your mind, nor any woman's."

"You are blind," she said, looking steadily into his eyes.

Wolf Runner's eyes widened in comprehension, and he instinctively stepped away from her. He was on dangerous ground here.

"Can you not see what is before your face?" Blue Dawn asked, punching him on the shoulder in frustration. "You have never looked at me as a woman."

Uneasiness tugged at his mind. "I do not understand."

"It is you I want to be with."

Wolf Runner's brow rose. He was shocked.

Do I want her in the way a man wants his life mate? Blue Dawn is right, I have never thought of her in that way.

There was certainly no other maiden he felt close to. "I did not know you felt that way about me," he admitted.

"No. You have never noticed me, when I yearn for only a word or a nod from you. Everyone in the village knows how I feel, but not you." Blue Dawn lowered her head and angrily brushed away tears. "I am ashamed that I have confessed this to you and still you do not respond."

Wolf Runner was becoming more uncomfortable by the moment. Trying to sooth her hurt feelings, he spoke gently. "Do not cry. Someone might see you," he cautioned.

"You do not even care how many tears I have cried for you," Blue Dawn said, grasping his upper arm. "It is your fault. You let me believe you cared for me."

"I did—I do." His confusion deepened. Would it be so bad if he took her for his woman? He liked her and had always been comfortable in her company. "You have given me much to ponder. When I return, we shall speak of a life together." He tilted her chin and looked her in the eyes. "Will that please you?"

She smiled at him flirtatiously, her eyes bright with triumph. "It is I who will please you—I will give you many sons."

Sons? He had not even grown accustomed to the idea of Blue Dawn as his woman and she was already talking about children.

"While you are gone, I shall make preparations and that will make the time pass quicker." She looked troubled when she caught his gaze. "Promise me only I will be your wife and that you will not touch another woman. Give me your pledge now." Her fingers tightened on his hand. "I could not bear to share you with another woman."

He laughed at her plea. "That is a promise easy to make and easy to keep. Like my father, I will only have one wife."

"It is a vow of honor?" she pressed him urgently.

"It is. When I return, I shall speak to your father." Wolf Runner wondered if he should say something more to her. He had not intended to ask her to be his woman, it had just happened. Should not his heart be bursting with happiness? He remembered Firethorn's great joy when he spoke of Spring Maiden.

Should he not feel the same joy?

When Blue Dawn pressed her cheek to his and he felt her smooth skin, he considered it might be pleasant to have his own woman.

Then he was assailed by doubts. After they were joined, would she object to him spending time in the mountains? She had never liked the high country, or understood why he spent so much time there.

He was conflicted.

It would be a good thing to walk through life with a friend who was also a lover. Why had he not thought to ask Blue Dawn to be his woman before now?

"Must you go away?" she pouted.

"I must."

Her lower lip quivered. "Why does your white mother want you to leave?"

Wolf Runner frowned. "No one in our tribe has ever called my mother white," he said in anger. "Do not do it again."

She must have seen her mistake because she was immediately contrite. "It was a mistake—of course your mother is no longer white."

Thinking he might have been too hasty in asking Blue Dawn to be his woman, he put her away from him. "I will not see you in the morning. I leave before dawn."

He turned and walked toward his own tipi knowing she was staring after him.

That night as he lay upon his robe, Wolf Runner wondered how he had become tied to Blue Dawn. It had never been his intention, or even crossed his mind. Satanta flopped down by his side, and the other three wolves joined him.

Why did he feel such emptiness inside?

His hand reached out to rest on Satanta's head. "You are loyal to your mate. She never questions if you look at another wolf."

Satanta raised his head and looked into Wolf Runner's eyes as if he understood his words.

It was a long time before he fell asleep.

Chapter Four

The train steamed and hissed, chugging up the last steep incline that took the passengers within sight of Santa Fe.

Wolf Runner stared at the sheer drop-off on either side of the train and smiled in amusement at the two women across from him who were clutching each other's hands and turning their gazes away from the deep gully below. With the exception of his mother and Aunt Cora, he believed all white women were weak and too easily frightened.

His thoughts went back to the last time he had been in Santa Fe. He had forgotten how excited he had been to ride with the ranch hands and learn from them the working of a cattle ranch. He remembered sitting around a campfire and listening to their tales of wild New Mexico, while one of the hands had strummed a guitar and sung plaintive songs.

Funny, he thought, how he had pushed those pleasant memories out of his mind.

He wondered why that was.

The train let off more steam and slowed. There had been no train to take his family to Santa Fe the last time they had visited the ranch—they had made the journey by boat, stage, and horseback.

In the distance the Sangre de Cristo Mountains rose ghostlike through the fog, dominating the land, the peaks shrouded by clouds. He closed his eyes, trying to imagine his grandparents, who had lost their lives in those mountains in a landslide.

As if he read Wolf Runner's mind, Cullen nodded out the window. "It's a pity your never knew your grandparents. For that matter, your mother doesn't remember them either."

"Yes. It is a pity."

Over the years Cullen had been a frequent visitor to the Blackfoot village. Discounting Uncle Matt, Cullen was the one white man Wolf Runner's father respected and called friend. Under Cullen's sharp eyes, their ranch had flourished.

Watching Cullen run a hand through his blond hair, Wolf Runner noticed for the first time Cullen was turning gray around the temples. He might be a rancher now, but Cullen still carried himself with the bearing and demeanor of an army officer.

In all the years Wolf Runner had known him, there had been a haunted look in his gray eyes. His mother had once explained that Cullen still grieved for his dead wife and probably always would. Wolf Runner wondered how a man could love a woman so much that he would dedicate his life to her memory.

Shifting in his seat, Cullen rubbed the back of his stiff neck. "You will find the ranch much changed since your last visit." Cullen spoke fluent Blackfoot, but it had been decided they would speak only English while Wolf Runner was in New Mexico.

"Mostly I remember the house. It seemed big to me at the time."

"It'll still seem big to you." Cullen thought of the two-story adobe that had become his home since the family was not in residence. "I find myself rambling around in all that space."

Wolf Runner straightened in his seat. "Now that the time is here, I find I look forward to seeing the place again."

Cullen glanced at his companion speculatively. Rain Song had seen to it that Wolf Runner was well educated, and he could mix very well in white society when he wished, but he was pure Blackfoot at heart. The white man's trappings he now wore were a thin veneer of civilization that barely masked the untamed warrior beneath.

Honor had been bred deep in the young warrior's heart, and he had benefited from the teachings of both his parents. In the past, he had had to walk a thin line between Washington political society and the Blackfoot roots he preferred.

Cullen had observed that Wolf Runner seemed as caged in as the wild wolf that now rode in the boxcar near the back of the train.

Wolf Runner, trying to blend in with the people he encountered, wore his buckskin trousers and a white dress shirt, with a fine broadcloth coat. His long black hair was tied back with a leather thong, and his skin was light enough that he could easily pass for Spanish. Women tossed admiring glances Wolf Runner's way, and Cullen wondered how they would react if they knew he was a Blackfoot.

Letting out a deep breath, Wolf Runner stood. "Since we are coming into the station, I need to see about Satanta. So far he has endured the cage better than I thought he would."

Yes, Cullen thought, *about as easy as you endure being pressed into this mission, my friend.*

When Wolf Runner returned Cullen was looking pensive. "How was the wolf?"

"Asleep, if you can believe that. When I approached him, he opened his eyes, regarded me for a moment and went back to sleep. I do not think he was too happy with me." Wolf Runner dropped down on his seat. "The conductor said Satanta snarls and bares his teeth if anyone else goes near his cage. No surprise there."

"Satanta sleeps because he trusts you, and his instincts tell him you would never put him in a harmful situation."

Smiling, Wolf Runner said, "You have become quite the deep thinker, Cullen. How long have you had this insight into the mind of a wolf?"

"I have learned much from the Blackfoot." Cullen smiled. "Do you recall how long it's been since you were last at the ranch?"

"A few years."

"It's been ten years since you've been here. Of course the rest of the family has been here several times since then."

Wolf Runner looked thoughtful. "Has it been that long?"

"It's hard to believe, isn't it? You will remember the old wrangler Doff and how he took to calling you Wolf and how the other hands began to call you Wolf as well?"

Wolf Runner grinned. "I remember."

"Don't be surprised if they still refer to you by that name. It probably makes them a little more comfortable to think of you as a wolf than an Indian."

"It is of little matter to me what they call me." Wolf Runner shrugged, and a smile touched his lips as he remembered trying to rope a steer and how long it took him to master the craft—but he had in the end, thanks to old Doff. "Is Hattie still the cook and housekeeper?"

"Indeed, she is. If you were to ask anyone at the ranch, they would say she's the real boss." Cullen gave a mock shudder. "I would not want to be the one to cross her."

Wolf Runner was pensive. "I remember her chasing me out of the kitchen with a wooden spoon."

"Be warned, she might still do it."

Wolf Runner had fallen silent, and Cullen could tell he had something on his mind.

"What about Ivy Gatlin, Cullen?"

"I'm not sure. She came to see me last spring and asked me to send word to your mother for help."

"What kind of help? And why my mother?"

"I don't know. She gave me a letter to get to your mother and I did. Mrs. Gatlin would not confide in me, and no one in Santa Fe can keep a secret like she can. She doesn't run on with gossip like some women. She is a breed apart. And that's putting it mildly."

"You know my mother has asked me to look in on her."

"She told me."

Wolf Runner retied the leather thong about his hair. "Perhaps the situation will turn out to be of little matter."

Cullen glanced out the window and noticed they were nearing the station, and he let out a long breath. He had not asked Wolf Runner what he had decided to do about selling the ranch. Cullen knew he would abide by whatever Wolf Runner decided without comment. The ranch had become such a part of him, and he did not want to see Mesa del Fuego go to strangers, but that was not his choice to make. He did not want to hold on to the ranch for selfish reasons.

"Cullen, may I ask you a personal question?"

"Of course."

"I know you still love your dead wife, but surely you get lonely sometimes."

The foreman was silent as he tried to think how to answer. "I have loved but one woman. She is dead and lost to me these many years, yet the memory of her smile is as real and fresh to me as the first time I saw her. Yes, I am lonely, but I would be more lonely with the wrong woman."

Wolf Runner did not really understand how the memory of a woman could stay with a man after she was gone.

Shaking himself out of the melancholy mood that threatened to swamp him every time he thought of Susan, Cullen managed a faint grin. "I heard you are going to take Blue Dawn for your woman."

"How did you hear that? I only decided myself the night before we left."

"I suspect Blue Dawn told the whole village because I heard many of your people discussing it that self-same night."

Frowning, Wolf Runner stared out the window, focusing on the cornfield rows that had tasseled. He did not feel as strongly about Blue Dawn as Cullen had about Susan. His own mother and father were very devoted to each other, and he had always thought that was how it should be when a warrior chose his woman. No great passion burned in his heart for Blue Dawn, but once they had lain together, surely that would change.

Would it not?

He pushed his nagging doubts aside. Blue Dawn would be his bride and he would do everything in his power to make her happy. In irritation, he pushed her out of his mind and turned back to Cullen. "What can you tell me about the family who wants to buy Mesa del Fuego?"

"I have met Juan Rivera on occasion. He is from a wealthy family in Albuquerque. He told me he'd had his eye on your ranch for some time." Cullen frowned. "He has offered a fair price and even agreed to buy every head of cattle at market price. I guess you could say he wants Mesa del Fuego real bad."

For some reason Wolf Runner did not like the idea that strangers would be living in his mother's house. But there was no time to dwell on it because the train was pulling up to the customs house. With a loud puff of steam it came to a jerking halt.

Wolf Runner stood to his full height, which was two inches over six feet, and waited for several women to move down the aisle before stepping into the aisle himself. When he took the last step onto the wooden platform, he drew in a breath of balmy air. People of all walks of life were either boarding or departing the train. His gaze went to the mountains in the distance, knowing Mesa del Fuego lay at their base.

First he sought the conductor and made arrangements for Satanta and his horse to be delivered to the ranch. Bending down beside the cage, Wolf Runner reached inside and rubbed the wolf's ear while speaking quietly to him. "You will not have to endure the cage for much longer. But you see I do not think the people of Santa Fe would take well to a wolf running among them. Even one so well trained as you."

Satanta licked Wolf Runner's fingers, showing there would be no recriminations for having been kept in the cage. At least that was the way Wolf Runner saw it.

He stood and pressed money into the conductor's hand. "Take care of my animals," he said.

The tall, gray-haired railroad worker looked concerned. "He won't bite, will he?"

"Not without cause. Whoever delivers him to Mesa del Fuego needs to handle the cage with great care." Wolf Runner adopted the white man's custom of shaking hands. "Special care."

When Wolf Runner joined Cullen he heard someone call out, "Wolf. Over here."

It took a moment for Wolf Runner to recognize the grizzled-haired man waving at him and holding the reins of three horses.

Wolf Runner smiled. "Doff has not changed much. But his hair hadn't been as white back then, and there was more of it."

Cullen lowered his voice because the old man was ambling toward them, leading the horses. "As you see, he is still just as bowlegged. The man must have been born on a horse. But I'll say this—no one knows more about cattle than he does."

By now the old man had drawn close enough to grab Wolf Runner's hand and pumped it in a vigorous handshake. "Wolf, I do declare you was a boy when I last saw you—now you're a man full growed."

"How are you, Doff?"

"I'm right well—thank'e for askin'."

Suddenly the old man stepped back, realizing the young man he had addressed so casually was now his boss. "I'm sorry. It's just that I'm so happy to see you. How's your ma?" He looked confused for a moment. "And what should I call you?"

Wolf Runner met Cullen's gaze and they both chuckled. "Call me Wolf, like always. And my mother is in good health. She sends her regards to you and the others."

"Bless you, young sir. I knowed your ma when she was a babe. Been riding for the Mesa del Fuego brand for nigh on to fifty years."

Another prickle of unease touched Wolf Runner's mind. If he sold the ranch, the new owner would surely let Doff and Cullen go. As eager as he was to have the matter settled, there was more here to consider than just the selling of a ranch—people's lives were involved and they depended on the work for their living.

Wolf Runner had a lot of thinking to do.

Cheyenne Gatlin, named for her mother's people, walked beside her grandmother, holding Ivy Gatlin's arm to help her down the boardwalk steps. Lately her gram had not been steady on her feet and had even fallen—luckily there had been no broken bones. Gram tried to hide the fact that she was forced to stop every few steps to catch her breath, and Cheyenne pretended not to notice.

"Mrs. Glass gave you a good price for your apple jam, Gram. And she told me if we made more she could sell it. We still have a bushel basket of apples in the root cellar."

"We'll have to cook up some more, won't we? Why I—" Ivy Gatlin broke off what she was about to say as three riders approached. Her gaze centered on the tall one in the middle. "From the look of him, I think I know who that is," she said in amazement. "I hope it's him—he'd be about the right age."

Cheyenne gazed at the three riders that had caught her grandmother's attention. Two of them she knew, they worked for the Mesa del Fuego ranch. The other man she did not know, but her eyes widened as he drew even with her. His dark gaze brushed Cheyenne for the briefest moment before he looked away. Old Doff tipped his battered hat to them and Cullen nodded.

Cheyenne's heart was thudding in her chest—not because the stranger was handsome—though he was—but because he was . . . different. Even though he wore the trappings of a white man there was no mistaking he had Indian blood in him.

He's a half-breed like me!

"Do you suppose he works for Cullen Worthington?"

Grinning as the three men rode out of sight, Ivy shook her head. "If I'm right about who he is, it would be Cullen who works for him." Her eyes took on a faraway look. "I wonder if Marianna told him—"

"Who, Gram?"

Ivy shook her head. "Never mind, child. Don't bother your head about it."

Cheyenne was puzzled by her grandmother's interest in the well-dressed half-breed. "Do you know his name?"

"Nope."

"I wonder what he's doing in Santa Fe."

"Family business, I suspect."

"What kind of business would bring him here?"

"Who can say?"

Cheyenne knew her gram was deliberately being vague, and she would get no more answers from her on the matter. She was still thinking about the beautiful half-breed as they approached their small house. Who was he, and why had her gram showed so much interest in him?

There was supper to cook and coffee to grind for the morning breakfast, and a garden to tend.

Soon the handsome stranger was forgotten and Cheyenne's mind moved on to other matters.

But as night fell, and she climbed into her bed, the image of the handsome stranger stayed with her until she fell asleep.

Chapter Five

It was the hour just before sunrise and the sky was tented with a soft rosy glow as Cheyenne Gatlin stepped out the back door and hurried toward the well to draw water. The day would be a scorcher because it was already hot. Pushing a damp tress of hair behind her ears, she dropped a wooden bucket into the well, watching it descend and hit the water with a splash.

A frown curved her lips. Her gram's health seemed to be worsening with each passing day. Yesterday Gram had not even risen from her bed, and today when Cheyenne had pressed her to eat, she had only taken a few bites of buttered bread. Desperate with worry, Cheyenne knew something was dreadfully wrong.

Against her gram's wishes, Cheyenne had gone for Dr. Taylor yesterday afternoon. The doctor had not been encouraging when he informed her that Ivy was suffering from a malady of the heart and that she was not likely to get any better.

Ivy Gatlin had stubbornly admonished Dr. Taylor, telling him she was merely tired and that he wasn't to make up some illness to pin on her.

Gram had always been a bundle of energy, either tending her garden or working about the house: canning fruits and vegetables, or baking pies and cakes to sell to Glass General Mercantile. Until lately, her hands had never been idle.

Cheyenne could not remember her mother, who had died when she had been an infant. Gram had said her mother had been crushed by a runaway wagon. Cheyenne had only been two years old when her father, a deputy sheriff, had attempted to break up a barroom brawl and had been severely wounded and died that very night.

Gram never liked to talk about Cheyenne's parents. She had once said her son, Grant, had met Whispering Wind when he had transported a prisoner to Fort Leavenworth. Whispering Wind had been attending school near the fort, and they met and fell in love, marrying before Grant returned to Santa Fe.

Gram had sadly admitted that she had never accepted the marriage. Was it because her mother was an Indian? Cheyenne assumed that was the reason, but had never asked, and Gram never said.

Gram was the only family Cheyenne had left, and she was desperately afraid of losing her too.

There were no living relatives on the Gatlin side of her family except an elderly great-uncle who lived in Kansas, and Gram had nothing to do with him because she said he was a cantankerous old fool.

If Cheyenne had any relatives left with her mother's side of the family she had no knowledge of them. Once she had inquired at the library, and had been told by the librarian, Mrs. Burns, that the Cheyenne tribe had been scattered to the four winds since the battle of the Little Bighorn and there was no way to trace them.

Cheyenne faced reality; being raised in the white world, she was certain the Indians would not accept her as one of their own, any more than the white people of Santa Fe did. She did not seem to belong to either race. Although she tried not to care how she was treated, it did hurt.

If Gram died, she would be left with no one.

Cranking the lever suspended above the brick well, she watched the bucket rise to the top with jerky motions. At times like this she wished she had someone to talk to—someone to advise her, other than Gram. Her only friend was Maria Mendoza, the daughter of the local blacksmith.

She smiled, thinking of the Mendoza family, whose house was always in chaos. With so many children there was hardly room to move around in the small space, but there was a warmth there that enveloped her every time she visited.

With a heavy sigh, she grasped the bucket and poured water into a clay jug. Pausing a moment, she observed Gram's three-room adobe house. It was located at the very edge of town, the last house on a dusty street. Gram liked to say it was within a good stiff walk of Santa Fe's town square. It was not a fancy house, but the walls were thick, and it kept them warm in the winter and cool in the summer months. Gram's garden was doing well because Cheyenne now kept it hoed and watered since Gram had become so ill. There were rows of corn and melons, and the tomato bushes were loaded. Some of the red peppers had already ripened, and she had hung them to dry.

The front of the house was beautiful because Gram had planted so many different varieties of flowers that the yard was awash with every color in the rainbow. This was the only home Cheyenne had ever known, and she loved it. Her earliest memories were of her loving grandmother taking care of her. Now Gram was ill and Cheyenne did not know what the future held for either of them.

About to enter the house, Cheyenne paused in the doorway when she heard a man call out to her.

"Good morning, Miss Gatlin."

Cheyenne's first emotion was annoyance. Her visitor was Mr. Nigel Sullivan, the owner of the End of Trail Hotel. Something about him always made Cheyenne feel uneasy, although she could not have said what it was. Lately, it seemed everywhere she went she would run into him. Cheyenne would not venture to say he followed her, but he did seem to dog her steps.

Mr. Sullivan was always friendly and never disrespected her. Why then, she wondered, did she want to shudder when he looked at her?

Nevertheless, she had to be courteous. "It is going to be a hot day," she said as she placed her jug of water on the doorstep and moved to the low adobe wall that served as a fence.

He smiled at her. "That it is, Miss Gatlin."

Nigel was not a tall man, but his shoulders were wide and he was good-looking, with brown hair and a thin mustache.

"If you came to see Gram, she is not feeling well enough for a visitor today."

Nigel's gray gaze swept up Cheyenne's body, pausing at her breasts, and lingering there long enough to make Cheyenne uncomfortable. There was something in his eyes, an expression that disturbed her.

The last thing Nigel wanted to do was tangle with Cheyenne's grandmother. Ivy Gatlin kept a close watch on the young woman and was fiercely protective of her. Ivy certainly kept all other men away from Cheyenne, and that was just the way Nigel wanted it. She was his—or she would be very soon—he was determined on that. It had been a long time since any woman had stirred his blood the way Cheyenne Gatlin did.

"In all truth, I came to speak to you, Miss Gatlin."

She stepped back a few paces and braced her hand against the rough trunk of a piñon tree, feeling a prickle of unease that soon turned into alarm because he was staring at her in the strangest way. She chided herself for distrusting him. After all, he had a wife and three children, and was well respected in Santa Fe. "What do you want to speak to me about?"

Nigel dragged his gaze from the sight of her firm, young breasts, and concentrated on her face. He had been watching her for some time, and that lovely face appeared in his mind when he was making love to his wife or some whore he frequented. By now the sunlight washed across the land and painted Cheyenne's skin the color of wild honey—her eyes, which sometimes appeared to be brown, had turned to a pure amber color in the sunlight. Her full lips were shaped for a man's kiss, and he was certain no man had ever had that pleasure. She was an innocent, and that thought fired his blood even more. It was not just that she was beautiful, or that her soft, curved body made him crazed with lust—he wanted her all to himself— if he did not have her soon, he would never sate the ache that tormented him day and night.

Becoming uncomfortable because he was staring at her with the most peculiar expression, Cheyenne spoke, "Mr. Sullivan?"

Nigel came out of his trance and took a deep breath. "I wanted to let you know I'm aware that you and your grandmother are having a difficult time and I want to help in any way I can."

Pride ran deep in Cheyenne's veins and she raised

her chin, meeting his glittering gaze. "Thank you for your concern, sir, but Gram and I are just fine," she avowed. "We don't need anyone's help."

Before she could say more he held up his hand to silence her. "Let me finish. My regular woman who cleans the rooms at my hotel has quit, and I wondered if you would like to have her job."

Cheyenne was stunned by his offer. They needed money desperately, but she did not want to work for him. "I hardly know what to say. I would have to talk it over with Gram. I can already tell you her answer will be no," she declared.

He nodded, knowing the old lady would most certainly object to her granddaughter working for him. But if he had Cheyenne under his roof, she would be his to take. "I suppose you will have to get her permission. But be strong in your resolve to be independent—know what you want and go after it. Your grandmother has probably forgotten what it's like to be young and to have money to buy pretty trinkets." His eyes darkened. "I'd be very generous to you."

She did not comprehend his meaning. "If you will excuse me, it is time for Gram's tea."

He dipped his head. "Why don't you come by the hotel tomorrow and I'll show you around."

Again she said, "I'll ask Gram."

"Perhaps you shouldn't tell her. You know how guarded she is where you are concerned."

Cheyenne moved farther away from him, troubled by his boldness. "I never keep secrets from Gram." Knowing Mr. Sullivan was still watching her, Cheyenne turned away, refusing to look back at him.

When she reached the back door she lifted the water jug and entered the house, placing the wooden bar securely into place.

Cheyenne poured water into a kettle and placed it to boil on the back of the stove. The kitchen was a cheery sight with yellow curtains at the window and the green-and-white dishes displayed in a glass breakfront that Gram said had been in her family for generations.

Pouring water into a dishpan, Cheyenne placed the breakfast dishes to soak while she went back outside to gather eggs. Later she would milk the cow.

Once her outside chores were done, she made Gram's tea and placed it on a tray with a slice of buttered bread. Gram was seated in her favorite rocking chair by the window that faced the front of the house. Cheyenne smiled as she watched her grandmother reach into a basket, pull out a tangle of white yarn, and roll it into a ball.

Cheyenne placed the tray on a small table, handing the teacup to her grandmother. "Do you feel well enough to be out of bed?"

Ivy took the tea, grumbling to herself, and then said out loud, "If you are brittle you will break."

"I don't understand what you mean," Cheyenne said, looking puzzled.

Ivy fixed her faded gaze on her granddaughter and took a sip of tea before answering. "What I mean is hard times are coming and I won't always be here to hold you up. If you are strong, you will bend in the wind and life will not defeat you."

Cheyenne was hit with a renewed fear of loss. "Gram, you will always be with me." She had to change the subject or the tears behind her eyes would fall, and that would distress Gram. "Would you like to go back to bed and rest?"

"No," she said, placing her teacup back on the tray and picking up her yarn. "I feel just as well sitting here as I would in bed, child. I need to be doing something, and knitting takes my mind off my ills."

"Gram, please let me go for the doctor again today. You still look sick to me."

"Nonsense. That old fool hasn't got a lick of sense. Why should we throw away what little money we have on his opinion?" Ivy looked over the top of her bifocals. She refused to tell Cheyenne that the doctor had informed her in private that nothing could be done for her condition and her heart could give out at any time.

Ivy had no fear of death, but she did fear leaving her granddaughter without protection. Something had to be done as soon as possible.

Cheyenne lowered herself onto a stool and took her grandmother's frail hand in hers. Even though the day was hot, Gram's fingers were cold. "Drink more of your tea, and try to eat a little of the bread. I will make your favorite corn soup for dinner."

"The tea is all I want for now. I can't seem to get warm these days. But the tea always helps."

"Gram," Cheyenne began, "Mr. Sullivan stopped by this morning. He offered me a job at his hotel."

Just the mention of that man's name made Ivy's temper flare and her frail body shake with anger. Her eyes snapped with a fierce expression as she shook her head. Forcefully casting her yarn back in the basket, it took a moment for her to catch her breath so she could speak. "You will not go anywhere near that man! Any young woman who gets tangled up with him soon loses her virtue. I've seen him watching you—don't think I haven't. Keep your distance from him."

Cheyenne was shocked by Gram's anger as much as she was about Gram's assessment of Mr. Sullivan's character. "If I worked for him, I would stay out of his way."

"You couldn't. He would be everywhere you were." Ivy hung her head for a moment. When her son had married Cheyenne's mother, Ivy had not wanted anything to do with her because she was an Indian. But when Whispering Wind died, it took only a short time to love the motherless child. Cheyenne had given Ivy's life purpose and a reason to go on after her son, Grant, died.

The problem was that Cheyenne was too beautiful and her body too seductive, so that men often watched her with longing in their eyes and lust in their hearts that they would have tried to conceal had she not been half Indian. The women had noticed how their husbands reacted to Cheyenne, and that gave them more reason to treat her with disdain.

And that made Ivy's blood boil.

Cheyenne had her father's gift for laughter, and she had always been happy—until lately. Ivy knew Cheyenne was worried about her, but not nearly as worried as Ivy was about her granddaughter's future.

The people in Santa Fe had never bothered to look into Cheyenne's heart and see the goodness there. Cheyenne had never been invited to dances or socials like the other young women in town, and Ivy knew she was lonely. Ivy wanted to weep for Cheyenne's situation, but what good would that do?

Closing her eyes, Ivy remembered the day she had discovered Nigel Sullivan had bought the mortgage on her house from the bank. Even then she knew he had something in mind for Cheyenne. Today he had shown his hand, and she saw how he was further trying to wheedle his way into her granddaughter's life.

What could she do to make sure he didn't get his hands on Cheyenne? she wondered in desperation.

Ivy felt that Cheyenne was like a fly caught in a spiderweb, and Nigel was just waiting to pounce.

Time was against Ivy. She laid her hand on Cheyenne's dark head. "Promise me you will not have anything to do with that man. Promise me," she urged.

"But if we had money—"

Interrupting Cheyenne, Ivy frowned and shook her head. "I don't want his kind of money and neither do you. The truth is, he brings women who are no better than they should be into the hotel and puts them up right in front of his wife and children. He is not to be trusted."

Cheyenne's face whitened and she put a new interpretation on Mr. Sullivan's offer to hire her. Remembering the way he'd looked at her made her shiver with dread. "I promise," she agreed, knowing Gram was not the kind of woman who would spread gossip about anyone unless it was true. "I will not go near him."

With her mind in a quandary, Cheyenne stood. "I'll put the soup on now. You need to eat."

"Child, you do not have to pander to my every need. Get out in the sunshine. Visit Maria."

"Gram, you took care of me all the years I was a child." She pressed her cheek to the old woman. "Now it's time I took care of you."

When Cheyenne left the room, Ivy hung her head. There was trouble coming for that dear girl and she had to do something to forestall it.

But what?

Chapter Six

Later in the afternoon, after Cheyenne had finished her chores, she found her grandmother still sitting in her rocking chair, her head bent over her knitting, her gnarled fingers struggling to loop the yarn.

"I promised Maria I would help hem her gown today. You should see it, Gram! It is pink, with white lace on the bodice. She will be the best-dressed girl at the dance tomorrow night, and the prettiest."

Ivy felt a stabbing pain in her chest and gripped the arms of her chair, hoping Cheyenne did not notice. When she could speak, she asked, "Are you never disappointed, child, that you aren't invited to the young people's gatherings?"

Cheyenne lifted her shoulders in a shrug. "I don't know how to dance, so if I went I would just have to stand around watching everyone else have fun."

There was self-recrimination in Ivy's voice when she said, "I should have taught you how to dance. I should have done a lot of things."

"I learned long ago that people here will not accept me. Don't distress yourself over it. It matters but little to me."

Ivy reached out her hand and clasped Cheyenne's, knowing it did matter. Even now tears gathered in her granddaughter's eyes. "You are a lovely young woman filled with goodness. I pray for the day when some special man will come along and see you for who you are." Something had to be done to help Cheyenne while she was still able to do it. "Of late, I have come to understand that you came from two proud races. I wish I had made an effort to know your mother better—but that is a wrong I have to live with. She must have been wonderful for my son to love her as much as he did."

Cheyenne could see her grandmother was upset and decided to change the subject. "Gram, Maria told me the owner of Mesa del Fuego is a half-breed like me. Remember we saw him when he rode into town? People seem to accept him for who he is. According to Maria he went to school in Washington, and even dined at the White House with the president!"

Ivy managed to smile. "It seems your friend certainly has lots of information about the young man. I'm sure he is the talk of the town."

"Mr. Mendoza talks to everyone and he hears things that he passes on to Maria, and she tells me."

Ivy looked pensive. "The young man would be the son of Marianna Bryant. I don't think I ever told you she was captured by Indians when she was but a child, and married one of them. Cullen Worthington once told me she is happy with her life among the Blackfoot and even has an Indian name." Her gaze wondered out the window to the lilac bush in full bloom. "I wonder what her son could be doing here?"

"Maria said the older ranch hands call him Wolf. Did you not think him handsome?" Cheyenne did not know her eyes were sparkling with excitement, but her grandmother noticed. "At least he appeared handsome from a distance. Maria told me that he speaks English as if he had been born to it—at least that's what Mr. Mendoza told her."

Ivy was lost in thought for a moment; then her gaze settled on her granddaughter. "Of course I recall seeing him. Sometimes I forget things, but I didn't forget about him." Her hands trembled as she clutched them together. "It is a frightful thing to get old, child."

Feeling pain in her heart Cheyenne touched her grandmother's hands to help still them. "Gram, I will always be here to help you. Don't be afraid."

Ivy's quaking hand touched Cheyenne's cheek. "Sweet child, it is I who should have taken better care of you. But never fear, I will rectify that."

"Gram, I don't understand. You have been the best grandmother a girl could ask for."

Ivy shook her head and sighed. "What else does Señor Mendoza have to say about Marianna's son?"

"He says the young man came to Santa Fe on some business for the ranch—he didn't know what it was. He said Wolf would not be staying long because he wanted to return to Blackfoot country." Cheyenne sank back on the stool. "I wish I could meet him. He would know how it feels to have an Indian and a white parent."

"I would think he does—but he has some very powerful friends if he dined at the White House and probably never experienced prejudice as you have."

Ivy fell silent for a moment, deep in thought as a plan grew in her mind. Daring as it might be, it just might work. She wondered if Marianna had received her message. And if she had, would she act on it?

"Hadn't you better be leaving, child," she said, "if you want to help Maria with her gown? I have something I must do." She tapped her finger on the arm of the chair. "Ask Señor Mendoza if he'll come by the house tomorrow with his horse and wagon—I want either him or one of his sons to drive me somewhere. Make sure you tell him I will pay him for his trouble."

Cheyenne looked puzzled for a moment, wondering who her grandmother would be visiting.

"Hurry on, child," Ivy urged. "You haven't got all day."

Kissing Gram's cheek, Cheyenne rushed to the back door, then quickly returned, smiling. "I forgot my bonnet." She grabbed up the green-and-white-checked bonnet suspended from a hook and settled it on her head, tying the ribbons beneath her chin.

Ivy smiled. "You always forget your bonnet."

Turning at the door, Cheyenne glanced back and smiled, arching her eyebrow. "Are you concerned that my skin will be darkened by the sun?" she giggled. "Hmm?"

Ivy laughed at her granddaughter's antics and watched her leave. Silence soon settled around her. It seemed when Cheyenne left the house she took the sunshine with her. Gripping the arms of her chair, Ivy stood on shaky legs and braced her hand against the wall. Slowly making her way to the bedroom, she opened the trunk at the foot of her bed and withdrew a small chest that held all her savings. Two hundred dollars was a lot of money to her—but would it be enough for the young half-breed called Wolf?

Sitting on the Mendozas' brick floor with pins in her mouth, Cheyenne motioned for Maria to turn around. She held up her hand for Maria to stop and slipped a pin in the hem of the gown.

Removing the pins from her mouth, Cheyenne exclaimed, "It's perfect for you!" The pale pink of the dress accentuated Maria's long black hair and shining brown eyes. They had been friends since childhood—

they knew and kept each other's deepest secrets. "You are going to have such fun."

Maria shook her head. "I will not have as much fun as I would if you were going to be there."

"Yes, you will. Now take off that gown so I can hem it."

At that moment Señora Mendoza entered the room, her arms full of laundry. "Maria is right. You should go with her."

Señora Mendoza was everything Cheyenne imagined a mother should be. She ruled her family with her kind heart. Not that she couldn't be strict—she certainly could put the fear of God in her children when the situation called for it. Although the señora was no more than forty-six, her hair was mostly white. She was short and plump, but her voice was soft when she spoke to her children, and husband, and to Cheyenne.

"I don't know how to dance, and Maria would not have any fun for watching me standing around without a partner."

"I have told you over and over, I can teach you to dance," Maria said with feeling.

Cheyenne knew she would not be welcome at the dance, but she smiled. "As I told Gram when she asked me the same thing, I have no wish to attend the dance." She watched Señora Mendoza place the folded laundry into a trunk at the foot of Maria's bed. "What about Francisco? Will you dance with him?"

Maria's face brightened. "I will save all my dances for him. I believe he will soon ask me to be his wife—if he were not so shy, he would already have done so."

Watching her friend's glowing face, Cheyenne wondered what it would feel like to love a man the way her friend loved Francisco Manual.

"Only this morning Francisco asked your father if he could talk to him," Maria's mother said, pausing in the door. "What do you suppose that can be about?"

Cheyenne laughed and Maria blushed. "So he is finding his courage after all," Cheyenne said, glancing about the tiny bedroom. Three small beds were crammed in the room, and there was hardly space to walk. Since there were six children in the Mendoza family, Cheyenne often wondered where they all slept with only two bedrooms in the small house.

After she finished hemming the gown, Cheyenne gathered her sewing basket. "I must hurry along. I have bread to bake, and I think I'll make Gram an apple pie. I want to make something special for her to tempt her to eat."

Señora Mendoza reentered the room with another armload of laundry, and nodded sadly. "You need not bake a pie today. I will send several of my apple tarts for the two of you."

Cheyenne hugged the dear woman. "I'm worried about Gram."

"I know you are. We all are," Maria's mother said, hugging Cheyenne back. "Come with me to the kitchen while I wrap the tarts."

After leaving the Mendozas' house, Cheyenne hurried home. These days it worried her to leave Gram alone for very long.

She sighed, thinking of Maria dancing in the arms of the man she loved. Cheyenne had never had a man's attention, other than the lustful glances that were usually followed by crude comments.

What would it feel like to have a man's arms about her?

"Nonsense," she mumbled opening the gate and

hurrying up the rock pathway to the front door, the delicious scent of Señora Mendoza's apple tarts tempting her.

Still, to whirl and dance in a beautiful gown in the arms of a man looking at her with love in his eyes would be a dream come true.

Chapter Seven

With Satanta keeping in step with his horse, Wolf Runner rode over the uneven ground, watching the sun strike the mountains and turning them the color of glittering gold.

No matter how he tried, Wolf Runner felt no kinship with this land that was so far away from his own beloved mountains. Yet here in the shadow of the majestic Sangre de Cristos he had discovered honor among the white man in the cowhands who had loyally served the ranch for years. Across the meadow the wild sunflowers had turned their yellow petals toward the sun, and he tried to view the land as his mother's white parents must have seen it when they settled there.

He thought back to the time he had spent in Washington—except for the company of his aunt and uncle he had found the society there false. There had been little honor in the people who had been mere social climbers and tried to win his powerful uncle's notice.

Here, on the ranch, the cowhands worked with the sweat of their brow from sunup until sundown. Some of their dedication Wolf Runner attributed to Cullen's management. Wolf Runner smiled. Cullen ran the ranch as if ordering troops into battle.

Homesickness crept into his soul as he felt the cool breeze on his face. High grass covered the rolling hills where fat cattle grazed contentedly in the shadow of the mountain. In the distance he could see the ranch house with its red tile roof and earth-colored adobe walls. His white grandparents had built the home, but there was no warmth of family connected to it—not for Wolf Runner.

The opposite was true. When he was younger, he had felt that the ranch would destroy his family.

He had not liked the change that came over his mother whenever they visited the ranch. She always put aside her buckskin gown and moccasins and donned the trappings of a white woman as soon as they left the Blackfoot village. At those times, she had worn her beautiful golden hair in a bun, rather than in braids, and had answered to the name "Marianna" instead of her real name, Rain Song. She had made him don the white man's clothes as well and speak only English.

At the time he had feared his mother would not return to their home in Montana. He had been too young to understand then, as he did now, she could not have gone about the country dressed as an Indian.

As Satanta circled him, Wolf Runner laid his hand on the animal's head, thinking of the twenty-four ranch hands who depended on Mesa del Fuego for their living. Five of those hands had worked for his grandparents and were too old to get employment elsewhere. His brow furrowed—this ranch was the only home those men had.

A sudden gust of wind whipped down the gullies that cut deeply into the foothills, stirring the knee-high grass, and suddenly the land called to him. It was peaceful here when he was alone. And if he closed his eyes, the smells of rain on the high grass reminded him of Blackfoot land.

Staring into the distance, he felt an urgency to
leave this place and sell the ranch because he did
not want to feel attached to this land. But what if
his brother or his sister one day decided to live
here? Did he have the right to deprive them of that
decision?

Wolf Runner had a lot of thinking to do.

Hearing someone approaching from the north, he
waited for whoever it was to come into sight. When the
man cleared the hill Wolf Runner saw that it was Doff.

Drawing even with Wolf Runner, the old man
leaned forward in the saddle and grinned. "You got
a caller up to the big house, Mr. Wolf."

Doff wasn't usually one to stand on ceremony, but
Wolf Runner could see he was still having trouble
trying to decide what to call him now that he was
grown. "Who is it?"

"It's Mrs. Ivy Gatlin, in person. Says she needs to
see you pronto."

Feeling guilty because he had not yet called on the
woman his mother asked him to find out about, Wolf
Runner frowned. "Did she say what she wanted?"

"No, sir, Mr. Wolf—she didn't tell me nothin'."

"Doff, just call me Wolf. It makes me uncomfortable when a man of your experience refers to me
with such formality."

"Well, sir, that don't zactly seem right, you being
the boss and all."

"Doff, it is my wish." Wolf Runner glanced in the
direction of the house. "What do you know about this
Ivy Gatlin?"

"She was once a friend of your grandma and
grandpa. Her and her husband ran one of the first
newspapers in Santa Fe. She's mighty respected in
these parts, and she's a woman who always speaks

her mind. You won't never be in question of where you stand with her." The old man frowned, shifting in his saddle. "She seemed like she was real sick to me. 'Course, I'm not a doc, so I can't say for sure."

As the man rattled on, Wolf Runner mounted his horse. "Then let us not keep her waiting."

Ivy slumped back against the oversize chair, her hands trembling, her eyes damp. There were memories in this room—memories that had come rushing back to her the moment she had come through the door. It was as if time stood still and she was a younger woman, holding a baby in her arms. In those troubled days Ivy had been weighted down with sorrow—as a friend of the family she had come to the ranch the moment she learned the Bryants had been buried in a landslide. She had taken their infant daughter in her arms and cried for the child's loss.

She tried to shake off sad memories, but they clung to her like a second skin.

Ivy was reaching her own mortality and had provisions to make for her granddaughter's future.

Still, her mind took her back to the day her dear friends had died. Ivy had taken Marianna Bryant home with her and cared for her until the baby's aunt could come for her. In the months it had taken the aunt to receive word of the tragedy and arrive in Santa Fe, Ivy had become attached to the child—more than attached. The lovely little girl had wrapped herself around Ivy's heart. Ivy remembered rocking Marianna to sleep each night as the child cried for her mother. She had sung her songs and read her stories. After several weeks Marianna had stopped asking for her mother and father and settled easily into a life with Ivy.

Ivy saw little of the child after her aunt had arrived. For a time Marianna had remained on the ranch with her aunt Cora. After a year Cora had married an officer from a nearby fort. Her husband had eventually been assigned to Fort Benton in Missouri, and they moved away.

In a few years word had sifted down to Ivy that a Blackfoot raiding party had kidnapped Marianna, and Ivy had feared for the child—prayed for her nightly.

Again she tried to free her mind of ghosts of the past. She glanced at the bookshelves, then reached out to run her hand over the heavy pine furniture that smelled of lemon oil. This was a house for a family to live in, but they were all gone now. All except the son who had returned.

Yes, there were memories in this room.

Lately the whole world had turned sad.

Folding her hands in her lap, Ivy lowered her head because it took too much effort to hold it upright. She did not hear the man who silently entered the room until he spoke to her.

"I am told you wanted to see me, Mrs. Gatlin."

Slowly she raised her head and stared at Marianna's son. He was dressed in what any ranch hand would wear: rough-out chaps, boots, and a blue shirt, rolled up to the elbow. Ivy looked for any sign of Marianna in his face. He was a half-breed all right, and a handsome one at that. His hair was tied back with a rawhide strip, and his eyes—she could not discern their real color from the distance and of course her eyesight wasn't much good anymore.

But those eyes were studying her intently.

Nodding, she settled back in the soft chair. "I am Ivy Gatlin—I'm sorry I don't know your name. I should have asked the housekeeper when she showed me to this room."

He settled on a chair near hers, an amused smile curving his lips. "Here it seems to suit everyone to call me Wolf."

"That must be part of your Blackfoot name. What's your whole name?"

He quickly drew the conclusion that the elderly Mrs. Gatlin was astute, and sharp witted. And she certainly was not a woman to waste words on pleasantries. He shrugged. "Not everyone is as observant as you, Mrs. Gatlin. My name is Wolf Runner."

Ivy nodded. "You are lucky to be accepted for who you are since you are a breed."

She watched those eyes narrow and she knew she had made him angry.

"And you don't like to be called that," she said quietly, watching his reaction. "But you mistake me. I meant no disrespect. I was just making comparisons and reminding myself what wealth can buy." She waved a frail, blue-veined hand in his direction. "I'll get to that later."

Baffled, Wolf Runner waited for her to continue.

"I was a friend of your grandparents. I knew your mother as a baby. I was at your aunt's wedding when she married your uncle—I guess if I was to be accurate I'd have to say they are your great-aunt and great-uncle." She blinked and refocused her eyes. "How are they faring?"

"Very well. When Uncle Matt retired, they remained in Washington."

"They were a lovely couple."

"Yes. They still are. But that is not the reason you wanted to see me. What can I do for you, Mrs. Gatlin?"

Chapter Eight

Wolf Runner watched pale blue eyes sweep across his face as if Mrs. Gatlin was searching for something in his expression.

"I know your mother's been back to Santa Fe several times, but she always left before I could see her. Tell me—is she happy living among the Blackfoot?"

The more Ivy Gatlin talked, the more puzzled Wolf Runner became. "My mother is beloved by our people."

"But does she ever want to return to her life here at the ranch? Is she forced to remain in the Blackfoot village?"

Wolf Runner felt a prickle of anger. "My mother can do what she wants. She is free to live where she wishes, but she will not be parted from my father, and he would not want to live here."

"Cullen has told me that Marianna is happy. It seems he's a good friend to both your parents."

The woman looked ill, her face a pasty color—he did not miss the trembling of her hands. "May I get you something to drink, Mrs. Gatlin, water perhaps?"

"No—I want nothing. And I didn't come here to waste your time with unnecessary shenanigans, so I'll get right to the point." She ran her hand down her gray gown as if she were pressing out a wrinkle. "Are you here to live on the ranch or to sell it?"

He couldn't imagine why it would matter to her what he decided about the ranch. "I do not intend to live here, but I have not yet decided whether I will sell."

She nodded. "Good, then you will be retuning to your village."

"Yes."

She studied him for a moment. "What they say about you is true—you are well educated. You speak with very little accent. I'm sure the ladies find it charming."

"Excuse me, madam?"

"Nothing. I was merely making an observation. Some people find me nosy, but I worked with my husband for many years on his newspaper. I can't break the habit of sticking my nose into anything that might be newsworthy."

No matter how Ivy Gatlin explained her prodding, Wolf Runner was beginning to lose patience. "What can I do for you, Mrs. Gatlin?"

She took a shuddering breath. "I'm here begging a favor." She met his gaze. "A big one. I am banking on you helping me because I was a friend of your grandparents."

"Do you need money?"

"No. It's nothing like that. Will you help me?"

"First I would have to hear what you are asking of me."

"I'm in poor health, Wolf Runner." She leaned back and took a deep breath. "More than that, I'm dying."

Wolf Runner hardly knew what to say. He did not know her well enough to feel sadness. She was an old woman who had lived her life. If she thought to ask for a favor from him on the thin thread of once knowing his grandparents, she was mistaken. Of course he would hear her out for his mother's sake.

He waited for her to continue.

"As I mentioned, some years back my husband and I ran the newspaper here in town. I sold it after he died—it just wasn't fun anymore. Even though my son lived in Santa Fe, I never saw much of him. After his wife died, I agreed to look after their young daughter. She doesn't remember her mother, like I'm sure your mother doesn't remember her parents."

She paused, as if expecting him to make a comment. When he didn't, she continued: "My son's wife was from the Cheyenne tribe, you see. My granddaughter was named for her mother's people."

This woman had no way of knowing that his bitterest enemy was a Cheyenne. Did she think because he was an Indian and her granddaughter was Indian that they were alike? But his mother had been concerned for this woman, so he would hear her out.

In an attempt to sound interested in what she was telling him, he asked, "Your granddaughter's name is Cheyenne?"

"That's right." Ivy nodded.

Wolf Runner waited while she stopped to catch her breath.

"I never met Cheyenne's mother, although I saw her from a distance often enough." Ivy dropped her head. "I'm sorry now I didn't make the effort to know her." She met Wolf Runner's gaze, as if she expected him to comment on her prejudice. When he said nothing, she continued. "Since I am about to face eternity, I regret many things I did or didn't do. Too late, though—it's too late for a lot of things I wished I'd done."

He was still wondering if she was trying to make

the connection between him and her granddaughter because they both had Indian blood.

"If you could just meet Cheyenne," she continued, "talk to her, you would see that she is a lovely young woman."

His mouth eased into a grin. "Mrs. Gatlin, are you trying to make a match for me with your granddaughter?"

"No, no." She shook her head vigorously. "Nothing like that! I want—I beg you to take Cheyenne with you when you leave Santa Fe."

He could not have been more shocked if she'd just sprouted another head. "You . . . want me to take her with me?"

She raised her hands in a hopeless gesture. "Cheyenne has not had an easy life—very few people here in town accept her because she is half Indian—like you are. Surely you can understand what that feels like? But then no, you wouldn't be shunned as Cheyenne is—money being the great equalizer."

"Have you thought about sending her to her mother's people?" Wolf Runner suggested.

Ivy looked haggard and very ill. "I once received a letter from an Indian agent in Indian Territory. The letter stated Cheyenne's grandfather wanted to know how to find her." She raised a troubled gaze to him. "I never answered. And I didn't tell my granddaughter about it either. If you were to meet Cheyenne, you would know she does not belong on a reservation." Ivy reached out her hand beseechingly. "With your mother she would be cared for—I know this in my heart."

While Wolf Runner's mother had asked him to find out what was troubling Mrs. Gatlin, surely she

had not intended for him to bring the woman home
with him. "What you suggest is impossible. I cannot
take you and your granddaughter with me, Mrs.
Gatlin. Surely the young woman would not agree to
leave her home for a land where she would be a
stranger. And surely you are too ill to make such a
journey."

"I won't be going. And you're right; Cheyenne
would not agree to leave me. But I plead with you to
consider what I have said. Don't say no until you meet
her and talk to her."

Desperation was written on every plane of her
face.

"Cheyenne is in danger here. Ask Cullen and he'll
substantiate what I have told you." She looked at him
pleadingly. "When I'm gone, there will be no one to
protect her." Ivy's tear-bright eyes sought his. "There
is this man in town who would dishonor her." She
clasped her hands so tightly her knuckles whitened.
"Nigel Sullivan will stop at nothing to get his hands
on Cheyenne when I'm gone. I have no one to turn
to—no one to protect her but you."

Wolf Runner shook his head, suspecting the woman
was trying to enlist his aid in ridding her granddaughter of an unwelcome suitor. "This seems to be
a family matter. I cannot help you in this. But is there
something else I can do for you?"

Her lips tightened. "There is nothing else that can
help me."

"Let me see you to your wagon, then," Wolf Runner said in a way of dismissing her.

She waved him aside and attempted to stand and
then fell back against the chair. "I got here on my
own," she said coldly. "I will leave the same way."

At a loss, Wolf Runner offered her his arm, but Ivy

shook her head. After a moment she was able to stand on her own. "Don't say no just yet."

Ivy handed him a crumpled envelope and tottered toward the door. Stopping in the doorway, she glanced back at him. "Think about it. Take my granddaughter to your mother."

Wolf Runner listened to her hesitating steps, and when he heard the wagon pull away, he opened the envelope.

Two hundred dollars!

He shook his head and went in search of Cullen. He needed answers, and he needed Cullen to return Ivy Gatlin's money to her.

As it happened, Cullen was at the neighboring ranch, delivering a bull and Wolf Runner didn't get to talk to him until suppertime.

The two men sat at the table, Cullen drinking coffee, Wolf Runner trying to think how to explain his encounter with Ivy Gatlin. He glanced down at Satanta, who was curled up at his feet. Shoving the envelope of money across the table to Cullen, he watched his friend's brow crease in puzzlement.

"What is this?"

"I was hoping you could tell me."

"It's money. But what's it for?"

"I don't know. Mrs. Gatlin was here today and left this with me. She wanted me to take her granddaughter with me when I leave, and she gave me this money."

"Ah. Ivy. It's a sad story. She is not well and she's worried about Cheyenne, and with good reason."

"She seems to think I owed her because she was a friend of my grandparents."

"She was more than that," Cullen told him. "When

your grandparents were killed, Ivy took your mother in until your aunt could arrive from somewhere in Europe. I heard she kept your mother for about six months. She once told me she became so attached to your mother that she grieved when your aunt Cora took her away."

Wolf Runner was quiet for a moment, while he stared at Cullen. "Then I do owe her. My people do not believe a debt should ever go unpaid."

"Ivy is just not the kind of person who would ask a favor from someone she doesn't know—unless she was desperate."

"Tell me about her granddaughter."

"I don't actually know Cheyenne Gatlin, although I have often observed her from a distance. She is a stunningly beautiful young woman, and that could be her problem. I've seen how some of the men in town disrespect her. But that old woman watches her like a hawk. I've heard the unkind gossip about her. Some women say she can have no morals since she's a half-breed—they walk on the other side of the street when they see her coming and would never allow her to associate with their daughters." Cullen shoved the money back toward Wolf Runner. "It's a sad situation. I have often felt pity for the young woman."

"I have to think what my mother would want me to do, and at this moment I do not know," Wolf Runner admitted.

Cullen fell quiet as if he was forming his words, and then he asked, "What have you decided to do about the ranch?"

"I have been thinking about that." Cullen was from Philadelphia and had often talked of returning there, but Wolf Runner doubted he ever would. "It is a more difficult decision than I expected. Let me ask you this—If I do keep the ranch in the family, will you agree to stay on as foreman?"

Cullen nodded. "I will be glad to stay on if it is your family's wish."

Wolf Runner nodded. "I will make my decision soon. There is more to consider than I thought there would be."

"You are thinking about the older cowhands."

"Yes. But that is not the entire reason. When my brother and sister are older they may like to come to the ranch."

"Possibly."

Wolf Runner became lost in thought. Even when he decided what to do about the ranch, there was still the problem of the young Gatlin woman. The last thing he wanted was to be responsible for her, but it appeared he was. He was sympathetic to Ivy Gatlin's plight, and now that he knew what she had done for his mother, he would not turn his back on her.

He knew in his heart his mother would want him to make certain that the girl was safe before he left Santa Fe. Suddenly, he sat forward, smiling as the solution came to him. "If I don't sell the ranch, Ivy's granddaughter could come here. What do you think if I offered to pay her to help Hattie around the house?"

Cullen thought it might solve Wolf Runner's problem, but not Cheyenne Gatlin's. "I don't know," he said doubtfully. "Hattie can be mighty cantankerous. She might think Miss Gatlin was here to replace her."

"Hattie's getting older and could use the extra help," Wolf Runner said dismissively.

"Maybe."

"No one on the ranch would be unkind to Miss Gatlin. You could make sure of that, Cullen."

"Wolf Runner, Cheyenne Gatlin is young. She may not want to be isolated on the ranch."

"We will not know until I ask her." Wolf Runner nodded, feeling relieved. "It is a good plan."

Chapter Nine

Summer was giving way to autumn and already the trees at the higher elevation were flushed with nature's brilliant colors of crimson, yellow, and gold.

By now, Wolf Runner had expected to be back home—but something kept him from making the final decision on whether to sell the ranch. He would lean one way, then reconsider and think in the opposite direction.

He knew all the reasons he should let it go; his family was not connected to the place and probably never would be. But his mother had made it his responsibility, and he had to consider what selling it would mean for all the people who rode for the brand.

Leaning against his horse, he gazed at the lazy, fat cattle grazing on the sweet grass while Satanta was off in the bushes somewhere, probably chasing a luckless jackrabbit. At first the cattle had been nervous around Satanta, but they soon settled down when they saw he was not interested in them and now they hardly noticed the wolf.

Cullen had told him they were ready to ship to market, and he was assured that the herd would bring a good price this year. In three weeks they would begin the cattle drive to the railhead in Santa Fe, and from there the cattle would be shipped to Kansas City; then the cycle would begin all over again.

Wolf Runner smiled as a white-faced calf chased a butterfly. How different cattle were from the wild game that the Blackfoot depended on for food—cattle had to be fed and watered, branded, and sometimes helped in the birthing process, while the antelope and the deer roamed free and were there for the taking.

His thoughts turned to Blue Dawn and he felt guilty because she had not entered his mind in weeks. Most probably she was making plans for their joining. His mother had once said Blue Dawn did some of the finest beadwork in the village, so she was probably sewing beads on her wedding dress.

Restlessly, Wolf Runner gazed at the white-hot sky. He had made his decision about Mesa del Fuego—his mother would not be surprised; it was what she had intended all along.

A smile suddenly broke out on his face—he had not seen it at the time, but his mother had brilliantly played him. She had known he would be conflicted about selling the ranch. She probably also knew he could not sell when it came right down to it. Everyone in his village thought it was Wolf Runner's father who was the mystic, but his mother was wise indeed when it came to knowing her eldest son's mind.

Casting an uncertain glance at the dark clouds to the east, Wolf Runner hoped the rain would hold off until he reached the house. He mounted and spun his horse around, nudging it into a gallop. Before Wolf Runner descended the hill, Satanta joined him, loping beside his horse. When he reached the barn, the first drops of rain fell.

He could return home and leave Mesa del Fuego in Cullen's capable hands.

* * *

That night as Wolf Runner stood at the window looking out at the rain, Cullen came up behind him.

"We needed the rain to green the grass so we can put a few more pounds on the cattle before we drive them to the railhead."

"I was just thinking today how strange it is that the white man carefully raises his cattle and then ships them off for others to enjoy the beef. It is very different with the Blackfoot."

Cullen nodded. "But the buffalo herds have all but disappeared—perhaps it will be the same with the other game. I remember your grandfather, Broken Lance, telling me of a time when the ground trembled hours before the buffalo herds arrived, and they would move across the land from sunup until sundown in an unbroken mass. I can't even imagine such a sight."

Turning from the window Wolf Runner met Cullen's gaze. "Yes. Sadly that is the way of it."

Cullen sat in the high-back chair and took a sip of coffee he'd brought in the room with him. "I was told that Ivy Gatlin died yesterday. She was buried today."

Wolf Runner felt a sudden rush of pain. The old woman had struck at his heart, although he didn't really know her. Letting out an irritated breath, he said, "This means I will have to approach her granddaughter and invite her to live on the ranch."

Cullen stilled with his coffee cup halfway to his lips. "Then you have decided to keep the ranch?"

"I have, if you still agree to remain as foreman."

Breathing in a relieved breath, Cullen nodded. "I would be glad to."

Wolf Runner paced to the window and back to the fireplace. "You gave Ivy Gatlin her two hundred dollars before she died?"

"I did, although she was reluctant to take it back. Ivy told me if she died while you were still here, to remind you of your conversation with her."

"I suppose I should go into town and see the young woman for myself." Wolf Runner gave him a wry smile. "If I do not, I can imagine the old woman haunting me from her grave."

Tears mixed with rain as Cheyenne stood over Gram's grave; the lilac bouquet she had placed there had already begun to wilt.

Although she had known her gram was gravely ill, the end had come so quickly it took her by surprise. One moment Gram had been laughing about some story from her past, and the next moment she just slumped forward, grabbing her chest and sliding out of her chair onto the floor.

Grief lay heavily on Cheyenne's heart.

How could someone so full of life, so vibrant, just cease to exist? she wondered in desperation.

For a long time Cheyenne stood there dreading the thought of going back to the empty house. There had been many people who had come to the service, and some had even approached Cheyenne and offered her their sympathy. But at the end of the service, dark clouds boiled in the sky and made the mourners scurry for their wagons.

With no knowledge of how long she had been standing in the rain, Cheyenne pulled her shawl about her. Gram had knitted it for her and given it to her last Christmas.

That had been such a short time ago, really.

The wind stirred the nearby oak tree and scattered the leaves, making a sound almost like her grandmother calling to her.

"Oh, Gram," she whispered. "How will I get along without you? I wish . . . you could have stayed with me for a while longer. Forever."

Cheyenne shook her head, knowing she was being selfish because Gram had been in pain. She had to let her go. But it was so hard.

The rain did not let up as Cheyenne made the long trek home—if anything it was raining harder.

Once inside the house, she hung her wet shawl on a hook and took a towel, drying her damp hair. There was no longer any light in the world—with the dark clouds hanging overhead, the day could have passed for night, and no one would know the difference.

Without lighting a lamp, Cheyenne slowly changed out of her wet clothing. When she returned to the small parlor, she eased down in her grandmother's rocking chair and watched the rain hit against the window. She picked up the knitting Gram had been working on—it would never be finished now.

Señor Mendoza knocked on the door and handed her a covered dish. "I will not intrude, but my wife wants to make sure you have something warm to eat."

"Thank you, and tell Señora Mendoza I thank her."

He tipped his hat, his eyes sad. "Do you want one of the girls to stay with you tonight—Maria would, but she is running a fever."

"No thank you. I'll be fine."

He turned and walked slowly away, soon to be lost in the rain.

Cheyenne's heart was broken, and she doubted it would ever mend.

"What do I do now, Gram?" she said to the empty room. "What would you have me do?"

She jumped nervously at a heavy rap on the door. Cheyenne knew it was not anyone from the Mendoza family, so she wished whoever it was would just go away. And when she saw who was standing on the stoop, she wished she had not opened the door. Nigel Sullivan had not seen fit to attend Gram's service and was the last person she wanted to see.

Gripping the door handle tightly, she refused to step aside so he could enter. "I would ask you in, but I'm not very good company today, Mr. Sullivan."

Removing his hat, he stood dripping on the doorstep, then moved her aside and entered anyway.

"I know about your sorrow," he said, gripping her shoulders. "What you need is someone to look after you." He walked over to the small table and lit the oil lamp. "There. Isn't that better?"

Remembering her manners, Cheyenne forced a smile. "Yes, it is."

. The poor man was soaked to the skin, so she added a log to the fire. "I'm sorry I can't offer you a cup of coffee because I didn't make coffee today . . . because . . . because I don't drink coffee." Her eyes welled with tears. "Would you like a glass of water?"

He stared at her for so long it made her grip her hands and squirm uncomfortably.

"I didn't come for food or drink—I came to see how you're making out."

"About how you would expect."

"Why are you alone? Someone should be with you."

His concern sounded false to her ears. "The Mendozas were with me at the funeral and offered to stay with me."

"The blacksmith and his family."

"Yes. My friends." She returned to the door, her

hand on the doorknob. "If you'll forgive me, I don't feel much like talking."

"What I have to say will only take a few moments," Nigel told her. "I want you to know I'm your friend." He studied her closely. "Did your grandmother tell you I hold the mortgage on this house?"

Gasping, Cheyenne could feel the color drain from her face and her heart plummeted. "I . . . no. Gram didn't mention it. I know she had to mortgage the house last year, but she didn't tell me you held the note."

"Maybe she didn't know." He shrugged. "I allowed you and your grandmother to live here without charge, knowing she was sick and the two of you were having a hard time." He looked pleased with himself. "It was the least I could do."

"I don't know what to say." And she didn't. Cheyenne certainly did not want to owe this man for anything. She remembered Gram's warning and shuddered.

"It's no big matter. I merely mention it because as a young girl alone, it would not be seemly for you to remain here by yourself."

"I wouldn't want to." Cheyenne tried to think where she could go. After his revelation that he held the mortgage, she knew she would have to leave this house.

"Do you have friends you can stay with?" Nigel asked, looking at the way her black hair glowed in the lamplight.

Raising her head, she met his gaze, her world was crumbling around her. "The Mendoza family. But I can't stay with them in their small house. It is hardly big enough for their family."

"I'm truly worried about you." Nigel shoved his hands in his pockets and rocked back on his heels, warming himself in front of the fireplace. "Maybe there's something I can do to help."

"My problems are not yours, Mr. Sullivan. If you will give me a few days I will vacate this house."

His gaze dropped to the front of her gown and he stared at the way her breasts pressed against the dark material. "I wonder if you have thought about the talk we had some time back? You will be welcome to a room at my hotel—you could pay for the room by working for me and doing little chores around the place."

Cheyenne shook her head. "I can't do that."

His gaze hardened. "Why not? You could be a big help to my wife, Nancy. Wouldn't that make it all right?"

Cheyenne ducked her head, wishing he would leave. "I can't think about anything but Gram right now. I don't mean to be rude, but would you leave?" She opened the door a crack to enforce her wishes.

He approached her and shoved the door shut. "It's like I said before, you can clean the rooms for spending money. How does that sound to you?"

It sounded like her worst nightmare. "Can I let you know later?" she asked, stalling for time.

He reached for his hat and twisted the brim with his huge hands. "Of course. But don't take too long; you're not likely to get a better offer in this town."

"I do need to be alone," Cheyenne said, ducking her head. "Please understand."

His eyes darted over her with the coldness of a snake's. "Come to see me when you're feeling better."

He took her hand and she jerked away, clasping them behind her, and he pretended not to notice.

"Do you have a key for this door?"

She wasn't sure, but she hoped there was one so she could lock him out. "I believe so. Gram probably put it somewhere."

"You'll want to keep your door locked, being a woman alone."

He was frightening her now, because he was staring into her eyes in a way that made her cringe. "I have a gun, Mr. Sullivan, and I know how to use it."

He clamped his hat on his head and narrowed his gaze. "Come to see me soon."

After he had gone, Cheyenne pressed her weight against the door, her whole body shaking.

The one thing she would *never* do—no matter how desperate she became—was to move into his hotel. She had to think of some other way to earn a living.

But how?

Mr. Sullivan would never leave her alone. She would have to leave Santa Fe. Tomorrow she would talk to Señor Mendoza and he might have some ideas for her.

Cheyenne had not eaten all day, but she doubted she would be able to keep anything down. Already she could taste bile in the back of her throat.

Frantically, she scooted a chair across the room and propped it beneath the door handle, hoping it would keep any intruder out, or at least alert her if someone tried to open the door. Cheyenne raced to the kitchen and slid the wooden latch in place, wishing there was one on the front door as well.

Walking through the empty house, she felt a chill. Climbing onto the middle of Gram's bed, Cheyenne grasped her grandmother's pillow and sank her face into it. It smelled so painfully familiar with just the hint of lilacs.

Shaking uncontrollably, she cried until she was exhausted.

"Gram, I need you."

Her gram could not answer.

Cheyenne was alone.

Chapter Ten

Cheyenne glanced out the window, relieved that the rain had finally stopped and a weak sun poked through scattered clouds.

Grabbing up her still-damp shawl, she left the house and made her way to Señor Mendoza's blacksmith shop. It was impossible to miss all the mud puddles as she stepped onto the street, her shoes already wet and muddy.

Why hadn't she worn her leather boots? She chided herself, wading through a puddle that seeped through her thin-soled shoes.

When she approached the blacksmith shop she heard the clanging of a hammer striking an anvil and was comforted by the familiar sound. When Señor Mendoza saw her, he wiped sweat from his brow and gave her his full attention.

"How are you today, *pequeña*?" His soft eyes were filled with sympathy.

Señor Mendoza had called her his "little one" since she was a child, and she was comforted by the familiar endearment. "I'm making out. Thank you for asking."

"Margareta said if I saw you today I was to invite you to supper, señorita. You should not be alone at a time like this."

She smiled at the man she admired above all others. His dark hair was dusted with gray, and his brown eyes radiated warmth. His arms were muscled from the heavy smithy work he did, but he was a gentle man, who loved his family, and he had always included her in that number.

"I have so much to do, I haven't thought about eating," she admitted. "I need to be moved out of the house as soon as possible. I found out yesterday that Mr. Sullivan holds the mortgage. Do you think you could store a few of Gram's belongings in your loft until I can decide what to do with them?"

He stilled. "Of course, but why must you leave?"

She lowered her head. "It's Mr. Sullivan. He has always made me uncomfortable, but when he came by the house last night . . . I really can't explain why, but I was frightened."

The blacksmith's jaw tightened. "Just say when you want your things moved and I will bring a wagon and my sons to help. Meantime, you must stay with us."

Cheyenne shook her head, knowing he was worried about her, and she didn't want that. "I need to stay in the house until I pack away Gram's belongings. Everything should be ready day after tomorrow. Can you come late in the afternoon?"

"I will be there," he told her with feeling. "How are you fixed for money, Señorita Cheyenne?"

"I have enough to get me by until I find work."

He continued to look at her worriedly, and she was sure he did not believe her.

"I wonder if you would accept the chickens and the milk cow?" she asked hurriedly, hoping to take his mind off her money situation.

He nodded, feeling her heartbreak. "I can take them and even pay you a little for them."

"No. I don't want money from you. I just want you to have them."

He lowered his head, feeling ashamed that he could give Cheyenne so little in her time of need. He had nothing to offer.

"Señor Mendoza, I believe Gram would have liked Señora Mendoza to have her furniture. I have no use for it anymore. But I could not bear to get rid of Gram's personal belongings. They are what I would like you to store for me."

"It is too much," he said, shaking his head. "I cannot pay you what the furniture is worth."

"I could never sell Gram's furniture. They are a gift to your family, for all your kindnesses."

"Kindness is not for sale, *pequeña*."

"No, it isn't. I wouldn't even try. It would mean so much for me to know your family is using Gram's furniture. I couldn't bear for anyone else to have the breakfront that has been in our family for generations. It was Gram's pride and joy."

He watched her for a moment and saw tears swimming in her eyes. "I know Margareta will take care of it for you, and for the rest, I thank you."

She smiled. "You will never know how much your family means to me."

He picked up his bellows and started fanning the flame in the forge, too choked up to speak at first. When the fire leaped high, he turned back to her. "Señorita Cheyenne, remember, you will always have a home with us."

"Thank you. I may spend a night or two with you, but I have to make my own way, Señor Mendoza."

He had known her since childhood and he knew about her pride. "The offer is there for you if you should ever change your mind."

She reached up and kissed his rough cheek. "Thank you."

He watched Cheyenne turn and walk away—she was such a lonely figure that it tugged at his heart. The "good" people of this town treated her no better than the dust beneath their feet. She was a sweet young girl, and she had so many troubles. He wanted to help her, but she would not accept his help. The pride of the young was often their undoing, he thought sorrowfully.

The sun had poked through the clouds again and it had stopped raining. Sitting cross-legged in the middle of the floor surrounded by wooden crates and crumpled paper, Cheyenne lovingly wrapped each item before carefully placing it inside the crate. It was heartbreaking enough to pack up her gram's meager belongings without the day being dark and gloomy.

Time was of the essence. She had to be out of this house before Mr. Sullivan returned. And she wanted to have everything ready by the time Señor Mendoza came by with his wagon.

Cheyenne found a packet of old letters wrapped in blue ribbon and she smiled—they were to Gram from her grandfather. She would not read them now, but she could not throw them away. They would be packed with the other things she was keeping and stored in Señor Mendoza's loft.

She lifted a faded tintype of her father and tears spilled down her cheeks. The world was a lonely place without family, without a home, without anyone who really cared about her.

Frowning, Cheyenne saw something tucked behind the frame—an envelope. She carefully slid it out and stared at it for a long moment. It was from Indian Territory, from a Mr. Samuel Dickens.

"Hmm," she said aloud, wondering whom the letter was from, and why her gram had hidden it away.

Removing the letter from the envelope she held it to the lamp and began to read:

Dear Mrs. Gatlin,

Allow me to introduce myself. I am the Indian agent for the Cheyenne tribe in Indian Territory. Chief Bold Eagle has asked me to make inquiries about his daughter's child, whom he has reason to believe is your granddaughter. He is most anxious to hear about the child and would appreciate any words of comfort you can offer him about his deceased daughter's child.

Sincerely,
Mr. Samuel Dickens

P.S. Since writing the above the Cheyenne people have been relocated to Montana. If you will write to me, I will make certain the letter reaches Chief Bold Eagle.

I have told him that it is unlikely he will ever find the child. But this does not dampen his spirits. If he cannot see her, he would like to know if she is thriving. If you can help set his mind at ease, you will have his gratitude, as well as mine.

Cheyenne held the letter to her breast as fresh tears washed down her cheeks.

She had family, a grandfather!

And he wanted to see her.

Of course, the letter was dated three years earlier. Bold Eagle might be dead by now.

Why had her grandmother never mentioned to her that she had family looking for her?

Had Gram ever answered the letter?

Cheyenne did not think so.

If anything, Gram would have gone to great lengths to keep her granddaughter away from the Cheyenne tribe.

Someone knocked on the door and Cheyenne's head jerked up. She wiped her tears on her apron before she went to answer it. Maria was still sick with a fever, so it would not be her, and Señor Mendoza was not coming with the wagon for a couple of days.

When she opened the door shock registered in her mind—she had never spoken to the woman who stood on the doorstep staring back at her, but she recognized Mrs. Sullivan. She wondered if the woman had come to ask her to vacate her husband's property.

"Would you like to come in?" Cheyenne asked, stepping aside.

"Indeed I do," the woman ground out. "I certainly want to talk to you."

Nancy Sullivan was a small-boned woman with thin, light brown hair. She was pretty despite the dark circles underneath her eyes. Her blue-and-white gingham gown was made of the finest quality material and not store-bought, but probably ordered from some fancy dress shop back East.

"If you like coffee, I could make some," Cheyenne offered.

Looking about the cluttered room Nancy Sullivan's thin lips curled in distaste. "No. I don't want any."

Quickly removing a stack of books from a chair and placing them on the floor, Cheyenne said, "Please forgive the mess. As you see, I'm packing. If you have come to inquire when I will be leaving, I will have most of the things out in two days."

Nancy Sullivan glared at the young woman, casting her a smug glance. "I have not come to ask you to vacate the house. I came with a warning."

Mr. Sullivan's wife was plainly angry and Cheyenne could not understand why. "A warning?"

"Yes, my girl. I'm warning you to stay away from my husband. Don't deny you are after him, 'cause I know you are."

Feeling her face pale, Cheyenne stared at her uninvited guest as if she had lost her mind. "I do deny it! I don't want anything to do with your husband. Why would I?"

"Of course you'd say that to throw me off track." The woman gave Cheyenne a wintery smile. "Do you deny he was with you the very night your grandmother was buried?" the woman asked, glaring at Cheyenne. "He was seen coming in here."

"He came to tell me he owned this house and to offer me a job. He said you would approve—I didn't believe him."

Mrs. Sullivan's face reddened. "And I suppose he offered you a room at the End of Trail."

"He did. But I can assure you, Mrs. Sullivan, I have no intentions of moving to your hotel or working for your husband." She gave a sweep of her hand. "As you can see, I am packing to move out of this house."

Nancy Sullivan stood and began pacing the room, which was no easy task since she had to weave her steps around wooden crates that littered her way. "I can always tell when my husband forms a new attachment for some woman." Her lip curled in distaste. "But you," she said with disgust. "A half-breed Indian, it sickens me that Nigel would take up with the likes of you."

Cheyenne felt the woman's harsh words like a physical blow. "I'm not responsible for your husband's actions. Mr. Sullivan is the last man I would allow to touch me," she said, going to the door and holding it open wide. "Just go and leave me alone."

"My girl, you can't order me out of a house my husband owns. But I am prepared to help you leave town."

"I wouldn't accept help from you."

Opening her drawstring reticule, Mrs. Sullivan pursed her lips and removed a wad of bills and thrust them at Cheyenne. "There is enough here for you to take a train out of Santa Fe and to even keep you in food and lodging until you can find work." She nodded at Cheyenne. "Take it!"

"I pity you. Do you have enough money to buy off every woman your husband looks at?"

"How dare you . . . you half-breed."

"You have insulted me in every way possible, and my pity grows thin. I just want you to leave."

"Don't try to play innocent with me. I've seen you sashaying about town, drawing all the men's interest. You aren't fit to live around decent people."

Trying to keep a tight rein on her temper, Cheyenne took a deep breath. "You don't know me well enough to make any kind of assumption. Your husband is the one who should not be allowed to be around decent young women. He has but one thing on his mind—the ruination of any woman who falls into his hands. You can tell him that for me."

The woman looked doubtful for a moment and then she shook her head, cramming her money back into her reticule. She had met Nigel's women before and they all claimed to be innocent, but they had all taken her money. "If you think my husband will give you more than I offered, in that you are mistaken. I control the money, not him."

Angry and hurt to the heart, Cheyenne felt her lips quiver. "I would not touch your money. I'll be leaving soon, and you and your husband will never see me again."

The woman's eyes flickered with uncertainty. "When? And where will you go?"

"When I leave and where I go is no concern of yours. I'm going to ask you this one last time to get out!"

Sweeping to the door, the short woman's head came only to the tip of Cheyenne's nose. "I don't have to take such talk from a dirty half-breed. If you aren't gone by the end of the week, I'll have the sheriff throw you out."

"I will be gone, but not because of your threats."

"I don't care what the reason is. Leave Santa Fe or you will regret it, my girl."

Feeling tears gathering behind her eyes, Cheyenne was determined this woman would not see her cry. She gave Nancy Sullivan a wide berth so she could move out of the house.

She flinched when Mrs. Sullivan slammed the door so hard the windows rattled. For a long moment Cheyenne stood in shocked silence and could no longer stop the tears from coursing down her cheeks. Whatever she decided to do about her future, she must do it quickly.

Listening to the mantel clock ticking away the seconds of her life, Cheyenne knew what she must do, but she was afraid to take that first step into an unknown future.

A storm struck at midnight with lightning and thunder shattering her sleep. She sat up in bed, her heart pounding with fear. She heard a banging and thought someone was trying to break in before she realized the noise was a broken shutter slamming against the house. Grabbing her shawl, she rushed outside and fumbled with the shutter until she finally latched it.

Cheyenne was drenched by the time she got back inside, and when she changed into a dry nightgown, she was still shivering. It was doubtful she would be able to sleep for the rest of the night. And she heard every sound—the creaking of the house, and the occasional barking of a dog.

Her eyes grew heavy, but she could not sleep for thinking of what Mrs. Sullivan had said to her, and for fear Mr. Sullivan would break down the door to get to her.

Her loaded gun lay at her side, so she could reach it if she needed to.

Chapter Eleven

When morning came, Cheyenne rose, feeling exhausted. She laid a fire in the fireplace and tried not to think of Mrs. Sullivan and her harsh accusations. But she could not get the woman's cruel words out of her head.

Thinking back to her meetings with Mr. Sullivan, Cheyenne wondered if she had ever done or said anything to encourage him.

No.

She had not.

In fact she had always attempted to discourage that loathsome man who apparently preyed on women who had no protection.

At the moment she did not know whom she despised the most, him or his sharp-tongued wife.

But she did know she was in trouble.

There was no doubt in her mind that Mrs. Sullivan would make good her threat and have the sheriff order her out of the house if she did not vacate as soon as possible.

The timbers in the old house creaked and groaned as Cheyenne spent the rest of the day packing. By the time she crawled into bed, she was too weary and heartsick to even remove her clothing. She finally dozed off listening to the familiar sounds of the house settling around her. This would be her last night to spend in the only home she had ever known.

Sliding out of bed the next morning, she had to make sure everything was in order so Señor Mendoza would not have to wait when he arrived with the wagon. She was facing a hard situation, but there was no time to waste feeling sorry for herself.

It was late afternoon before she hammered the nails in the last crate. Standing back, she surveyed the remnants of Gram's life. How sad that everything Cheyenne was going to keep fit into four small crates. She grabbed up her bonnet and was on her way out the front door when she stopped dead still, watching Mr. Sullivan come up the walk.

It was too late to retreat into the house, so she stood her ground. "Good afternoon, Mr. Sullivan," she said, closing the door firmly behind her, knowing she would not allow him inside the house. "If you are here to make sure I'm leaving, I can assure you I'll be out before the day is over."

"There was no need for you to rush," he said, stopping in front of her. "I just spoke with Mendoza and he told me he would be moving your belongings out today. I have to say I didn't like the man's attitude."

He was standing much too close to suit Cheyenne, so she stepped around him and moved toward the gate. "Señor Mendoza is a very dear friend and he feels protective of me."

Nigel's light-colored brows met across his nose in a frown. "Just how close a friend is he?"

Whirling on him with overwhelming disdain, Cheyenne said angrily, "How dare you ask me such a question! Señor Mendoza is like a father to me. He is nothing like you."

"You have the wrong idea about me, Cheyenne," he protested.

"I don't think so," she snapped, "and don't call me by my given name, *Mr.* Sullivan."

"Don't be so unfriendly. I only want to help you."

Taking Cheyenne's arm, he led her back toward the house, but she pulled away from him with a glare.

"Now, now, don't take offense. There are things I need to talk to you about."

She jerked her arm free of his grasp and said in desperation, "There is nothing left to say between us."

"There you are wrong." Nigel Sullivan loomed over her. "Do you think I don't know that my wife paid you a visit yesterday? I know what she said to you. Do not imagine I would ever let Nancy dictate to me."

"She's your wife."

He waved his hand dismissively. "That don't mean nothing to you and me. Don't worry, I took care of her this morning, and she won't be bothering you anymore."

"Get. Away. From. Me," Cheyenne said between clenched teeth, enunciating each word carefully.

"You won't want me to go when you hear that I've decided you can unpack those crates and remain in this house. How would you like that? I'll even sign over the deed to you if it will make you feel better." His voice took on a silken quality, and he touched her cheek. "I will be real good to you, Cheyenne." His voice became lower. "I'll see that you want for nothing."

Mr. and Mrs. Glass, the owners of Glass General Mercantile, were passing by and both paused to gawk at them. Mrs. Glass's mouth curved into a disapproving line. Her voice carried to Cheyenne. "I told you that half-breed was no good and you can see for yourself I was right," she told her husband.

Shame washed down Cheyenne's face and she stepped around Mr. Sullivan—she could only imagine what the Glasses thought was going on between her and this man.

"We can't talk here," Nigel said, grasping her hand and leading her toward the house. Opening the door, he pulled her resisting body inside and slammed the door shut before Cheyenne could protest.

She turned on him, her hands fisting at her side. "You have no right to be here," she said, breaking away from his grasp. "And you have no right to treat me with such disrespect."

"I respect you. If you'll just give me half a chance, I'll show you how much."

Terrified of being alone with him, she tried another tactic. "You should leave now. Señor Mendoza will be here at any moment with his three sons."

Wolf Runner dismounted in front of the small adobe house. He had seen the man and woman in the yard as he approached, and he had watched them enter the house, drawing the obvious conclusion.

He had come by to talk to Cheyenne Gatlin so he could make provision for her future. Guilt had been his motivation today, but he could have saved himself the trouble. It seemed she already had a man to take care of her. He had just gripped the reins, with the intention of remounting his horse, when he heard scuffling sounds coming from inside the house and then a woman screamed.

Nigel grabbed Cheyenne and pulled her into his arms. When she cried out and tried to turn her head, he held her so tightly the buttons on his coat bit into her skin. She pushed against him when he tried to nuzzle her neck.

"I have waited a long time for this moment. I want you and I'll have you, you can make sure of that."

"Please, no, Mr. Sullivan," Cheyenne pleaded, sounding helpless when she wanted to sound decisive. "Leave me alone! I can't abide to have you near me."

The more she struggled, the tighter he held her, and he was much stronger. When he backed her into a corner and pressed his body against hers, she screamed, even though she knew no one would hear her, or even care if they did.

"Fight me—bite and scratch me—it will make your surrender all the sweeter."

"You are an animal!" Cheyenne cried, trying to wedge her arm between their bodies. "I despise you!"

Sullivan groped for her breasts and she bit his hand so hard he cried out in pain. "You little bitch," he said, slapping her so hard her head hit the wall and she crumpled to her knees.

Neither of them had heard Wolf Runner enter until he spoke from the open doorway. "I believe the lady told you to leave her alone," he said in a dangerously calm voice.

Nigel's head whipped around and he stared at the stranger. "Get out. This is none of your business."

Cheyenne's eyes widened. She didn't know why the owner of Mesa del Fuego was there, but she reached out to him. "Don't go," she pleaded. "Please help me."

"Who do you think you are?" Nigel demanded as he turned to face the stranger. "You're on private property and I could have you arrested."

Wolf Runner saw the young woman reach out her hand to him with terror in her eyes. "And you are pressing your attentions on a lady who doesn't want them. I could have you arrested. Or . . . I could take care of you myself."

"She isn't a lady—she's an Indian." Nigel looked Wolf Runner over carefully. "But then so are you, aren't you?"

Wolf Runner ignored the man's comment. "Miss, do you want me to make him leave?"

"Yes, please."

Wolf Runner towered threateningly over the man. Nigel felt the first inkling of fear when he looked into dark, menacing eyes—for a moment he thought he saw his own death reflected in their depths.

"The lady wants you to go. So go."

Sullivan inched around Wolf Runner and made his way to the door. "This isn't over," he said to Cheyenne. "I'll be back."

She cringed as he left and slammed the door. Trembling, she gazed up at her rescuer, wondering why he was there. "I don't know how to thank you," she said, standing, and bracing herself against the wall for a moment. "I don't know what I would have done if you hadn't come along when you did."

"Am I right in assuming you are Ivy Gatlin's granddaughter?"

She nodded slowly as grief etched her face. "Gram is . . . dead."

"I know. I spoke to her a few weeks ago. We have to talk."

Chapter Twelve

Still shaking from her encounter with Mr. Sullivan, and more than a little confused because the owner of Mesa del Fuego had come to her rescue, Cheyenne asked the first question that popped into her head, "You spoke to Gram?"

"Briefly."

It was now clear to Cheyenne where Señor Mendoza had taken Gram that day she wanted his wagon. "What did she want with you?"

Wolf Runner stared into the face of the young woman who was causing him no end of trouble. Her Indian heritage was apparent in her high cheekbones and her darker skin. Her amber eyes were remarkable. Having only seen her from a distance, he had not known she was so beautiful, although Cullen had said she was. Ivy Gatlin had been right; her unprotected granddaughter would become a target for every unsavory man who crossed her path.

"I have seen you before," she said. "The day you came into town. But I don't know your name."

As if coming out of a daze, he said, "To the Blackfoot people I am known as Wolf Runner."

Cheyenne saw green flecks in his otherwise brown eyes, and knew either his mother or father was white. "You are Blackfoot and a half-breed as I am."

He turned to observe the crates stacked near the

door. "I never consider that I am a half-breed until I walk in the white world. Never think that my heart is not fully Blackfoot."

"I am half white and half Cheyenne—nothing I do and no amount of wishing can change that. The day I was born marked who I am and how people react to me. You saw how Mr. Sullivan treated me."

"Your grandmother said you had never met your own people, the Cheyenne."

Tears glittered on long, silky lashes, and she wiped them away on the tips of her fingers. "What did Gram say about me?"

"Did Mrs. Gatlin not tell you she came to see me at the ranch?"

Cheyenne's brow furrowed. "No. Why did she go to see you?"

"She told me about your circumstances and that there was a man who was pursuing you."

Shame washed over Cheyenne. "Tell me she didn't do that."

"She was worried about you, and from what I saw here today she had good reason."

His voice was deep, his words cultured, and he spoke with only a slight accent. His face was as beautiful as any of the statues she had seen in one of Gram's books on ancient Greece. Making a hopeless gesture, she shook her head. "I'm sorry Gram dragged you into this." She stared at him for a moment before breaking off eye contact. "I wish she hadn't."

Wolf Runner did not know how much to tell her since Ivy Gatlin had not mentioned her visit to his ranch. "Your grandmother knew my mother in the past so she came to me and asked if I could help you."

How like Gram to worry about her when she had been so sick. Cheyenne was still reeling with grief and she could hardly follow Wolf Runner's reasoning. "As you can see, I am packed to move out of this house since it belongs to Mr. Sullivan."

"Do you have plans?"

"No." She avoided his eyes. "Not yet."

"Then I can help. How would you like to move to Mesa del Fuego?"

Gasping, Cheyenne stepped away from him, her eyes narrowed. "How dare you! I just had a similar offer, and I turned it down."

Anger flashed in his all-seeing eyes.

"Miss Gatlin, do not mistake my intentions with those of the man who just left here. I have no interest in you whatsoever, other than to help you for your grandmother's sake."

Confused and embarrassed by her outburst, Cheyenne realized she had mistaken his intentions. "Thank you for helping me today. But as you see, I have much to do."

"Where will you go?" he pressed.

She regarded him silently for a moment before she shook her head. Her gaze reflected caution, for she did not fully trust any man after today. "You need not be concerned."

"Mrs. Gatlin asked me to take you to my village and place you under the care of my mother." He turned away from her and gazed out the window. "That, or living in safety on Mesa del Fuego is all I can offer you."

Her mouth flew open in shock. Hurt pride and shame battled inside Cheyenne. "I'm not going with you to your Indian village or your ranch. I can take care of myself," she said in anger.

Wolf Runner stared down at her, wanting to walk away. She was ungrateful and obstinate, two traits he did not admire in women. "You were not doing very well at it a moment ago."

When he saw hurt pour into her eyes, he was sorry for his sharp words. She had just lost her grandmother and been accosted by a man—she did not need his criticism. For reasons he did not care to examine, he felt the need to offer this young woman words of comfort. "In times of great grief," he said, looking deeply into her eyes, "it may seem that hope has deserted you, but with the passing of time, grief lessens."

Cheyenne stood frozen in place for a long moment. Then she broke eye contact with him and turned away. "Good day." She walked to the door and held it open. "Thank you for your concern."

Wolf Runner was reluctant to leave. If it were not for her dark skin and the slant of her beautiful eyes, she would pass for a white woman and would not be as vulnerable as she was now. Her honey-colored eyes seemed to pull him into their depths, but he resisted.

"If you are certain—I will not make the offer again." He expected to be relieved because she was releasing him from the obligation Ivy Gatlin had placed on his shoulders, but he still hesitated.

"Thank you again," Cheyenne said stiffly, opening the door wider and looking at him pointedly.

Wolf Runner had good instincts, and at the moment he knew that this woman who stood so bravely before him was terrified. He could do nothing for her if she would not accept his help.

"I will leave you, if that is your wish." He paused at the door. "I will be departing Santa Fe tomorrow. Should you need anything at all, I will instruct Cullen Worthington to help you. Do not hesitate to go to him; he is trustworthy and honorable."

Cheyenne's hand trembled as her grasp on the

doorknob tightened. "I will not need anything," she said proudly.

Wolf Runner nodded. "Then good day to you, Miss Gatlin. And accept my sympathy on your grandmother's passing."

Watching him leave and smoothly mount his horse, Cheyenne wished she could call him back. But what would she say to him? She had been humiliated that her grandmother had involved him in her troubles. She would always be grateful he had arrived in time to make Mr. Sullivan leave, but she didn't know him, and wasn't going to trust a stranger.

As Wolf Runner rode away he could not get the problems of the young woman out of his mind. She said she was going to be all right, but he did not believe it, and he did not think she did either.

Cheyenne Gatlin was in no way his responsibility. He had offered to help, and she had refused. That settled the matter, as far as he was concerned.

Romero and Ricardo Mendoza had just finished lifting the last crate in the loft of the blacksmith shop, and the oldest, Romero, who was fifteen, came down the ladder to stand before Cheyenne. "That is the last of it, Señorita Cheyenne. Will you need anything else?"

She pressed a coin in each of their hands. "There is nothing else. Thank you both for your help."

Señor Mendoza had been watching the exchange and looked at each of his sons sternly. "Do we take money from our friends?"

Both boys looked ashamed and handed Cheyenne back her coins.

"But Señor Mendoza, I want to pay the boys for their work."

"Say nothing more about it." He turned back to his sons. "Do you not have chores to do for your mother?"

Both nodded and dashed out of the blacksmith shop.

"They are good boys," Señor Mendoza said with pride.

"Yes, they are," Cheyenne agreed.

"Your belongings will be safe in the loft until you have need of them."

"I seem to always be thanking you for your many kindnesses."

"It is a pleasure to be of help." His brown eyes took on a serious expression. "But the family wishes to do more."

"You have already been a great help to me. I don't know what I would have done without your family."

"We had a meeting last night and we all decided we would like you to come and live with us. The boys have agreed to sleep here in the shop. In fact, they are most eager to do so; I suspect they would enjoy the freedom away from their mother's watchful eye. You can bunk in with Maria and her sisters. They are eager to have you with them."

Cheyenne smiled. "Life can't be so hard when I have friends like you and your family. I would like to stay the night with you—then I will be leaving for Albuquerque on the morning train."

He frowned. "What will you do there?" he asked in concern. "You have no friends in that town, while you have us here in Santa Fe."

"There might be an advantage to being unknown," Cheyenne said, putting on a brave front. "Besides that, Albuquerque is a larger town and perhaps it will be easier to find employment."

"What kind of job will you seek," he asked worriedly.

"I would prefer to be a housekeeper or a shop clerk, if I can find someone who will employ me."

"I see your mind is made up, so go with God, señorita. He will keep you safe." He looped a rope around his hand and hung it on a hook. "Should you find it does not work out for you in Albuquerque, come home to us."

She touched his arm and he clasped her hand. "You will see me again."

Wolf Runner reached through the rungs of the boxcar and rubbed his horse's neck. "He is always nervous and high-strung," he told the conductor who stood beside him.

"Most of them are like that before they settle down." The man reached in and touched the horse's sleek neck. "This is a fine animal."

"A little bit of home," Wolf Runner said, turning away. "He's from my father's breed." He glanced back at the conductor. The man was tall, with a thin face and long black hair. "You will see that he has food and water. Of course, I will tend to the wolf."

The older man laughed at Wolf Runner's words. "I've been working on the Atchison, Topeka, and Santa Fe Railroad since it first reached Santa Fe. In all that time I have never lost a horse, and I have never fed a wolf." He looked warily at Satanta. "And I hope to keep my clean record. On both counts."

Wolf Runner laughed. "Satanta will not trouble you."

"I understand you are only going as far as Albuquerque today."

"What time will we arrive?"

The conductor took out his pocket watch. "I should think we would be there by noon."

Wolf Runner found a seat near the window and stared at the people on the platform. They scurried about like mice looking for a hole. Life was much simpler in his village. He could not breathe among so many people. He yearned for the open spaces of his homeland, and blue skies that stretched on forever.

He only planned to be in Albuquerque for a few days. He would meet with the man who had offered to buy Mesa del Fuego and tell him the ranch was not for sale. Then he would purchase some equipment Cullen had asked for, and then he would be on his way home.

Home.

Still gazing out the window, Running Wolf's eyes suddenly centered on a young woman carrying a valise much too heavy for her—but no one offered to help her with it. Although her bonnet covered most of her face, he knew it was Cheyenne Gatlin.

His eyes narrowed with skepticism. Was she following him? He became even more suspicious when she took the seat right across the aisle from him.

The train started forward with a hiss and a jerk and Cheyenne Gatlin raised her head, looking uncertain.

From the grip she had on the back of the seat in front of her, Wolf Runner assumed she had never before ridden a train. As they pulled away from the platform, she glanced over at him. From the widening of her eyes, she appeared to be surprised—or was that only a trick?

Perhaps.

Deciding to ignore her, Wolf Runner leaned back in the seat and closed his eyes.

His thoughts were on home when he fell asleep. And he dreamed of running up the Sweet Grass Hill with his wolves trailing behind him. There was a woman with him, and when she lifted her face to him, it was not Blue Dawn, but Cheyenne Gatlin.

And in his mind, he was home.

Chapter Thirteen

Much to Cheyenne's mortification, Wolf Runner had not even acknowledged her, so she could only conclude she had made him angry.

Well, what do I care?

She had forgotten he had said he was leaving town today. If she had known he would be taking the train, she would have left town the next morning.

Despite her determination to ignore him, Cheyenne's gaze kept going back to him. He remained perfectly still in sleep, his arms crossed over his broad chest. She looked at his hands because Gram had told her she could usually gain insight into a man's character by the appearance of his hands. Wolf Runner's fingers were long and well shaped, callused, no doubt by working on his family's ranch and doing whatever a Blackfoot did in his tribe.

Cheyenne wondered what his day-to-day life was like living in an Indian village. From his manner of speaking one might think he had been raised to be a gentleman; someone had honed his manners—probably his white mother.

She noticed his skin was not as dark as the Navaho or Zuni who could be found selling their wares in Santa Fe's market square.

But then, neither was hers.

His face was smooth, so he had no need to shave—

that would be from his Blackfoot heritage. His mouth was firm and well shaped, and Cheyenne suddenly blushed as she imagined pressing her lips to his.

Turning away quickly, she gazed out the window until her heartbeat returned to normal. She had never had such thoughts about a man before. What was the matter with her?

Gazing at the passing countryside, she saw the brittle grass waving in the breeze. Most of the trees were small and misshaped, almost ghostlike, because of the harsh wind that rushed down the mountains and constantly pelted them. This was the land of her birth, but she felt no kinship with it—the land and its people had never accepted her. The only part that meant anything to her was the small plot where Gram had been buried.

Drawing in a deep breath, Cheyenne closed her eyes. She was weary because she had hardly closed her eyes all night. Maria had cried and begged her to stay, but she could not put her burdens on the Mendozas. Her mind turned back to Wolf Runner's hands, and she imagined them caressing her skin.

Try as she might, she could not get him out of her mind. Something about him called to her and she did not know what it was, unless it was their shared Indian heritage.

The train hissed steam and jostled Wolf Runner awoke. He stretched, glancing out the window.

Apparently they had reached the outskirts of Albuquerque. Glancing over at Cheyenne Gatlin, he saw she was looking out the window and paid him not the slightest heed. He remembered her invading his dream, and he wanted to get as far away from her as possible.

When the train came to a full stop at the railroad station, Wolf Runner watched Cheyenne struggle once more with her heavy valise, knowing he should help her. He did not offer because he was not inclined to renew their acquaintance.

Apparently she felt the same because she did not even glance in his direction. He wondered what she might be doing in Albuquerque.

Perhaps the two of them being on the same train was accidental, after all.

Cheyenne steered clear of the fancy hotels on the square and found a small hotel around the corner and down the street. It bothered her that it was located next door to a cantina, but she must conserve what money she had left of the $200 Gram had left her. There was no way of knowing how long it would take her to find employment, or even if she would.

The desk clerk was a Mexican, somewhere in his fifties. He was a balding, coarse-looking man with a long, thin nose and eyes set close together.

The man looked her over carefully from head to toe and asked in Spanish, "How long will you be staying with us, señora?"

Cheyenne answered him in Spanish, relieved that the man had mistaken her for a Mexican woman.

However, when she signed her name in the registration book, he glanced at her signature and his high forehead wrinkled. "You are traveling alone, Señora Gatlin?"

"*Sí*, señor," she replied.

"I see here," he said, pointing to the ledger she had just signed, "that your name isn't Spanish."

She looked at him a moment before deciding that a lie would serve her well in this hotel. "No," she said, ducking her head, fearing he would read the truth in her eyes. She had already learned how vulnerable a woman alone could be. "My husband is a gringo."

"He will be joining you?"

She had already told one lie; why not tell another to prop it up? *"Sí."*

"What is your business in Albuquerque?"

Cheyenne glared at the inquisitive man. "My business is my own." She raised her head and met his gaze. "May I have the key please," she said, extending her hand toward him.

Hesitating for a moment, he handed her the key.

"Will you have someone retrieve my valise from the railroad station," she said, opening her reticule and taking out some coins and handing them to the man.

"I will have my grandson bring them to your room when he returns," he assured her, looking her over carefully. "Can I help you in any other way?"

Cheyenne recognized the gleam in the man's eyes and glared at him. "I want only to be left alone," she told him, thinking he was asking too many personal questions.

As she climbed the rickety stairs Cheyenne could feel the desk clerk's eyes on her. Her room was at the end of a dimly lit hallway. Inserting the key in the lock, she entered cautiously, not knowing what she would find. To her delight and surprise the room was clean and it smelled fresh. There was a colorful quilt on the bed, a stand with a pitcher of water, and a straight-back chair.

Going to the window, she pulled the cheap lace curtains aside and felt a cool breeze on her face. Cheyenne had no notion what turn her future would take, but at least she was safely away from Mr. Sullivan's lascivious pursuit. No one, with the exception of the Mendoza family, knew where she was, and none of them would tell anyone, especially not Mr. Sullivan.

Tomorrow she would start looking for employment. She had no qualifications, but she could clean house as well as anyone, and if they weren't too particular, she could also cook.

Removing her bonnet with a sigh, Cheyenne went to the ewer and poured water in a porcelain pan. She glanced in the oval mirror and was shocked to see her face was smudged with soot from the train smoke. For that matter her traveling suit was covered with black specks as well.

After dusting off her traveling gown and washing her face and hands, she went back to the window. She stood looking down on the street below until daylight gave way to darkness.

Chapter Fourteen

For three dreary days Cheyenne trudged the streets of Albuquerque, searching for work without success. Her feet hurt and she was bone-weary, but she had to keep trying.

She hurried across the street, leaving the general store behind, where the woman had told Cheyenne they had no need of help from the likes of her, and the woman went on insulting Cheyenne, until she walked out the door.

How can people strike out at someone they don't even know, just because they are different?

Cheyenne knew she would never treat anyone with such disrespect. Was there no one in this town who would look past who she was and give her a chance?

On entering her hotel room, she laid her money out on the bed and counted it, then recounted it. She had $123 left, and there would be less than that after she paid for her hotel room.

Her stomach growled to remind her she had not eaten all day. Maybe she could have a piece of toast and something warm to drink. She could not really afford to spend money, but she must keep up her strength so she could hunt for work.

Later, she hoped to move to a more respectable rooming house where they offered room and board.

She had seen several unsavory-looking characters hanging around out front. And at night when she went to bed, she could hear the raucous noise coming from the cantina next door.

That afternoon she was back on the streets, looking for employment. After three hours of disappointment, she trudged back toward her hotel, feeling heartsick and lonely. And to make matters worse, it had begun to rain.

Cheyenne's head was down so she did not notice the man who stepped in front of her.

"Miss Gatlin?"

Seeing it was Wolf Runner, she stepped beneath a tattered awning that did little to protect her from the rain. She'd had a miserable day and talking to him would only make it worse. He was arrogant and when he looked at her it was as if he was criticizing her in some way.

"I saw you on the train, but I did not know you were going to remain in Albuquerque."

"This was my destination," she said shortly.

He took her arm and pulled her farther against the building to protect her from the rain. "What are you doing here?" he asked, frowning. "Do you have friends in town?"

Tilting her head upward, she looked into his eyes. There was no reason she should confide in him, but what did it matter? "I had to leave Santa Fe, to get away from Mr. Sullivan."

He lifted his brow, frowning. "Yes. I saw how he was a problem for you. But do you have somewhere to stay? Have you any plans?"

Cheyenne pushed a wet strand of hair out of her face. "I have been looking for work."

She was soaked to the skin and looked so forlorn

that it touched a note of pity within Wolf Runner. She seemed so young and so alone. "What will you do?" he asked.

Cheyenne shook her head, about to tell him it was none of his concern. Then she capitulated because she needed to talk to someone. She would never see Wolf Runner again, so she could tell him her troubles. "The last place I tried"—she nodded down the street toward the general store—"the woman there told me I should try the saloon."

He stiffened. "You would not consider that, would you? It is unthinkable."

Cheyenne's chin went up. Talking to Wolf Runner had been a mistake. "How does anyone know what they would do if they were desperate enough?" She stepped away from him. "Now, if you'll excuse me, I was just on my way back to the hotel."

Before she knew what he was doing, Wolf Runner took her arm and was guiding her back across the street toward an elegant eating establishment where delicious smells wafted through the open windows. When she tried to pull away from him, his grip only tightened. "You look like you could use something hot to eat. I know I would be the better for it."

Cheyenne jerked her arm away from him. "No thank you."

No woman had ever irritated Wolf Runner as much as this one did. Her pride was making her foolish. But she was a woman alone and in trouble, and he could not abandon her. "Miss Gatlin, you would be doing me a favor. I do not like to eat alone." He would not tell her he had just come from eating in that same restaurant—alone.

She looked at him with a strange expression, realizing he was the only person who had shown her kindness since she arrived in Albuquerque. It would be rude to refuse his request.

Anyway, she was so cold her teeth chattered, so she agreed with a nod. "Something hot to drink would be nice, but I'm not hungry," she said, too proud to accept food from him.

His strong hand against the small of her back guided her through the crowded dining room and to a round table near the hearth, where a warm fire blazed.

A waiter approached, and looking surprised, started to say something to Wolf Runner. Fearing the man would mention he had just eaten there, he said quickly, "I am hungry. Bring me a platter of fried chicken, a bowl of stew, and six tamales, with a dish of corn and mashed potatoes as well. I will want corn bread and biscuits. We will both have a mug of hot apple cider."

The waiter, who was well trained, said, "Of course, sir. I'll be right back with your drinks."

Cheyenne's eyes widened. "You have a hearty appetite, sir."

Wolf Runner's gaze dropped to her. "I often order more food than I can eat. Maybe you can help me with it."

She gave her head a quick shake. "I will just take the cider."

A short time later she had wrapped her hands around a hot cup of cider and took small sips, looking longingly at the platter of fried chicken.

Wolf Runner pushed the platter toward her. "I do not really like fried chicken. I do not know why I ordered it. It would be a shame to let it go to waste. Are you sure you will not reconsider eating?"

"I . . . no. I won't," she answered, hoping he had not

heard her stomach rumbling. Licking her lips, she focused on the butter dripping from the hot corn bread.

"Would you like me to tell you what most Indians do," Wolf Runner asked, trying to put her at ease, "if a child refuses to eat something his mother serves?"

Cheyenne, no longer able to resist temptation, reached for a chicken leg. "What do they do?"

He smiled inwardly. "The father will place the serving pot in front of the child and force him to eat not only the food he left, but every morsel in the pot, even if it takes hours."

She licked her fingers after she'd devoured a chicken leg, and reached for another. Pride was one thing, but desperation trampled her pride in the dirt. "Why is that?" Cheyenne found she was not only hungry for food, but also for any knowledge of the Indian customs.

"Because the child needs to learn not to waste food. When they have to eat a lot of something they do not like, they rarely leave food uneaten."

"Has that ever happened to you?" she asked.

"Only once. I learned my lesson well."

"Not very well, it seems," she said, nodding at the mounds of food in front of him that were uneaten.

Wolf Runner merely smiled.

At the moment, Cheyenne did not think she would ever have too much to eat. "Tell me again about your visit with Gram," she said, taking a sip of cider and setting her mug on the patterned tablecloth. She listened while he explained more about his encounter with her grandmother.

Cheyenne stared at him in stunned silence, then shook her head. "I don't understand why she would do such a thing. And no matter what Gram said to you—I am not your responsibility."

"No, you are not. All the same, your troubles seem to have become mine."

She recognized leashed power behind those dark eyes that gazed into hers. Taking a steadying breath did nothing to quiet her racing heart. "You are mistaken. My troubles are my own. I have given myself two weeks to find employment here," she said, thinking he deserved an answer since he'd shared his food with her. "If I don't have work by that time, I have other plans."

Wolf Runner looked at her inquiringly.

She reached into her pocket and laid coins on the table. "I will be going now."

Forestalling her, he grabbed her hand and forced her to look into his eyes. His tone sounded patient, but those eyes told a different story. "You do not really have anything else planned, do you? Why not reconsider and allow me to take you to my mother as your grandmother wished?"

She tried to bury her emotions, hoping she could hold back the tears that threatened to choke her. He had a way of stripping away her defenses and seeing past her vulnerability.

People were beginning to stare at them, and Cheyenne lowered her voice. "I'm not going with you to live with your mother," she said decisively. After a long pause, she raised her head and stared into those dark eyes that seemed to know everything she was thinking. "Besides, it wouldn't be proper for me to travel with you."

"Proper?"

"Yes. Proper."

"I imagine your money will soon be gone; then what will you do?"

She reached into her pocket and withdrew a crumpled envelope and stared down at it. "I have this letter about my grandfather. I will go to him if I have no other choice."

Wolf Runner studied her face for a moment. "Who is your grandfather?" he asked abruptly, remembering Ivy Gatlin had said he was from the Cheyenne tribe.

She considered a sharp retort, but he had been kind to her, so she answered him politely. "I don't really know him. But he is family—my mother's father."

"From the Cheyenne tribe."

"Yes. Perhaps you know him, since you're an Indian."

Wolf Runner's eyes became piercing. "Not all Indians are the same," he explained, surprised at her naïveté about her mother's people. "Blackfoot and Cheyenne are different tribes and sometimes bitter enemies, but tell me about him. I may know of him."

"I . . . am not quite sure—this letter was written years ago." Cheyenne gazed down at the crumpled paper, a faint thread of hope lingering in her mind. "The Indian agent who wrote this was a Mr. Dickens. He says in his letter that my grandfather lives on Cheyenne land in Montana."

Tensing, Wolf Runner stared at her. "His name?"

"I . . ." She glanced down at the letter. "It says here he is Chief Bold Eagle."

Wolf Runner's fists curled. Here across from him sat a blood relative of his enemy, Night Fighter, for Night Fighter was Chief Bold Eagle's nephew. Surely this woman had been sent to test his fortitude, and he was failing the test. "I know of your grandfather," he finally said.

Her eyes lit up. "And he is alive?"

"The last time I heard he was. But you must understand he is not a young man."

"I don't care!" Cheyenne exclaimed, clutching the letter to her breasts. "He is my mother's father."

Wolf Runner's lip curled with disgust as he thought of her blood ties to a cowardly warrior such as Night Fighter. "How would you like to live in an Indian village?" he asked, waiting for her to object to the notion.

"I don't know," Cheyenne remarked in all honesty. She raised her chin, feeling it tremble. "I intend to find my grandfather. You can't imagine how alone you can feel when you have no family."

Letting out his breath, Wolf Runner gathered his thoughts. Here across the table from him sat the very person who would become his instrument to bring down his enemy. If he escorted Cheyenne to her grandfather's village, he would finally be able to face Night Fighter.

"If you are set on going to Montana," he said carefully, "I will take you. It is not that far from Blackfoot land."

Cheyenne sat forward excitedly, for she'd had no idea how to find her grandfather on her own. She still did not think it was proper to travel in the company of a man, but since her grandmother had trusted Wolf Runner, she would too.

He had been watching her indecision and then her excitement. He knew what she was going to say before she said it.

"Thank you. I would appreciate it, and I won't be any trouble to you."

"You do understand there will be no comforts on this journey?"

"I am not a creature of comfort. Gram and I lived very simply."

Shaking his head, Wolf Runner was doubtful, but

it would get him what he wanted in the end—Night Fighter.

"Understand this, where we are going you will ride until you think you are too weary to continue, but you will. At night you will sleep on the ground. Your food will not be what you are accustomed to. You will not complain about how difficult the journey is. If you do, I will leave you behind."

"I will not complain," Cheyenne said indignantly.

"It is a long way from here, and winter is likely to overtake us before we arrive. We will go by horseback, and most of the time the roads will be trails, and sometimes, there will not even be a pathway. You will have to ride through thickets with thorns, dangers lurk at each turn."

"But the train—"

"The train," he interrupted, "will only take us on the first part of our journey. You will likely curse me before we reach our destination."

"If you are trying to make me change my mind, it won't work."

"Very well. We will be traveling light, so leave everything behind that is not absolutely necessary. A packhorse can only carry so much."

She thought about how heavy her valise was. "I understand."

"Where are you staying here in town?"

"At that small hotel near the cantina."

Wolf Runner looked startled, until he realized she had chosen her hotel to save money. "Do you have a gun to protect yourself?"

"Yes." She took a sip of her apple cider, which had grown cold. "But I hope I don't ever have to use it."

Wondering what he had gotten himself into, Wolf

Runner let out an irritated breath. "I will call for you just before sunrise. Be ready."

"I will." She touched his hand and he pulled back. "How much money does it cost for a horse and saddle? I want to pay my own way."

Wolf Runner wondered why he avoided the touch of her hand, and at the same time, he could not look away from her golden eyes. "We will discuss that later," he said with a finality that left her nothing else to say on the matter. Standing, he nodded toward the window. "It has stopped raining. You might want to take this opportunity to leave before it starts again."

He was so tall she had to look up to see his eyes. He did not look at her the way Mr. Sullivan and other men did—he looked at her with irritation. She preferred to be an annoyance rather than the object of a man's lust.

"Thank you."

Wolf Runner nodded curtly to her, and watched as she moved out the door. She walked with an easy grace, her shoulders straight, her chin tilted upward. There was pride in the young woman, but he feared pride would not sustain her. Life had not been kind to her, and he was sure it was about to get a lot more unkind.

Chapter Fifteen

Cheyenne thought she would have difficulty falling asleep, but the moment her head hit the pillow she knew nothing else. She slept the first dreamless sleep she had had since her gram's death.

Always having been an early riser, she awoke well before daylight and gathered what she thought she would need for the journey. Wolf Runner had told her to travel light, so she would accommodate him. Her comb and brush she tucked into the corner pocket of her valise. She gently wrapped her father's picture and placed it in the bag.

Digging in her valise, she removed her black leather dress shoes and placed them on the floor. She was wearing her boots that laced up her ankle—they would serve her well where she was going.

Achingly she touched the white lace her gram had sewn onto her green gown. Shaking her head regretfully, she put it with the other gowns she was leaving behind, hoping the maid would get some use out of them. Next she unpacked her extra stays and petticoats. She would make do with the ones she was wearing.

Cheyenne picked up the gun that had been Gram's, holding it gingerly by the ivory handle. It was loaded, but it had probably been years since anyone had fired it, and would probably blow up in her face if she pulled the trigger. Tucking it back inside her valise, she shook her head. She had just enough time to write a letter to Maria, telling her all that had happened. The Mendoza family would be upset to learn she was setting off for the unknown, but she wrote about her grandfather, hoping they would understand her need to be with family. She thought it wise not to mention Wolf Runner. She promised to write them when she reached her destination.

Cheyenne quickly braided her hair and wrapped it about the back of her head, as she usually did.

She kept her sewing kit and a few other treasured mementos that would mean nothing to anyone but her. Lastly, she packed the shawl Gram had knitted her and placed it lovingly into the valise.

Recounting her money, Cheyenne kept out enough for postage for Maria's letter.

How much does a good horse cost? she wondered. She would also need a saddle and tack. *Can I buy them with the money I have left?* She wasn't sure.

Then there would be food and supplies for the journey. She certainly did not want Wolf Runner to buy what she needed, although he said they would settle up later.

Gram had taken care of their expenses, and Cheyenne was beginning to understand just how little she knew of finances. Gram had raised her for a life of privilege, while she was headed for a life of great want.

With a resigned sigh, she lifted her valise, which was now considerably lighter. Stopping by the front desk, she paid her bill and gave the clerk Maria's letter and the money for postage.

Stepping outside, into the clear light of dawn, Cheyenne questioned her sanity for attempting such a journey.

*I must be out of my mind to start on such an excursion
with a man I hardly know.*

Still, what else could she do?

Like Gram always said, "Let Providence take care
of today, and let tomorrow take care of tomorrow."

Wolf Runner watched Cheyenne come down the steps
in front of her hotel, feeling a slight pull at his heart
because she looked so forlorn. Who wouldn't feel
pity for a young woman who faced such an uncertain
future? The life she had led with her white grandmother had not prepared her for what awaited her
among the Cheyenne in Montana.

When she paused on the bottom step, he drew in
his breath as the sun shimmered across her face, and
he could not help but think how delicate she appeared.

When their gazes met, he could tell that she did
not entirely trust him. In fact, he could feel the chill
of her gaze all the way to his bones. If she only knew
how safe she would be with him. He was not attracted
to her—she was too much like a white woman to interest him. She was much too opinionated—always
saying the first thing that came to her mind. She was
going to give him trouble, he knew it.

Yet he had never seen a woman with such a stead-
fast fortitude, other than his mother. If he had been a
betting man, he would wager Ivy Gatlin had had iron
in her backbone, and had passed it on to her granddaughter. He would just see if Cheyenne Gatlin's fortitude lasted throughout the rigorous journey ahead
of them. The first part would not be difficult—but
the true test would come when they left all comforts
behind and traveled through the mountainous wilderness.

As Cheyenne approached, he noticed her valise was lighter. He recalled when she boarded the train she had had trouble lifting it. He was satisfied she would do as she was told.

"Let us go. The train is due any moment."

In no time they were seated on the train with her valise between them. Wolf Runner watched her as she glanced out the window.

"I can guess what you are thinking."

"I imagine not," she said, turning to him.

"You are thinking you are leaving everything behind that is dear and familiar to you."

Her eyes widened. "How did you know?"

"I had somewhat the same feelings when I left home to go to school in Washington. I wanted the days to pass quickly so I could return home. I still have those feelings whenever I am away."

She turned back to the window and said so quietly he could hardly catch her words, "But you had a home and a family to return to. I will not be coming back."

Through the day, the train chugged up steep hills and passed wide mesas. Cheyenne watched the countryside roll by, feeling numb inside as the familiar scenery changed to flat bushes and hilly land.

When night descended, Cheyenne closed her eyes and slept, gripping her shawl tightly, not knowing Wolf Runner watched her in the dimly lit car.

He wondered what she looked like with her hair loose. She always wore it braided and twisted around the back of her head primly. Her long lashes lay like shadows against her cheeks. Her features caught and held his attention—she was perfect in every way, her nose just the right size, her lips full and beautifully shaped. He had seen many pretty women in his life, but none with Cheyenne's haunting beauty.

He shook his head and turned away from her. He was promised to Blue Dawn, and he should not be thinking of another woman in such a way—especially not this woman, who carried the blood of his enemy in her veins.

Three days later found them in Silverland, Colorado, and the mountain air had a bite to it.

Wolf Runner had left Cheyenne in the lobby of a hotel while he went to the blacksmith shop to buy a packhorse, and Cheyenne a horse and saddle. Then he went into the general store and purchased the supplies they would need.

Cheyenne watched out the front window of the hotel as the town of Silverland came to life. The day was overcast and it looked like it might rain. She hoped not.

Glancing down at her heavy muslin traveling gown, she wondered if it was appropriate for a journey where she would be spending hours in the saddle. It must do—she had nothing else to wear.

The lobby clock chimed the eleventh hour and still Wolf Runner had not returned for her. For just a moment she panicked. What if he abandoned her—what would she do? Placing her hand on the windowpane, Cheyenne glanced nervously down the dusty road. She breathed a sigh of relief when she saw Wolf Runner leading a packhorse loaded with supplies, and two other horses.

Her eyes widened in surprise as she saw a large dog lumbering along beside him. She had known his horse traveled in the stock car, but he did not tell her anything about a dog.

Breathing deeply, she stepped out of the hotel and waited for him on the steps. Her heart was beating wildly—it was one thing to be with Wolf Runner on a train where there were people about, and quite another to be alone with him on the trail.

As he approached, Cheyenne noticed he was appraising her, no doubt speculating how serviceable her wearing apparel was for a trek in the wilderness. Then he stared straight into her eyes, and she dropped her gaze against his intense gaze, so dark and seeking.

They had been together for three days, and in that time he had said very little to her, but his eyes said much—she just did not know how to interpret his moods.

Cheyenne told herself she could still back out and return to New Mexico.

She shook herself mentally; no she could not. She would only go forward, so she walked down the steps toward Wolf Runner.

Chapter Sixteen

"I insist on paying for my horse and my share of the supplies," Cheyenne said as she came down the wooden steps, eyeing the dog that had come to heel at Wolf Runner's feet.

Wolf Runner cast her a quelling glance. "We will speak of that later. Let us hope you know how to ride a horse," he stated calmly.

Cheyenne's eyes flashed with irritation. "Of course I can ride. Every woman in New Mexico Territory knows how to ride a horse."

Taking her valise and securing it to the packhorse, he nodded at the pinto. "That will be your mount," he prompted, swinging onto his own mount, which he rode without a saddle. "I hope you can handle him."

"Just because I wasn't born in an Indian village, doesn't mean I can't handle a spirited horse."

"We shall see about that."

Though angered by his tone, Cheyenne chose not to reply. That was when she noticed Wolf Runner's attention was centered on her traveling gown, and she could tell he thought she was improperly dressed for the journey.

Cheyenne touched a pleat on her traveling gown. "I have no proper riding habit." Why hadn't he gotten her a sidesaddle?

"Where we are going no one has even heard of a 'proper' riding habit," he said. "Mount up."

Cheyenne had the feeling he was testing her in some way, and she did not intend to rise to the bait.

"Will your dog follow us?" she asked, kneeling beside the animal and rubbing the stiff hair on its back.

"Don't touch him!" Wolf Runner warned. "Move back slowly."

But it was too late—Cheyenne had already laid her face against Satanta's head. Wolf Runner tensed. Satanta had never taken well to strangers.

Wolf Runner dismounted and moved closer to Satanta, placing a hand on the wolf's head.

"Stand back, Miss Gatlin. Slowly. Satanta is not a dog, he is a wolf."

Cheyenne knew Wolf Runner expected her to pull away in fright, but she merely glanced into the animal's eyes and rubbed his ear. In truth Cheyenne felt sudden fear riveting through her body, but she refused to let him see how afraid she was, even when the bitter bile of panic rose in her throat.

A wolf!

She was touching a wolf.

She attempted to make her voice sound normal, but she did not quite succeed. "I have never been this near a real wolf before," she said, hoping Wolf Runner had not seen her hands shaking. "He seems as gentle as a dog."

"Miss Gatlin, Satanta is a wild animal, and if he took it in his head not to like you, he could tear your head off."

She stood, hoping her legs would not collapse beneath her. "But he didn't attack me."

Giving the animal's head a final pat, she moved

slowly away from him, while instinct urged her to run.

Wolf Runner was still shaken by what could have happened to Cheyenne if Satanta had objected to her touching him. "Miss Gatlin, in the future you should not go bounding headlong into danger without thinking."

Cheyenne's sorely tried patience finally crumbled. Throwing her hands up in the air in frustration, she gave him a glacier look, saying, "Well, who would expect someone to bring a wild wolf into a town where there are people about? It just doesn't make any sense to me."

He was startled by her outburst. Wolf Runner was not accustomed to being questioned or chastised. All he could do was frown at Cheyenne as she crammed her boot into the stirrup and mounted her horse, showing a fair amount of petticoat.

When she was settled comfortably in the saddle, she said airily, "I am ready to leave when you are."

His dark gaze pierced hers. "One of the first things I want you to do when we stop today is get out of those petticoats. You cannot ride well with so much heavy clothing."

"No. I certainly will not. And you should not be discussing a woman's undergarments."

His dark eyes smoldered as he mounted his horse, and she sensed danger. She wanted to say more, but the determined expression on his face sealed her lips. She reminded herself she wanted to cause him as little trouble as possible. So far that was not working out so well.

"Did you hear me, Miss Gatlin?"

Cheyenne gritted her teeth. If removing her petticoats would satisfy him, what choice had she? "I heard."

"Well?"

She bit back the words she wanted to say and murmured, "I'll do it."

As they rode out of town, the few people who were up and about seemed to take no notice of them or the giant silver-white wolf running beside Wolf Runner's horse.

"You do know where we are going?" Cheyenne asked because she could not resist provoking him after the petticoat incident.

He gave her a disgruntled nod. "Did you think I would just start in a direction and hope to end up where I wanted to be?"

Her courage left her. "No . . . I—"

"Miss Gatlin," he interrupted. "Where we are going is as familiar to me as Santa Fe is to you."

She bit her lip to keep from delivering the hot retort that came to mind. Wolf Runner perplexed her. Sometimes he seemed to make an effort to be kind to her, and other times he treated her as if he didn't like her at all.

As they left the town behind Wolf Runner ignored Cheyenne and she lapsed into silence.

It was going to be a long journey.

They had been traveling through a deep mesa with terra-cotta-colored bluffs rising on both sides. Half turning in her saddle, Cheyenne watched a thin serpentine curl of smoke evaporate among the low clouds that hovered across the valley. Although it seemed they were traveling in an isolated and inhospitable countryside, she supposed there was a ranch nearby, maybe more than one.

Wolf Runner kept a close eye on the darkening clouds overhead. So far the rain had held off, but he knew it was but a matter of time before they had a downpour. A good soaking would be Miss Gatlin's first discomfort—there would be other challenges before too many days had passed. Her grandmother had raised her to be a lady. He would soon know if she had the courage and stamina of an Indian, or if she would fall apart at the first hardship.

They had been riding quietly until late morning, when Wolf Runner finally called a halt to rest the horses. He uncapped his canteen and handed it to Cheyenne, while Satanta streaked off into the bushes.

Out of the corner of his eye Wolf Runner saw Cheyenne grimace as she dismounted. "Are you doing all right?" he inquired, watching her closely, waiting for her to complain.

Cheyenne would never admit to him that she was weary, or that she ached in the places where her body came in contact with the stiff saddle. "I'm fine." Taking a deep drink, she handed the canteen back to him and wiped her mouth on the back of her hand. "How long will it take to reach my grandfather?"

He took a drink and then gazed into the distance. "I cannot be certain, since I do not know exactly where he is located. What I do know is we will be going through rough country. And we must be alert to danger at all times."

Cheyenne gathered her horse's reins and almost groaned in pain when she settled back into the saddle. "What do you mean by rough and dangerous country?" she asked.

"Outlaws, renegade Indians who have broken away from the reservation, among other dangers."

"Do you mean to frighten me?" She raised her

chin and gave him a haughty glance. "If you are, it's not working."

"Miss Gatlin, you had better be afraid—it could save your life. The country we will be traveling in is harsh and unsettled. Just make certain you do everything I tell you. Stay close to me and do not take it into your head to wander off on your own."

"There will be times when I need privacy."

"I understand that," he bit out, watching her chin go a bit higher.

Wolf Runner suddenly chuckled, his shoulders shaking. "Then again, you might just frighten anyone we meet up with, if you glare at them the way you are glaring at me."

His humor surprised her. She was not accustomed to banter between a man and woman and hardly knew how to react to his lighter mood. Her confusion must have shown on her face because his laughter deepened.

"I need privacy now," she told him with a scowl.

Wolf Runner halted his horse. "This would be a good time for you to remove your petticoats."

Sliding off her horse, she wordlessly stalked off behind a clump of cedar bushes and unhooked, unsnapped, and stepped out of her petticoats and stays, letting the offending garments lay where they landed.

When she returned, Wolf Runner looked at her in satisfaction. Then he noticed the soft outline of her body as her gown fell in soft pleats across rounded hips. His body tightened unexpectedly and he looked away from her.

"Mount up. We do not have all day."

Cheyenne ground her teeth. His light mood had left him. He was as sour as before.

* * *

The rain held off until it was almost sundown, and then it came down in torrents. Lightning split the sky and thunder rumbled in the distance, shaking the ground and echoing off canyon walls.

"We will camp here," Wolf Runner said, swinging off his horse. "I will hobble the horses," he yelled to be heard above the rain. "It would help if you unloaded the packhorse. We will need the blankets and the pouch of dried food. Be sure you cover the rest with the tarp."

Cheyenne quickly complied. With rain peppering against her face and dripping off her chin, she untied the ropes and stacked the supplies against the canyon wall. Removing what they needed, she covered the rest with a heavy tarpaulin, weighing it down with stones.

After Wolf Runner secured the horses Cheyenne watched him cut branches from nearby pine trees. In no time at all, he had fashioned a lean-to with branches and canvas. Pushing a damp strand of hair out of her face, she gratefully crawled beneath the shelter. She was cold, hungry, and miserable, but she would rather have her tongue cut out than admit it.

When Wolf Runner joined her moments later, she could see him clearly in the flickering lightning. She gripped her hands, fearful of being so close to him. In horror, she realized he had stripped off all his clothing except for a breechcloth. Never having seen a man so scantily clad, she turned her back and closed her eyes tightly.

Is he like all the others? Have I been a fool to trust him?

Unaware of her feelings, Wolf Runner brushed Cheyenne's shoulder as he reached up to cover an opening where water was dripping through. "I had hoped the rain would hold off until we were in the high country where there will be more trees to shelter us."

"What you are wearing is not proper," she said, stiffening.

"Miss Gatlin, this is what a Blackfoot warrior wears. And while we are on the subject, you need to get out of your wet clothing, or else you will catch a chill." He picked up one of the blankets and thrust it at her. "I have no intentions of nursing a sick woman."

She thrust the blanket back at him. "I certainly will not remove my clothing. As it is, you already have me down to the bare necessities." She shook her head. "I won't do it," she exclaimed unabashed, clutching her hands into fists. "How can you ask such a thing of me?"

"Shall I do it then?"

Cheyenne shrank away from him. "What are you going to do to me?"

"Miss Gatlin, let me put your mind at ease—you are not at all the kind of woman who draws my attention. And I would never take an unwilling woman. Does that answer all your fears?"

The only part she heard was that he was not attracted to her, and for some reason that brought a dull ache to her heart. "Turn your head," she said ungraciously.

Hearing his soft laughter when she tried to struggle out of her wet clothing while trying to hold the blanket up so he could not see her. It was frustrating. When she finally managed to drape herself in the blanket, she asked, "Shouldn't the wolf be in out of the weather?"

Wolf Runner listened for a moment as the rain peppered against the tarpaulin. "Like any of his kind, Satanta does not like to be confined."

Settling back as some of the chill left her body, Cheyenne asked, "His name—is it from the Blackfoot language?"

He took her wet garment and hung it from one of the rough branches he had used to build the lean-to. "Satanta is actually Kiowa meaning 'white bear.'" He smiled. "When he was born he was a fluff of white. My mother gave Satanta his name."

"But she is white—does she speak Kiowa?"

Wolf Runner was quiet for so long she thought he might not answer. "I do not think of my mother as white, and neither does she. But to answer you, she is intelligent and learns languages quickly—she speaks several dialects."

"Your father must be an exceptional man if she gave up such a successful ranch to be with him."

"He is more than you can imagine," Wolf Runner said as he reached up to close another opening where rain had begun to pour in. "You must be hungry. Choose from any of the dried meat in the leather satchel."

She nodded and opened the bag, taking out two strips of dried meat, and handing one to him.

"Although I'm half Cheyenne, I am not proud of it. I have accepted it because I have no choice. Gram was a fine lady, having grown up on a plantation in North Carolina. She raised me in her traditions. That's why I don't know how to be an Indian."

"I have noticed that. You come from a line of Cheyenne chiefs, from a proud race and you should be proud of that."

She took a bite of the meat and chewed for a moment. "I don't know what waits for me at the end of this journey. The one thing I'm sure of is that life as I know it is over."

He was mystified by her acceptance of what life had handed her. So far she had not complained about anything other than removing her undergarments. "There is truth in that," he told her, watching her nod.

They both lapsed into silence.

At last she spoke, "I want to be of help to you, but I don't know how unless you show me what to do. Tomorrow you could start teaching me to tend the animals," she suggested. "I know I'm capable of that."

He considered her offer for a moment, then said, "I will tend the animals."

It was dim inside the lean-to and she could not see him, but she could certainly feel his presence. "Then tell me what else I can do."

He was not in a mood to teach a sheltered young woman about her Indian heritage. "Eat. Then you must sleep. Tomorrow will be a long day with hard riding. We will soon reach a part of the journey where the terrain is so treacherous we will have to lead the horses."

Cheyenne felt him becoming detached from her, his mind on other matters. She quietly finished her meat, took a drink of water, and lay down. Pulling the blanket tightly about her, she was determined to make sure she gave Wolf Runner no reason to criticize her.

Closing her eyes, Cheyenne listened to the drumming of the rain. "Should we worry about wild animals?"

Wolf Runner smiled, bemused. "We *have* a wild animal. He will let us know if danger approaches."

Baffled, she sighed and sunk heavily into her blanket, falling immediately to sleep.

* * *

Wolf Runner sat in the dark, for the first time feeling guilty that he was using Cheyenne to get to Night Fighter.

He could do nothing but go forward. His path was already set on a course and he would see it through.

Chapter Seventeen

The next morning the sun came out in all its glory, painting the damp land with a golden glow. Cheyenne came out of the lean-to after struggling into her still-damp clothing. She almost went back inside when she saw Wolf Runner was still wearing only his breechcloth. She squeezed her eyes shut tightly, but when he spoke, she glanced at him.

"You must be hungry," he observed, noticing her embarrassment, not that it affected him one way or another.

It felt like her heart flipped over inside her—all semblance of civilization had been stripped away from Wolf Runner. A Blackfoot warrior stood before her—the most handsome man she had ever seen. His muscles were honed and firm, his shoulders were broad, his stomach flat. Cheyenne was so stunned by his appearance she missed the way his eyes darkened and the frown that creased his brow.

"You must eat so we can leave," he said.

"Yes," she agreed, with a catch in her throat, as a jolt went through her body and slowed her breathing. Cheyenne was unable to turn her gaze away from his magnificent body. His long black hair flowed free across his shoulders and was now intertwined with three eagle feathers.

Thinking she was disturbed by his lack of clothing,

a slow grin tilted his mouth. "Cheyenne," he said, using her given name for the first time. "It is natural for a Blackfoot male to dress for the seasons."

Ducking her head, she nodded. "I understand. Please continue in the way of your customs," she told him. "I'm sorry if I made you feel uncomfortable."

He was retrieving the canvas from the lean-to. "I am not the one who is uncomfortable," he told her. Cheyenne had much to learn about Indian customs, but Wolf Runner had no intention of being her teacher. So he reached for his buckskin leggings.

She turned away, her heart beating rapidly. Deciding she needed something to do, she began folding the blankets and repacking their supplies.

With her gaze on her feet, Cheyenne ate two slices of fried bacon and a chunk of hardtack, and then she helped Wolf Runner secure the supplies to the packhorse. She was silent, her thoughts troubled. She was going into the great unknown and she had to be strong.

Quietly, she mounted her horse and they rode together toward the distant mountains, Satanta lumbering along beside them.

In the daytime the air was fresh and invigorating, but when the sun went down, it brought with it a chill that went right through Cheyenne's bones.

There were arduous days when she was so weary she had to hold on to the saddle horn to stay upright. The stalwart, sure-footed horses picked their way across rocky inclines, and sometimes they had to swim the horses across swollen creeks and rivers. The one blessing, Cheyenne assured herself, looking for something positive, was that it had not rained in the last week. She hoped the dry weather would continue.

But later in the day her hopes were dashed; dark clouds gathered on the horizon and a sudden thundershower pelted them. Cheyenne hunched in her saddle until it stopped raining and the clouds dissipated.

By late afternoon the wind whipped up, racing down the hills, spreading its icy fingers against her cheeks.

Now that they were traveling in a higher elevation, the leaves had turned colors, and it was growing colder.

Since they were traveling through clay hills, they often had to dismount and scrape mud off the horses' hooves before they could continue.

Cheyenne dismounted on Wolf Runner's command and went to her knees before Satanta, and patted his rough coat. "It is hard to think of him as a danger to anyone." The animal was affectionate, and she was growing attached to him. She glanced up at Wolf Runner, who was watching the way Satanta curled up beside her. She laughed. "He is more gentle than the dogs on the streets of Santa Fe."

Wolf Runner smiled with irony. "That is because you have charmed him. Believe me when I tell you, Satanta can be dangerous if he feels threatened, or if he thinks I am threatened."

When she smiled up at him, Wolf Runner caught his breath. Her eyes seemed to have picked up the gold of the sun, and her skin was glowing with health and vitality. He was suddenly caught by her beauty, and wondered why he had not felt the full effect of her charms until now. He had never seen her laugh, and it transformed her whole demeanor.

"I'm not afraid of him." Cheyenne's smile turned to laughter. "Although I will admit I was at first."

Wolf Runner knew he had deliberately pushed her hard in the beginning in an attempt to find her breaking point, but she had not broken. He admired that about her.

"How did you get Satanta?" she asked, rubbing the wolf's ear.

"He is one of a pack that belongs to my family. Satanta is the alpha male."

She stood, her eyes wide with surprise. "You have a pack of wolves?"

"It would be more correct to say they belong to my mother. All of them are descendants from a she-wolf my father gave her before I was born—in fact, before they were husband and wife."

"You are fortunate to have such animals. This one is devoted to you."

"He was devoted to me before you came along." Wolf Runner ruffled Satanta's fur. "I believe he has deserted me for you."

Laughter bubbled out of her mouth. "I don't think that could happen. He tolerates me because you do." She met his gaze. "You do tolerate me, don't you?"

"It seems the fates have thrown us together, Miss Gatlin," Wolf Runner answered evasively, reverting to her formal title. "And that same fate will part us when you are safe with your family."

Cheyenne turned her back to him, suddenly struck with a pain she could not understand. For now, Wolf Runner was the only person she had in her life who was familiar to her. The thought of being parted from him was almost unbearable. He was the rock she depended on, and at the same time, her tormentor.

"How much farther until we make camp?" she asked, forcing her mind in a different direction.

Glancing skyward, he judged the time. "We have another two hours of daylight left. Tomorrow we come to the most dangerous part of our journey. We will walk most of the day."

Although she was no longer sore from riding, walking sounded like a good change to her.

"Are you a good walker, Miss Gatlin?" he asked, uncapping his canteen and handing it to her.

There had been a bite to his tone and she resented his testing her at every turn. Certainly the softness she had felt for him moments ago had all but disappeared. "Gram said I learned to walk before I was nine months old." She raised her gaze to his. "I have been walking ever since."

Wolf Runner threw back his head and laughed. The way she could suddenly disarm him took him by surprise.

That night they found a narrow cave halfway up a cliff. Outside the wind howled and pitched, and rain drove into the front of the cave. But for the first time since leaving Colorado, they were safe from the elements, if only for this one night.

By now Cheyenne was becoming adept at lighting the campfire and she had a fire going when Wolf Runner entered with a rabbit he had already skinned and gutted. He handed it to her and she slipped it onto a spit, her mouth already watering for the taste of fresh roasted meat.

Dusting her hands, she stood. "Am I not becoming a Cheyenne maiden?" she asked, smiling.

He could not look away. She drew him to her in a way that he could not explain, and he did not like it. She was almost childlike now as she waited for him to compliment her on her accomplishments. But something inside him kept him from praising her. "You still have much to learn. Living in the white world for so long robbed you of the instincts any Indian maiden is born with."

Cheyenne ducked her head, feeling the sting of his words. "It is true, I do have much to learn."

"Give it time."

"What will it be like in the Cheyenne village?"

"Since the Cheyenne escaped from the reservation in Indian Territory some years back, they live much as they always have."

"They escaped the reservation?"

"They did. And they stubbornly hung on to what was theirs. In the end, they were allowed to stay on their land in Montana, even though they are under government supervision."

"That's admirable."

"You may well think so. But their life is hard, and their women and children are often malnourished when game is scarce. They are a proud people and decided not to live under the white man's yoke, but they are often without hope."

Cheyenne's eyes widened with horror. "Do you think my grandfather lives without hope?"

"I cannot speak about him personally." Wolf Runner had been thinking he needed to explain some things to her, and now was a good time. "Have you considered your grandfather might not be alive?"

Cheyenne nodded. "I have considered that. If he is dead, surely my mother's people will welcome me to live with them."

Wolf Runner thought of how her beauty would stir the heart of many young warriors, and she would be unprotected and innocent of their ways. He did not like the thought of her becoming the woman of one of the Cheyenne warriors. He bedded down near the entrance and watched her place her bedroll in the back of the cave. It was good that she was some distance from him tonight because she was beginning to trouble his mind.

Cheyenne had a lot to think about. The campfire had died down and turned to glowing embers before she finally slept.

Chapter Eighteen

For most of the morning they rode over steep hills, and the horses had to go slow as they picked their way through the razor-sharp rocks.

By midafternoon they left the hills behind and began their ascent into the high country. As they climbed, the horses slowed, and Wolf Runner instructed Cheyenne to dismount. They walked the horses across a narrow ledge where if they strayed but an inch either way they would tumble into a deep precipice.

Breathing with relief, she was glad when they left the steep cliffs behind, but that was before they came upon volcanic hills.

As they walked along, Cheyenne could feel every pebble and stone through the thin soles of her boots, which were falling apart. When one of her laces broke, she found it doubly hard to walk, but she dared not ask Wolf Runner to stop so she could mend her lace.

Cheyenne chided herself for not purchasing another pair of boots. She had been totally unprepared for this journey and could not have guessed the hardships they would endure, even though Wolf Runner had warned her what to expect.

However, he seemed to take the hardships all in stride, and she was sure he expected her to as well.

Weariness tore at Cheyenne's muscles. When she stumbled, she barely managed to keep her feet.

Glancing over at Wolf Runner, she would not have known him for the same man she'd met in Santa Fe. Gone was the veneer of civilization he had adopted in town. He seemed as one with this harsh, rugged land. His dark hair flowed loosely about his shoulders. He walked with the grace of a predatory cat and Cheyenne could see by the tilt of his chin that it was his pride that gave him an edge of arrogance.

When they remounted their horses, a feeling of kinship swelled Cheyenne's heart. Something inside reached that part of her that was Indian—her spirit cried out to Wolf Runner's, but his did not answer.

He glanced back at her and nodded indifferently. "Keep up. You are lagging behind."

She kicked her horse in the flanks and the spirited animal leaped forward.

When she rode even with Wolf Runner, he turned to her abruptly. "Let us hurry so we can be out of this canyon before dark. There is nowhere to camp among the lava rocks."

Wolf Runner saw how pale she was, and said with concern, "I know you are tired, but we cannot stop to rest here. It is raining in the mountains and this valley will become a rushing torrent of water in a few hours."

"I can manage," she assured him, hoping she could.

Cheyenne thought they would never reach the end of the valley, but at last the land sloped upward again. As they climbed higher, Cheyenne could see wide stretches of prairie far into the distance.

"Are you now able to tell me how far it is to the place my grandfather lives?" she asked, wishing the long trek were over.

He regarded her pensively. "It will take as long as it takes."

Satanta came bounding out of the bushes and trotted alongside Cheyenne, staying even with her horse.

"Traitor," Wolf Runner said, smiling.

Cheyenne gave Wolf Runner a mischievous grin. "He goes to the one who feeds him the most often." She tried not to laugh at the condemning expression on Wolf Runner's face, but the laugh came out in a choking sound. "I have been sneaking him food."

"It is not food that buys his loyalty—give him the sight of a beautiful face and he forgets all about loyalty."

Cheyenne looked at Wolf Runner quickly. Did that mean *he* thought she was beautiful?

Reaching behind him, Wolf Runner pulled his rifle out of the saddle holster and pointed it toward a misshaped pine tree that clung to the rock face of the mountainside. "Rest there for a while," he said, dismounting. "I am going to hunt game. I fancy fresh meat tonight instead of the salted pork."

Nodding, Cheyenne dismounted, so weary she could hardly make her legs move. When Wolf Runner and Satanta were out of sight, she sagged down on a flat boulder, and groaned in pain when her backside came in contact with the hard stone.

She glanced hopelessly at her boots, which were beyond help, with holes in the soles and a broken lace. Setting her jaw stubbornly, she retied the short lace in a double knot.

The sun had dropped behind the mountain and a cold wind now whipped down the gulley. Sliding down, Cheyenne huddled against the cliff, closing her eyes, almost drifting off to sleep.

Her eyes flew open when she heard a horse's whinny from the bend in the trail behind her. Her newly budding instincts took over. Whoever it was wore heavy boots, so it was not an Indian. She had no time to hide before two men came into sight.

But it was too late—they were already upon her before she could react.

One was an older man, perhaps in his early fifties, with a shaggy beard and whiskers. He wore a battered hat and buckskin trousers. The second man was probably ten years younger—he was thin and his beard was scraggly. They both wore heavy buffalo coats, and she could see little of their faces in the gathering dusk.

"Well, lookee what we've got here," the older man said, leading his horse forward. "A pretty little gal."

The younger man grinned, showing brown-stained teeth. "What do you think we should do with her?"

Cheyenne knew she was in danger. Before she could get near enough to her saddlebag to get her gun, the younger man had grabbed her arm in a tight grip and brought her closer to him.

"What'cha doing out here alone?" he wanted to know. "Where's your man got off to?"

"I'm not alone and he'll be back soon," she warned. "You had better leave before he returns. He doesn't take kindly to strangers."

"Well, now don't you speak right good white man for an Injin? What do you think, Ezra?" the younger man asked. "Should we be scared of her man?"

"Willie, it's best if we don't wait 'round to find out. Tie her hands," his companion ordered. "We'll take her and the horses and her man won't be a'catching up with us on foot."

Cheyenne struggled, trying to free herself, but the man called Willie was too strong for her. She cried out when he tied her hands behind her with buck-skin strips.

Willie gave her a shove and prodded her forward with his rifle. "Let's get out'a here. I don't cotton to taking on an Indian buck." He gathered the reins of the horses and the packhorse.

"Let me go," Cheyenne pleaded. "If you don't, Wolf Runner will hunt you down!"

"Keep quiet," Ezra ordered. "And get a'goin'."

Willie looked over his shoulder worriedly. "She might be right."

"Let's ride," Ezra said, mounting his horse and look-ing nervously over his shoulder.

Before Wolf Runner approached the place where he had left Cheyenne he sensed something was wrong.

It was too quiet.

When he emerged from the thicket Cheyenne was nowhere to be seen, and neither were the horses. Bending, he examined the hard-packed ground. There were tracks of two shod horses and two men wearing boots.

The trees were too dense and the trail curved so he could not see anything up ahead. He was desper-ate, his heart beating in fear for Cheyenne. Climbing higher up the hill so he could see farther into the distance, his heart stopped when he located Cheyenne being taken away by two white men.

His lip curled in disgust.

Trappers. In their own way they were as bad as the buffalo hunters who had senselessly depleted the herds—trappers were after furs and cared nothing about the meat that sustained his people.

Feeling helpless when he watched Cheyenne strug-gling with one of the men, he could sense her fear like a knife in his heart. Her hands were tied behind her and she had no chance of escaping.

Sliding back down the hill, Wolf Runner knew he had to catch up with them, but they had horses, and he did not.

Satanta sensed something was wrong and circled Wolf Runner, his yellow eyes staring into Wolf Runner's as if he was waiting for a command to spring into action.

Those men would easily outdistance Wolf Runner if they were in open country, but their progress would be slowed because of the mountains. He must reach them before they came upon the open prairie or he would never catch them. Desperation gripped him, and he shuddered to think of Cheyenne being in the hands of those men. Clasping his rifle, he started off at a run, Satanta at his side.

They had not gone far when Ezra's horse stumbled on the steep incline and developed a limp, slowing them down considerably. With a string of loud curses, he removed his saddle and placed it on Wolf Runner's horse. Since the animal had never felt a saddle on his back, he immediately reared and kicked, drawing more curses from Ezra.

"What's wrong with this damned critter?" Ezra shouted.

Willie scratched his beard. "You're forgetting he belonged to an Injin. I'd say he's never been saddle broke. If you want to ride him, it'll have to be bareback."

"I ain't never rode without no saddle. It ain't civilized."

"Well," Willie speculated, "if'n you're planning on

riding that horse, you'd better learn right quick. Leave your saddle behind."

"Are you crazy? I ain't doing no such thing. That saddle cost me fifteen dollars."

"It ain't gonna do you no good. Both these Indian horses are better than these two of ours." Willie's gaze swept the steep incline they had just left, and he felt unease stir within him. "You'd better make up your mind quicklike. I don't want to give her man a chance to catch up to us."

Ezra mumbled as he tossed the saddle to the side of the trail and climbed onto Wolf Runner's horse, abandoning his own mount. "I'm gonna be sorry I done that," he gritted out, moving the horse on down the trail.

Cheyenne was having troubles of her own. Since her hands were tied behind her, she couldn't grip the reins and kept sliding sideways when her horse took a step. It was only the strength in her legs that allowed her to stay in the saddle.

"Like I said, it ain't civilized."

"Quit your damned griping. We gotta get out of these mountains." Willie glanced over at Cheyenne and took the reins of her horse, leading it forward. "Just think what we get to do to this little Injin gal when we camp tonight."

The trapper's words struck fear in Cheyenne. There was not a chance Wolf Runner would catch up with them on foot. If she were going to escape, she would have to watch for an opportunity.

Ezra was having a difficult time controlling Wolf Runner's spirited horse, and that could work to her advantage since his attention was centered on managing the animal.

It was only a short time later when Cheyenne finally got her chance. At a wide curve in the trail, she jabbed her heels into her horse's flanks and the animal tore the reins out of Willie's hand and shot forward down the narrow path. She figured it would be hard for them to overtake her since there was a sheer drop-off on one side of the trail and the rock face of a cliff on the other.

Cheyenne had not gone far when she realized her mistake—with her hands tied behind her, she couldn't control her horse, and she was having a difficult time remaining in the saddle. She stiffened her resolve, knowing what would happen to her if she did not escape. Her leg muscles ached from the pressure she was applying to her horse's flanks, but somehow she held on. Her horse was galloping now, and she slipped sideways. There was no way to catch herself when she pitched forward and fell to the ground.

Pain tore into her head as she struck the rocky cliff, and then slid to the ground, dazed. Cheyenne's head was spinning and she closed her eyes, hoping the world would right itself.

"Now lookee here what she's gone and done," Willie remarked in an agitated voice. Dismounting, he bent down beside Cheyenne, striking her hard with his open hand. "You was plumb stupid to think you could get away from us."

Although pain exploded in her head from the force of Willie's blow, she kept her eyes closed, pretending to be unconscious. She was aware that both men knelt down beside her because she could smell their foul stench.

"Sure is a little beauty, don't you think, Willie? I ain't never had me no Injin gal afore."

Willie shook his head. "Quit your thinking 'bout

that. We got to get her up and moving. Her man will be coming after her—don't you ever think he won't be. No matter what you heard to the contraire, those bucks value their women."

When Ezra tried to pick up Cheyenne, she made herself limp so he had a hard time holding her. "She can't ride—and neither can I—not on that devil horse."

Cheyenne gulped and drew in a deep breath when the older man uncapped his canteen and splashed water in her face. Her eyes flew open. "I figured you was just pretending," he said, his blue gaze cold.

When he stood Cheyenne on her feet, she tried to twist away from him.

Willie gripped her arm and shook her. "Gal, if you try anything like that again, it'll be the worse for you." He lowered his head, looking her straight into the eyes. "You're lucky I don't kill you here and now and leave you for buzzards' pickings."

To prove his point, he slammed his fist into her chin, and this time Cheyenne cried out in pain.

Now her head and her chin throbbed. But she was still determined to find a way to slow them down so Wolf Runner could catch them. Faking a sigh, she slid to the ground.

"Look what you've gone and done," Ezra said. "You didn't have to hit her so hard."

"She's faking again," the younger man stated. "Do with her what you want. I don't fancy having my scalp hanging on some Injin's lodge pole. She's yours to look after."

"I'll ride her horse and you hand her up to me. Don't know why I didn't think on that afore."

That certainly was not what Cheyenne wanted. She was revolted just thinking about being close to either one of the men. But she had no say in the matter.

She was soon settled in Ezra's arms, and the smell of him made bile rise in her throat. As they started off, she kept her eyes closed, even when his hand landed on her breast and he squeezed so hard it hurt. If her hands were not tied she would have fought him. Words of protest rose in her throat, but she didn't speak them. She was helpless and must endure his repulsive touch for the time being. Anger rose inside her, but she held it in check by the primal instinct to survive.

Wolf Runner, she cried silently, *find me!*

Chapter Nineteen

Night had fallen by the time they made it out of the mountains, and Cheyenne could no longer pretend to be unconsciousness. Ezra jabbed her hard in the ribs and she cried out in pain.

The motion of the horse made her dizzy and her stomach churned. Weak and aching, she was having difficulty holding up her head. She closed her eyes, hoping that when she opened them everything would not be spinning.

But it was.

The man was rubbing his hands over her breasts and she thought at that moment if she had a knife she would drive it into his heart. She tried to move away from him, but he only pulled her back to rest against his smelly buffalo hide coat. Wrinkling her nose in disgust, she knew she would have to bear him touching her. But it was hard.

Ezra whispered close to her ear. " 'Bout time you woke up," he said, jerking her head up and watching anger sparkle in her eyes. "I got me plans for you tonight. You're such a pretty gal, I might just decide to keep you for a spell."

She shuddered as his hand moved up her neck. "Take your hands off me," she said between clenched teeth.

"Damn, Willie, this here little Injin gal's got spunk. I'm gonna like doing things to her. You can have her after I'm through if you want."

"I ain't taking your leavings. Maybe I'll have a go at her first."

"You ain't having her first," Ezra protested. "I'll slit your throat from cleft to gullet if you was to try that."

"Wolf Runner will slit both your throats," Cheyenne said with a bravado she was far from feeling. She shouldered Ezra's hand away when it tightened about her. "I told you not to touch me."

"I ain't scared of no Injin. 'Sides, he can't catch up with us. Ain't no man can run this far or this fast for very long."

Cheyenne feared he was right—no human could catch them now. Even Wolf Runner would have to rest sometime.

Without hope of rescue, she feared what her fate would be at the hands of these men. She was even more frightened when they stopped for the day to make camp.

Willie pulled Cheyenne off the horse and set her on her feet. "Stay there and don't try nothin'."

Once Ezra had started the campfire, he removed a gold pocket watch from his coat and dangled it over the flames, watching it sparkle. "I've sure took a liking to this here timepiece," he said.

Willie snorted, "You didn't have to kill the sheepherder to get it—you could have just stole it."

"In the first place, I don't like sheepherders, and second of all, he made me plumb mad."

"Shut up, Ezra. I don't care if you are my brother, you had no call to take his wife to the woods and diddle around with her. That's what ain't right. I make me a habit of not fooling 'round with another man's wife. And there was no need to kill 'em both. You could have let that woman live."

Ezra nodded at Cheyenne. "What about her? She's got her a man. Should we let her go?"

Willie cut his gaze toward the older man and muttered a curse under his breath. "You ain't got the sense Mother Nature gave a peanut. You can't go 'round comparing any Injin with no sheepherder. Injins just don't count for much."

Cheyenne pulled at her restraints, but they held tight. She would not give up without a fight.

Wolf Runner was not even winded as he came down out of the mountains just as the sun sank low, painting the sky a deep purple. He was accustomed to running for hours without end, and it was no hardship for him to do so now.

But he had never been this desperate.

He paused beside the discarded saddle he found abandoned on the trail and struck a flint so he could examine the ground around it. There were four horses and his packhorse, one was Cheyenne's—the one not shod was his. One of the men's horses had gone lame.

Wolf Runner saw the signs that someone had tried to put a saddle on his mount. He smiled, knowing his horse would not allow anyone to put a saddle on him.

In the gathering darkness it was difficult to pick up the tracks, but it looked as though the men were staying on the trail—if they were, he would find them. "Come on, Satanta," he told the wolf. "Find Cheyenne."

As if he understood his master, Satanta put his nose to the ground and started off at a lope. Satanta could track anything with his keen sense of smell. And he was already on Cheyenne's trail.

The men were going about setting up camp and seemed unconcerned about being followed. Cheyenne kept twisting her hands, trying to work them free, but it was useless. Ezra had tied her to a scrub tree, and the rawhide was biting into her wrists.

With growing desperation, Cheyenne watched while Willie used his knife to open a can of beans, dumping them into an iron pot. They sizzled and the aroma immediately wafted toward Cheyenne and her stomach tightened with revulsion. Her head was throbbing and she was still sick to her stomach.

The world tilted and she closed her eyes. The fall from her horse must have hurt her more than she had at first thought. Or maybe it had been Willie's fist.

Her fate rested in the hands of these two men who had no honor.

Cheyenne slowly opened her eyes. Beyond the circle of light reflected by the glowing campfire, it was dark and foreboding. She wanted to cry, but she must show no fear. That would only feed Ezra's lust. She watched Ezra walk into the darkness and a short time later return with an armload of wood.

"Did you hear that wolf?" he asked his brother. "Sounds like it's nearby."

"I heard it," Willie said as he went through the stolen supplies from the packhorse.

"Don't you think we'd best keep the fire up all night?"

"It ain't gonna bother us, Ezra. Stop whining."

Cheyenne felt the first hope bloom in her heart. She had heard the wolf too, but had not considered it might be Satanta.

Was it possible?

No.

Even if Wolf Runner walked all night, he would not reach her in time. And no man could run for such a distance—it would be impossible.

There was grim desperation in Wolf Runner's hurried stride. He had been running full out for hours, and his chest burned from lack of air. But still he did not slow his pace, and neither did Satanta, although Wolf Runner knew the wolf was tiring.

Just ahead through a small clearing of trees, Wolf Runner glimpsed a flicker of light. And hope gave him new energy. He had to reach Cheyenne before those men did anything to her. She had been in his care and he had been negligent, allowing her to be captured.

It was his fault.

He was filled with anger and bloodlust. Too much time had passed—if they were going to harm Cheyenne, the deed was already done. Hatred burned in Wolf Runner's heart for the men who had taken her captive. If she had been a white woman, they may have merely robbed her and left her on the trail—but those men were trappers—he had smelled their stench—and they would have had no compunction about taking an Indian woman.

He knew their kind; when they looked at Cheyenne they would see only that she was an Indian.

At last he was near enough to see the campfire, and his gaze flickered over the crackling flames. The clouds had parted enough to let the quarter moon shine down upon the land with a faint light. Wolf Runner saw the horses had been hobbled, and he saw the faint outline of two men.

Falling on his stomach, he watched the camp, taking in every detail. Wolf Runner's lip curled in distaste as he watched one of them going through his supplies.

Frantically he looked for Cheyenne. When he saw her tied to a tree, he was relieved she was still alive. Stealthily moving closer, his gaze perused her face—she looked pale, and sick.

He was seething inside, and rage almost choked him. What had they done to her?

His eyes narrowed as he watched one of the men untie Cheyenne and drag her to her feet.

She struggled and tried to twist away, but with her hands tied behind her she could do nothing to help herself.

Wolf Runner rose in a rush when the man struck her with his fist doubled.

Cheyenne's knees buckled and she fell to the ground.

Shaking her head, she glared up at Ezra. "If you touch me, Wolf Runner will kill you!"

"Your man's way back there in the darkness and he ain't never gonna catch up with us, so just save your threats."

Cheyenne managed to stand, but she had to brace herself against the trunk of a pine tree. "He will find you."

The trapper grabbed her arm and yanked her forward and she spit in his face. Ezra merely laughed and wiped the back of his hand over his face. "Go ahead and fight me. I like it that way. Or you can come with me peaceful-like, but either way I'm gonna have you, pretty little Injin gal."

With grim determination, Wolf Runner silently moved forward, gripping his knife and carrying his rifle. When he and the wolf entered the encampment at a run, Wolf Runner yelled out an order in Blackfoot, "Kill, Satanta!"

The wolf was airborne, going for the throat of the man who had been tormenting Cheyenne.

Wolf Runner's attention centered on the other man, who was edging toward his rifle. "Do not try it," Wolf Runner warned him.

"What you want with us?" Willie cringed in terror. "Call off the wolf. We weren't going to hurt your woman any. We'd of left her for you when we was done with her."

A quick sideways glance told Wolf Runner that Satanta had the other man on the ground, tearing at his throat—the man thrashed about and a gurgling sound told Wolf Runner he was near death.

"That there's my brother. You're wolf's killing him. Call him off, mister. Do it now."

"Your brother is dead. And you will soon join him."

Cheyenne turned toward a tree and hid her eyes, not wanting to witness the horror of what was happening to Ezra. When it was quiet, she opened them again and saw blood pooled at the trapper's head, soaking into the ground around him.

"Are you all right, Cheyenne?" Wolf Runner asked, not taking his eyes off the white man.

"Yes," she answered with tears running down her face. "I am, now that you're here."

He saw Willie dive for his rifle, but before the man could even touch the stock, Wolf Runner's knife sailed through the air and struck the man in the heart. He did not even make a sound as he fell over dead, and Wolf Runner turned away, hurrying toward Cheyenne.

She ran to him and he caught her in his arms. He

felt her trembling and held her even closer. "Did they hurt you?" he asked, cutting her restraints with his spare knife.

She shivered. "Nothing I couldn't bear." She pressed her face against his shoulder. "He touched me. I want to wash my whole body."

Wolf Runner rested his chin on the top of her head. "I will find a stream and you can wash." He raised her face to his. "Did he—"

She smiled through her tears, knowing what he was asking. "No. I am no worse than I was except for the bumps and bruises."

Wolf Runner noticed her face was swollen and bruised. "I am sorry I left you to face those men alone. It was my fault they captured you."

Moving her head so she could look into his eyes, Cheyenne took his face in her hands, and it seemed the most natural thing in the world. "It is not your fault those men kidnapped me. You are the one who saved me."

She wanted him to hold her forever, but Wolf Runner dropped his arms and moved away from her.

The wolf came to her, his yellow eyes staring into Cheyenne's. When she bent down to Satanta, he flopped down on the ground as if nothing out of the ordinary had happened.

She laughed as Satanta continued to stare at her. "You are my hero," she told the wolf.

Cheyenne dropped to her knees beside the wolf, feeling almost lighthearted as relief still washed over her. "You are wonderful," she told Satanta, sliding her fingers lovingly through his thick fur and pressing her face against the wild animal that had just killed a man and was capable of killing her.

Satanta pressed against Cheyenne and laid his head

on her leg, while Wolf Runner looked on amazed that his wolf should so totally accept Cheyenne's overture, especially when he had just made a kill.

"We must leave this place as soon as possible," Wolf Runner said, pouring water onto the campfire and listening to it hiss. "We do not know who might have seen the campfire."

Cheyenne stood. Wolf Runner had killed for her today, and she was glad he had put an end to those evil men's lives. They would never be able to hurt anyone else as they had the sheepherder and his wife, or do to any woman what they had intended to do to her.

But she was safe now.

If only her head would stop aching, and the world would stop spinning.

Chapter Twenty

Wolf Runner hurriedly gathered their supplies and reloaded them onto the packhorse. He cut the hobble on the horse that had belonged to the trappers, turning it loose.

Cheyenne was still feeling light-headed and leaned against a tree for support. "Aren't we going to bury these men?" she asked dispassionately.

"They do not deserve it. By morning the buzzards will arrive and nature will take care of the remains."

Shaking and pale, Cheyenne braced her hand against a tree in an attempt to steady herself. "But we should—" Her voice trailed into silence as she considered if she really cared whether Willie and Ezra were buried or rotted where they lay. What was wrong with her—even if those men were evil they deserved to be buried. "Wolf Runner, why can't we just bury them in a shallow grave?"

Wolf Runner swung around and pinned her with a glare. "It is not the Blackfoot way. I will hear no more about this."

Cheyenne watched him retrieve his knife from Willie's carcass and wipe the blood off the blade on Willie's shirt. She looked into Wolf Runner's eyes, and they still held a hint of anger, so she made no further objection.

Tonight she had seen the real Wolf Runner. The

two white men had never stood a chance against him.

There was a part of Cheyenne that had been fascinated by his daring and courage, and another part of her had been frightened by his ruthlessness. She was sure her mother's people would be much the same. How would she ever fit into a culture where life had so little value?

Of course she was not sorry the men were dead—they had admitted to killing a man and a woman, and they would have done unspeakable things to her if Wolf Runner had not saved her.

Allowing the matter to drop, Cheyenne lifted her saddle and placed it on her horse, tightening the cinch. "Will we make camp nearby?"

Mentally Wolf Runner looked her over. Her eyes were wide with the horror she had witnessed and she seemed ready to collapse. "We must ride a distance," he said with a kindness she had not expected, considering his mood. "We do not know if these men had companions that will come along later. Do you feel you are up to going on?"

Under Wolf Runner's watchful gaze, she swung into the saddle. Managing a weak smile, she said, "I'm up to it." Cheyenne hoped she was, but she wasn't even sure she would be able to stay astride her horse because the dizziness was getting worse, and everything was whirling about her.

But Wolf Runner had not noticed. After mounting his horse, he glanced about to see if he had overlooked anything. His gaze skimmed over the two dead trappers with no more emotion than he would have felt for a flea on a dog. "Let us leave this place," he said, urging his horse forward.

Cheyenne was glad that clouds now covered the

moon so she could not see the scene of death and carnage they were leaving behind.

They had been riding for over an hour and Cheyenne was not sure how much longer she could go on.

She was relieved when Wolf Runner finally halted his horse beside a creek and turned to look at her.

"You said you wanted to wash. There is ice in the water and it will be cold. But it is neither swift nor deep, so there is no danger."

Resolutely, Cheyenne slid off her horse, already unlacing her dress. Despite feeling dizzy, she hurried toward the creek. "I don't care if it is cold." She ripped off the traveling gown and tossed it to the ground, knowing she would never wear it again.

Wolf Runner had turned away to gather wood for a campfire. "After you have rested and warmed yourself, we must ride farther before we stop for the night."

"I will hurry," Cheyenne said, testing the water with her toe and shivering.

After Wolf Runner had built a campfire, he stood with his back to the creek. He could hear Cheyenne splashing in the water and he closed his eyes, imagining his hands were touching her. When he heard her make a small shivering noise, he wished it was his kiss that had made her react in such a way.

Wolf Runner heard her come out of the water, and without turning, handed her a blanket. He did not look at her until she was wrapped in the blanket and sat trembling with cold before the fire.

Long, wet hair clung to the sides of her face and her lips were trembling with cold. "The water was so icy it was painful," she said, her teeth chattering. "But I'm glad I washed."

Wolf Runner's gaze dropped to her shapely legs, which were not entirely covered by the blanket, and he turned away, not wanting to think about her naked body beneath that covering.

"When you are warm, you should dress," he said huskily.

When Cheyenne nodded, the movement of her head sent the world spiraling around her. "I'll do that right away."

The pale moon cast very little light as they rode across the creek. They had been riding for some time when Cheyenne realized she could no longer sit her saddle. With a cry of alarm, she slid sideways and landed on the hard ground. She must have blacked out for a moment because when she came to her senses, Satanta was licking her face and Wolf Runner was bending down beside her.

She tried to rise. "I'm . . . sorry."

Wolf Runner gathered her in his arms, holding her as gently as he would have held a baby. "You should have told me you were ill," he whispered against her cheek. "I would not have pushed you so hard."

Then for a long moment he just held her, saying nothing.

Too weak to speak, Cheyenne nestled closer to him. She felt safe and warm in his arms and there was nowhere else she wanted to be.

When Cheyenne awoke, the sun was streaming through a pine grove. Sitting up quickly, she looked about her, but Wolf Runner was nowhere to be seen. She had a moment of unease, trying to remember what had happened. Then it all came back to her in a flash and she was momentarily terrified of being alone. That was when she saw the wolf, and he came to her, dropping down to rest his head on her lap.

She was not alone.

She gripped Satanta's face and made him look at her. "You are a wonderful animal. As mysterious and unpredictable as your master."

Satanta's eyes focused on her and she could see the intelligence in the golden depths. "You stayed here to guard me," she said, laying her cheek against his head.

"I am afraid you are going to spoil my wolf and he will be useless to me," Wolf Runner said, coming into camp and smiling.

Cheyenne watched him drop an armload of wood. "The wolf will always obey you."

"I am not so certain. Lately Satanta prefers your company to mine."

She smiled. "I am glad he has accepted me at all."

"His loyalty has turned to you," Wolf Runner said thoughtfully, wondering how such a thing could happen. "Satanta has become devoted to you." He tossed several logs on the campfire and made a neat stack with the rest.

Cheyenne watched him move toward her, and her heart stopped. When he knelt beside her she could not catch her breath.

He looked her over carefully. "How are you?"

Cheyenne met his worried gaze and reached out to him. "I feel strange."

He tilted her chin and looked into her eyes. "Such a thing sometimes happens when you have a blow to the head." He touched the knot on the back of her head. "Like the one you have."

Her lips curved slightly. "I am even more embarrassed to tell you how I got that knot. Although my hands were tied behind me, I tried to outrun them and fell off the horse."

Standing, Wolf Runner looked down at her, his expression unreadable. "You will rest for today. We will start out early tomorrow morning."

Scrambling to her feet, Cheyenne shook her head. "I can ride on now. I don't want to hold you up."

"You will rest," he reiterated in a strong voice that brooked no disagreement.

The morning was warm, and he had stripped off his shirt. Cheyenne watched Wolf Runner move away, the muscles rippling across his back.

A strong new feeling took hold of her and she did not know how to react. She wanted to be in his arms. She wanted him to hold her like he had when she had been hurt.

The difference between their two worlds yawned between them. In his case, that part of him that was Blackfoot was dominant, and she had been raised as white. She doubted the two of them would ever fully understand each other.

Pushing her troubled thoughts aside, she moved to the campfire where Wolf Runner had meat roasting on a spit and her mouth watered. She did not care what kind of meat it was—she was starved and would have eaten anything at the moment.

He swiveled and looked into her eyes. "Rest. I will bring you meat when it is done."

She nodded and returned to her blanket as a new and troubling thought took hold. Before long they would reach her grandfather's village, and Wolf Runner would leave her.

Turning her head away so Wolf Runner could not

see her face, tears of grief rolled down her cheeks.
With an angry wipe of her hand, Cheyenne gritted
her teeth.

She must not allow him to mean so much in her
life.

Chapter Twenty-one

Somehow Cheyenne's relationship with Wolf Runner had changed. She felt shy with him, especially when he watched her, which he often did. Unlike all the other men Cheyenne had known, with the exception of Señor Mendoza, Wolf Runner did not want anything from her.

Not wanting to think about how she had recently become so drawn to him, she examined her boots and scowled at the holes in the soles.

Wolf Runner knelt beside her, raising her foot, and examining the bottom of her boot.

His gaze met hers accusingly. "You should have told me before now that your boots had worn through," he said, turning the boot over and noticing how small it was. When he glanced back at Cheyenne, he saw her face redden, and he frowned. "Remove your boots and let me see the bottom of your feet," he said in that voice that made it a command and not a request.

Reluctantly she lifted the hem of her gown past her ankles and removed one boot and then the other. "It is of little matter."

Wolf Runner's brow lowered into a scowl when he saw that the bottoms of her feet were bleeding. Gripping her boots, he stood and went to his satchel, where he took out a strip of buckskin, which he placed on a boulder. Using his knife to trace the leather, he made it a fraction smaller than her boot so it would fit snugly inside. Seeing that the laces were broken he replaced them with thin rawhide strips.

When he returned to Cheyenne, he brought a tin of salve, which he rubbed on the bottom of one foot and then the other. At first she winced in pain, and he must have noticed because he gently massaged both feet. She shivered at the gentleness of his touch.

"Thank you," she said, putting on her boots and lacing them past her ankles.

"I know you are uneasy because I left you unprotected and the two men came upon you. I do not want you to worry anymore because if I have to leave you, Satanta will guard you."

"I'm not uneasy." She raised her gaze to his. "I feel safe when you are nearby."

Wolf Runner drew in his breath as he stared at Cheyenne's amber-colored eyes. He suddenly wanted to be the man who would always be responsible for her care and protection.

He was shocked by the new feelings that swamped him. The change in his attitude toward her had happened so suddenly, he had not been aware of it until now. Cheyenne was everything a man would want in his woman; she had beauty of face and of spirit. She had not complained although the journey had been difficult. Cheyenne would be the kind of wife who would go with him to his mountain and glory in the experience.

He was angry with himself for having such thoughts when he was promised to another. Setting his jaw in a hard line, he reminded himself that Cheyenne could be no more to him than the means to get to Night

Fighter. He must take her to her grandfather and be done with her.

There was no place in his life for a half-Indian girl who had been raised as a white woman.

He did not understand her, and he doubted she understood him. But his heart thudded inside him when he thought of lying beside her and holding her in his arms. But Wolf Runner could never hold Cheyenne to him—she was not his.

In an attempt to get his emotions under control, he stared up at the sky, watching a flock of geese migrating before winter set in.

"I will return soon," he said, moving away from the camp, leaving a puzzled Cheyenne staring after him.

It was midday when they crossed into Montana.

They had only been riding for a short time when Wolf Runner glanced up at the sky, focusing on the dark clouds gathering in the north. He sensed a storm was coming—a bad one—a "blue norther" that always descended without warning.

He found a cliff wall that would help protect them from some of the wind. But he had little time to prepare for the storm that would soon be upon them.

He held his hand up for Cheyenne to stop and he slid off his horse. "Cheyenne, find the rawhide among the supplies and cut it into slender strips to be used for ties."

Cheyenne dismounted and followed his instructions without plying him with useless questions.

Wolf Runner quickly hacked large pine branches from a tree and threw them in a pile to be used as lodge poles. After eight of the poles were deeply embedded in the soil, he reached for the leather strips

Cheyenne had cut for him. Then Wolf Runner began attaching a long canvas strip to the poles and secured it with the rawhide, his fingers deftly threading the knots.

Since the storm was coming out of the north, Wolf Runner faced the opening to the west. Lastly he drove wooden pegs through the canvas to keep it from flapping in the wind.

He instructed Cheyenne to gather what supplies they would need for warmth and place them inside the lean-to. They had hardly finished their tasks when the frigid wind struck, and struck hard.

It took Cheyenne's breath away as icy needles of sleet hammered against her face. She turned to ask Wolf Runner what else she could do, and he placed his hand on her shoulder and guided her inside the lean-to.

"I will see to the horses while you remain inside. This is going to be a bad storm and it is hard to tell how long it will last."

"How will the animals weather such a storm?"

"I will lead the horses to the side of the cliff that is facing away from the wind. They are sturdy and will press together for warmth. They will survive if the temperature does not drop too low. Do not be concerned if I do not return right away. It may take a while to see to the animals' well-being."

Cheyenne heard him give an order to the wolf, but she did not understand what he said because he spoke in Blackfoot.

A moment later Satanta entered the lean-to and flopped down beside Cheyenne. Without thinking, she rested her hand on his head. It seemed the wolf audibly sighed with contentment and he laid his head on her lap as he usually did.

Cheyenne heard a new sound—sleet pelting against the canvas and the wind whistling down the gullies with such a force the noise was deafening, sounding almost like a woman screaming. Satanta whined and she stroked his head while her heart constricted. "I know. He's cold out there and you want to be with him. So do I."

Suddenly Wolf Runner climbed inside and tossed a fur robe to Cheyenne. "There is not much help for the weather; it must merely be endured." He glanced down at his wolf and smiled. "You have turned Satanta into a tamed lapdog."

Cheyenne could not see his face in the darkness of the lean-to, but his voice sounded like he was teasing her. "I might agree had I not seen him attack Ezra. I believe the man would have died of fright if Satanta had not ripped his throat out."

"You are becoming a vicious little thing. We will make a Cheyenne out of you yet."

She fell silent, listening to the wind hitting the lean-to, and fearing it would rip their shelter from the stakes at any moment.

"We are fortunate it is this cold," Wolf Runner said, trying to offer her comfort. "If it were warmer, it would be raining and we would certainly get a good drenching in this wind."

Her teeth chattering, she pulled the fur about her shoulders. "I have never been this cold," she said. "Not even when I bathed in that icy creek."

Moving closer to her, Wolf Runner pulled her into his arms, and she did not object. "You must share mine and Satanta's warmth."

For a moment Cheyenne held herself stiff. She felt Wolf Runner's breath against her cheek and forgot about being cold. It was as if she were melting on the inside. Her body relaxed, and she sank nearer to Wolf Runner as the deep stirrings of womanhood awoke within her body.

"Do not fear," he whispered. "I want only to keep you warm and take a little of your warmth for myself."

"I don't distrust you, Wolf Runner." She pressed her face against his shoulder, loving the feel of him close to her. "I can't imagine now why I ever did."

It was the first time she had called him by name, and it pleased him mightily. For a long moment neither of them spoke. At last Cheyenne broke the silence with a question. "Will you tell me about your life in the Blackfoot village?"

She fit just right in his arms and he resisted the strong urge to nuzzle her neck. "There is not much to tell. I have a younger brother and sister. My father is the shaman of the tribe, and my mother is its heart. My grandfather, Broken Lance, is the chief, and rules the tribe." Wolf Runner laughed. "*He* is ruled by my grandmother, Tall Woman."

"Your mother is the heart of the tribe? What a wonderful tribute."

"My mother sings like an angel, and everyone wants to hear her song. Her gift has helped the passing of many who were drawing their last breath on this earth."

"She was brought to your tribe as a child."

"Yes."

"Against her will?"

Wolf Runner shifted his weight and brought her closer to him, hearing her soft sigh. "That is right."

"Will you teach me some Blackfoot words?"

His voice deepened and he found it hard to breathe with her in his arms. "If you would like." He thought it might be prudent to concentrate on something other than how right she felt in his arms.

He thought himself a pathetic specimen of his powerful tribe if he could not control his emotions. A strong yearning hit him so he quickly said, "*Ni't* means one."

"*Ni't.* One," she repeated.

"*Nããsi.* Two."

She repeated the words.

"*Nioõkska.* Three."

"What is the word for love?" she asked.

He was quiet for a moment. "There is no word for what you ask."

"But you feel love—surely you do."

Again he was quiet while he thought how to answer her. "What we feel cannot be put into one word. It is deep, meaningful, too powerful a feeling to be described in a single word."

"Oh."

He untangled his arms from about her. "You need to sleep if you can," he said, turning his back on her, but still able to feel the heat of her body next to his.

How could she be expected to sleep with him so near? How could a feeling be so powerful there was no word for it?

Her mind in turmoil, she listened to the howling wind and thought of the man who was so near, yet kept himself so closed off from her. She had never known a man with such integrity. He had risked danger to see her placed with her mother's people. She could not think of anyone else who would have made this journey for her.

But what of the day when he would leave her and she would never look upon his face again?

"*Ni't.* One," she said quietly, repeating the numbers he had taught her.

When Wolf Runner heard her, he smiled and turned over, dragging her into his arms. "Cheyenne, the world was not built in one day. You can learn more words tomorrow."

Grateful to be back in his arms, she nestled her cheek against his shoulder. "I have wasted so many years trying to forget my Indian heritage, when I should have embraced it."

"Then you will be all the more eager to learn about your Cheyenne culture, not Blackfoot."

She stiffened. He was reminding her that she had no place in his life.

Outside the small lean-to the weather was fierce, the wind building, the sleet heavy, but inside Cheyenne felt safe, and warm, yearning for something that was just out of reach.

"Sleep," Wolf Runner whispered, his hand touching her arm so gently it felt like a caress.

Chapter Twenty-two

Heat seared through Wolf Runner's body as he held Cheyenne close. He wanted her to belong to him, not just her body, but also her mind and her soul. She was asleep and would never know that he bent his head, his lips touching her forehead and lingering there for a long time. He was filled with the essence of her, and he ached, knowing he had to give her up.

The year he had spent in Washington, there had been many women to share his bed. He knew they sought him out because he was different. And it had not gone against him that his aunt and uncle were close friends with presidents and other high-ranking politicians. Those women were nameless and face-less, and had meant little to him at the time, and even less now. They had thought they were using him, but in truth he had used them, and they never guessed his disdain for them.

But this half-white woman was innocent and had not yet discovered the allures a woman can have over a man. She was young and helpless and she tugged at his heart.

He could not have her.

Had he not promised Blue Dawn he would be faith-ful to her alone? How could he have been so blind as to pledge himself to her when he knew he had no love for her? How could he have known that he would meet a golden-eyed woman who would tie him in knots?

Wolf Runner thought of the years he would spend with Blue Dawn—they would pass slowly because she was the wrong woman for him. He knew if he asked his father what he should do, his father would say as he always had, "honor first." Wolf Runner had bound himself to Blue Dawn and would take her as his wife, although he had nothing of himself to give her. He did not desire her; he never had.

He remembered Blue Dawn's tears as he prepared to leave for Santa Fe. His promise to her had been made in haste to dry her tears—but it was a promise nonetheless.

He swept his lips across Cheyenne's cheek, wishing he dared touch his mouth to hers. These stolen moments belonged to him. She must never know when he left her he would be dead inside.

Cheyenne sighed in her sleep and cuddled closer to him. Turning her toward him, he held her head against his chest, running his hand up and down her back, familiarizing himself with the feel of her.

He wanted more—he wanted the taste of her on his lips, he wanted to know all of her body. He wanted to know what she thought and what she felt.

Suddenly he felt something furry come between the two of them and Satanta reared his head.

Wolf Runner was grateful his wolf was reminding him that he must not go so far with Cheyenne that he could not pull back.

Untangling himself from Cheyenne, he gently laid her down and quietly left the lean-to, standing in the storm that raged about him, cooling his passion.

Blue Dawn would be cheated, for he would come to her with only half a heart. As Wolf Runner stood in the wind and sleet, he contemplated what Blue Dawn would feel if he told her he could not take her for his woman because he wanted Cheyenne. Blue Dawn was kind and gentle and had always looked up to him. He could not humiliate her by choosing Cheyenne for his woman.

His thoughts were in a jumble. What he wanted did not matter. It could be worse if Cheyenne returned his love. Then he would have to weigh her unhappiness against his honor.

Honor must always win.

He did not know if Cheyenne cared for him, but she trusted him. It would destroy her faith in him if she ever learned he had used her to get to her cousin, Night Fighter.

Cold and shivering, Wolf Runner glanced down at Satanta, who was watching him closely with those all-knowing eyes.

"You love her too."

A blast of icy wind hit as he turned away and trudged to where the horses were sheltered. Laying his hand on his horse's neck, he tried to clear his mind of tortured thoughts.

He was Blackfoot, a man of nature with ancient blood of warriors in his veins. He could sense the storm would soon play out. Tomorrow they would be able to continue their journey.

As Wolf Runner stood there in the cold, with a stiff wind tearing at his hair, hopelessness coiled inside him. It would have been better for him if he had never known Cheyenne.

And maybe better for her as well.

But, no—if he had never known her he would never have known love, the word he could not give her the meaning of in Blackfoot. A lump formed in his throat and he tried not to think about the moment when he would ride away and leave Cheyenne with strangers.

Until that day he must hide his feelings and not show how he felt about her by either word or deed.

That would be difficult since he wanted so badly to snatch her in his arms and hold her to his body. He wanted to capture her sweetness and take it with him whenever he left her, so he could remember her in the long years ahead.

He would still want her when he was a man so advanced in age that the passions of youth had passed away.

He could tell her his meaning of love in the Blackfoot language meant "torment," for he felt it in every fiber of his being.

Wolf Runner stiffened his resolve to get to the Cheyenne village as soon as possible. Every passing moment he spent with Cheyenne would be a temptation.

One he did not know if he was strong enough to resist.

Wolf Runner raised his head to the sky and cried out, "Why!"

Satanta stood beside Wolf Runner, raising his head and howling as if he knew what his master was suffering.

Perhaps he did.

Chapter Twenty-three

Crawling out of the lean-to, Cheyenne was greeted by a cloudless sky. Sometime during the night the storm had blown itself out, and she felt warmth creep into her body as a chinook wind moved across the land.

Smelling the delicious aroma of meat cooking, she was delighted to see Wolf Runner was roasting a fine fat rabbit.

Wolf Runner did not look up as he said, "I thought you were going to sleep the day away."

Cheyenne glanced at the sky and smiled, now knowing him well enough to recognize he was teasing her with his own dry humor. "It is barely past dawn."

"While I see to the animals, you must eat, then get ready to leave," he told her, his gaze shifting to her hair. Some of the long curls had escaped the braids and tumbled down her back—he was fascinated by the way the wind played in the dark strands.

Cheyenne dropped down on a log, enjoying the warmth of the campfire. A short time later she nibbled on a chunk of meat, savoring each bite.

"I wonder where we are now," she said, licking her fingers.

Wolf Runner turned to look at her, his eyes flaming as his gaze settled on her mouth. "If this weather holds, you will see your grandfather within the week."

Cheyenne dropped her gaze, feeling a stab of pain through her heart. She fought valiantly to hold on to her composure, but was not sure she succeeded. She had only a few days to spend with Wolf Runner before he rode out of her life forever.

Cheyenne was reluctant to leave this place. The closer she got to her grandfather, the sooner she would be parted from Wolf Runner and living with people she didn't know, who might not even welcome her. Her gaze feasted on Wolf Runner as he dismantled the lean-to.

She reached for another piece of meat, knowing very well why she lingered over her meal—she did not want Wolf Runner to leave her. Wherever he went, she wanted to go with him, even if she was merely a shadow in his life—even if he took no notice of her as a woman.

Feeling as if her heart would break, she took the last bite of meat and wiped her hands so she could fold the robes. Wolf Runner had not, by word or deed, suggested he cared anything for her—in fact, he had told her he was not attracted to her. Life had hard lessons to learn, but to be parted from Wolf Runner would be one of the hardest she had to endure.

With her arms loaded with blankets and robes, she watched Wolf Runner come striding toward her. Taking the blankets from her, his hand brushed hers and his green-flecked gaze settled on her, making Cheyenne quickly recoil, resisting the impulse to curl her fingers around his. She was afraid she would betray her feelings for him.

Cheyenne stepped back a pace, watching him roll the blankets into tight strips and secure them to the packhorse. Once the tarp was in place she saddled her horse.

Gathering the reins, she hoisted herself onto the saddle. Weary of heart and mind, she waited for Wolf Runner to douse the campfire with water. Sighing, Cheyenne decided she must cherish whatever time they had left—it was all she would ever have of him.

The days passed in quick succession, and the clear weather held, but the winds were biting and frigid. Cheyenne's fingers were stiff with cold and she could not even feel her feet.

In the last day the scenery had changed from open grassland prairie to forests of spruce, cedar, and fir trees that vied for pieces of the sky.

Wolf Runner was unusually quiet. He had hardly spoken two words to her since they had started out that morning. Satanta, however, had become her constant companion. Wherever she went, the wolf was beside her, and even now he loped along beside her horse.

She had lost count of the calendar days and could not decide if it was late autumn or if autumn had already passed into winter. In this part of the country it was difficult to tell one season from another. Wolf Runner had told her that sometimes in August it would snow in this land.

It was nearing sundown and the temperature had dropped as Cheyenne huddled beneath a warm blanket.

Wolf Runner halted his horse and Cheyenne did the same.

He rode back to her and handed her the reins of the packhorse. "Remain here while I scout ahead to find a place to shelter for the night. It will snow before morning and the weather will turn colder."

He did not give her the chance to reply before he

spun his horse and rode to the north. She thought how Wolf Runner had changed from the man she had first known; or perhaps she had changed her perception of him by knowing him better. He held his head at a proud tilt, his back straight, and his dark hair free of restraints flowing down his back.

Cheyenne's heart caught in her throat. Her spirit called to his, but his did not answer.

Glancing up at the clear blue sky, Cheyenne wondered how Wolf Runner always knew when the weather was going to turn. Perhaps his training as a Blackfoot warrior made his senses more attuned to the weather.

Cheyenne dismounted, then allowed the horses to go on a nearby quest for the wheat grass that still remained in the shadows of the trees. Before she took a drink from her canteen she poured some on a stone, where it pooled so Satanta could take a drink. The wolf gazed up at her expectantly and she laid her hand gently on his noble head.

"When the time comes for you and your master to leave me, I'll miss you."

Satanta flopped on the ground, closing his eyes. She knew, however, that the wolf was alert to everything around them because his ears were perked up, as if he was listening to sounds she could not hear with her human ears.

Bracing her back against the trunk of a spruce tree, Cheyenne closed her eyes for a moment. With the wind playing nature's song through the lacy branches of the trees, she thought she could stay in this place forever.

A moment, or an hour later, she could not be sure, she heard a rider approaching. Becoming tense at first, she relaxed when Satanta merely rose to his feet and yawned. It had to be Wolf Runner returning.

"I have found an abandoned cabin not too far ahead," he said, capturing the reins of the pack animal and leading him forward. "We will wait out the storm there."

After a brisk ride over a hill and across a small valley, Cheyenne saw the abandoned cabin and was heartened. To sleep beneath a roof would be sheer pleasure after being exposed to the brutal elements for so long.

She dismounted and started to step over a broken bottle when she felt Wolf Runner's hand at her waist, guiding her safely over the sharp glass shards. When she turned her head to look at Wolf Runner, his hand dropped and he turned away.

Stepping over the threshold, Cheyenne found the cabin only had one room, but it was dry and out of the wind. She turned to smile at Wolf Runner. "It's wonderful." Her eyes brightened and she stepped closer to the fire and held her hands out to warm them. "You already lit a fire."

Wolf Runner thought how little it took to make Cheyenne smile. "Remain inside. I will unload the packhorse," he said, turning to leave.

She held her hands closer to the flames, rubbing them together to restore the circulation. Glancing at the corners of the cabin, she saw spiderwebs. The floor was dirt, but the structure seemed sound, although there were cracks between some of the logs.

"I can make this livable," she said, smiling to herself. Finding a broom with a broken handle and with very few straws left, she swept the cobwebs out of the corners. Finding a broken lady's hand mirror, she wondered at the woman who had brought this treasure to this place and then left it after the glass was broken.

She dropped it and swept the scattered debris out the door and stood back to admire her own handiwork.

She wondered about the people who had built the structure; were they happy? Had they been forced to leave, or had they left of their own accord? There was no window, and when they closed the door, it would be dark inside if not for the fire.

Wolf Runner brought in their supplies and placed them out of the way in a corner and propped his rifle against the log wall. "Whoever built this place had a good hand. There are cracks in the walls, but the roof seems secure."

"That was just what I was thinking. We could pretend we built this house," she said, smiling. "I am mistress of this domain and you are the master."

He smiled down at her. "What would your orders to the master be, madam?" he asked, joining in her levity.

She playfully pushed him toward the door. "I would say, 'Husband, go fetch me some meat! I'm hungry.'"

They both froze and she realized what she had said. Ducking her head to hide her face, Cheyenne wished she could call the words back.

Wolf Runner nodded toward the rifle. "I leave that for you. If anyone comes, use it."

Cheyenne nodded mutely as he left, shoving the door closed behind him. She heard him speak to Satanta, and knew the wolf would remain on guard until he returned.

Burying her face in her hands, she felt totally humiliated. How could she have said such a thing to him? No wonder he had left so abruptly. Unwelcome sobs clogged her throat. She wished in that moment that Wolf Runner really were her husband.

But that would never be.

"'Busy hands are happy hands,'" she muttered to herself. "At least that is what Gram always said." She untied the pack of supplies and spread the tarp on the dirt floor and then placed the fur robe over that. Next she went outside to see if there was water for the horses.

After finding a well at the back of the house, she managed to send the rusted bucket down on a frayed rope. There was not much water, but she tasted it before watering the horses, and it seemed fresh.

After giving Satanta a drink, she gazed across the valley, suspecting some other woman had once stood as she was now, waiting for her man to return. Was there a great love between them? Probably, otherwise why would a woman follow a man to this harsh country?

Satanta trailed along beside her as she gathered wood. When she went inside the wolf followed, flopping down by the fireplace. She had become so accustomed to Satanta being at her side, how would she bear it when Wolf Runner took the wolf away with him?

Cheyenne thought she had never tasted anything as delicious as the haunch of elk that had been roasted on the hot stones Wolf Runner had placed in the fireplace. They had not spoken as they ate and Cheyenne imagined he must be displeased with her.

* * *

Wolf Runner's mind was in turmoil. The fireplace lit up the small cabin with a soft glow. He watched Cheyenne repack their supplies and felt a now-familiar ache in his heart.

While he had been stalking the elk he had thought what it would be like if he lived in that cabin with Cheyenne as his wife, to be bringing meat home for her to cook. But it would not be her hands that prepared his meals—it would be Blue Dawn's.

After he had skinned and sliced the meat, he had washed in a nearby creek. He ached for Cheyenne in a way he had never ached for any woman. When the time came, how would he be able to leave her? He had grown accustomed to her riding quietly beside him.

Raising his head to the sky, he gathered his thoughts. What had his father said to him before he left home? It was something like a decision he must make would seem like the right one, but it would be wrong. He could not remember the exact words and still wondered what they meant.

What if he was supposed to bring Cheyenne home with him? Yet his father's warning could have been about something else altogether—like not selling the ranch.

Now as he sat by the fire bracing his elbow against his knee, he watched fascinated as Cheyenne let down her hair. The beautiful mass fell about her shoulders like a silken waterfall.

Watching her work at a tangled knot at the back of her hair, Wolf Runner was frozen in place.

"I'll never get this tangle out," she said, fighting against a snarl at the back of her head.

She stopped when she felt a hand close around hers, and she twisted around to look up at Wolf Runner with a puzzled expression when he took the brush out of her hand.

"It will be much easier for me to get the tangle out, since you cannot reach it."

Cheyenne turned back to the fire, closing her eyes as he gently touched her hair, sending shivers through her body. His hand slid down her hair and then the brush followed.

She swallowed once, then twice, as his hand paused at the nape of her neck.

"Your hair is beautiful," he whispered. "I have never seen it down before."

She would have thanked him for the compliment but she could not find her voice.

His hand swept her hair forward and he ran the brush in that direction. At last the tangles were unsnarled and he handed her back the brush, moving as far away from her as the small space allowed. He settled along the wall, his arms folded over his chest.

"Thank you," Cheyenne said breathlessly.

She put her brush in her leather bag and turned to Wolf Runner. "I have been thinking."

He smiled. "Have you?"

She watched the way the firelight reflected off his face, and there was something in those green-flecked eyes she could not discern. "Yes . . . I . . . there is no way I can thank you for your kindness to me. You were under no obligation to help me, but you did. And I can never forget you saved my life."

"You do not need to thank me. Your grandfather's village is not far from my home."

Cheyenne shook her head. "You can make little of what you did, but I know better. If you had gone directly to your village, you would probably have been home by now."

He did not look at her, fearing she would see the guilt in his eyes. In the beginning he had not agreed to take her for any noble reason. "It is of no matter," Wolf Runner said dismissively.

"Please let me say what I have on my mind. I have learned so much from just watching you. You have given me something I never had before."

Wolf Runner's eyes half hooded lazily and his voice was deep as he asked, "What is that?"

"Pride in my Cheyenne blood." She could see his eyes glitter in the firelight, and she thought he might be displeased by what she said, but she was not finished. "You taught me to embrace who I am and not be ashamed, as I was in Santa Fe, where people turned away from me because I was different."

His feelings were raw and near the surface and Wolf Runner knew it would take very little from her to push him over the edge. "Cheyenne," he said, looking away from her eyes. "Now let me tell you about yourself. I have seen a young woman faced with heartbreak and sadness with no one but a stranger to turn to in her time of need. I have watched you face hardships and dangers, yet not once have I heard you complain. You should be proud of who you are—I certainly am proud of you."

Cheyenne was flustered, and she felt like a thousand butterflies were beating their wings in her stomach. She did not know how it happened, but she quickly stood and moved toward Wolf Runner and he opened his arms to her. As he embraced her against his body, she trembled with desire.

Chapter Twenty-four

Wolf Runner's breath was on her cheek; his lips followed her jawline and found her mouth. Feeling her lips tremble and then soften made him catch his breath.

Cheyenne tasted the saltiness of her tears when his lips touched hers ever so gently, as if he feared he would hurt her. She felt his hands move through her hair and she melted inside. Somewhere in the back of her mind a voice warned her to stop him, but another part of her was curious to explore the feelings he had awakened in her.

Pulling her tighter against him, he felt the softness of her body, and his hands moved over her curves.

Her heart was singing as he eased her back onto the fur robe and clasped her to him, his breathing heavy.

Reaching up, she touched his strong jaw and could tell he was clenching it tightly. He wanted to say something to her, Cheyenne could feel it, but instead he breathed her name.

"Cheyenne."

Then he lapsed into the Blackfoot language and she did not know what he said to her.

"I have wanted to hold you like this," he said, trembling. "You are in my heart," he admitted, as if the words were torn from his lips. He was confessing all because Cheyenne did not understand anything he said.

She slid her arms around his shoulders, and all his restraint broke. His hands were rough as he grabbed her to him, crushing his mouth against hers. His hands stopped at the curve of her waist, and he took advantage of exploring the soft curves that had enticed him almost from the beginning of their acquaintance.

"I want you," he murmured against her ear, and he did not just mean her body—he wanted the right to call her his woman. He wanted to take her to his village and build her a lodge where they would live together. He wanted to be inside her to make her moan with the same passion he was feeling and had been fighting against for so long.

She nibbled at his mouth and he let out a loud hiss. "This is wrong," he said in English, starting to move away.

But she took his hand and placed it on her breast. "It does not feel wrong to me."

In the flickering firelight Wolf Runner pulled back. "It is wrong for you," he said, his voice trembling with the restraint he kept over his equally shaking body. "I wish I could make you understand—to take you would fulfill my deepest desire. But I must not."

Cheyenne touched his face. "How many days until we reach my grandfather's village?"

He wondered where she was going with her question. "Two, maybe three. Why do you ask?"

"And after that we will never see each other again?"

He hesitated. "I do not believe we shall."

"I would like to give you a memory of me, so you might think of me sometime." She was shy as she looked into those blazing eyes. "I give it freely, asking nothing in return."

Wolf Runner's body swelled painfully. He ached to take what she offered. His hand moved over her breast and he eased open the top lace of her gown so he could touch her bare skin. Bending his head, Wolf Runner touched his mouth against her breast. When she drew in her breath, his breath came out in a groan.

"Cheyenne," he said, raising his head. "This is not fair to you. I am promised to another."

His words were like a dash of cold water in her face. She lay there beside him, staring into his eyes for a long moment, trying to fight her way out of the passion that ruled her thinking. It took her a moment to speak, and when she did, it was in a whisper.

"I never considered that. I should have." She pulled her gown together and sat up, tying the laces with trembling fingers. "Take no blame on yourself—the fault is all mine."

He stilled her hands, covering them with his. "It will be a marriage of honor, Cheyenne, not of love—although I have cared for Blue Dawn like a friend for many years."

Unshed tears glistened in Cheyenne's eyes, and her pain went right to his heart.

"I understand." But she did not really. He had said he cared for the woman, but did not love her. "Thank you for being honest with me. Your words prove you are a man of honor."

"Cheyenne," he said, reaching out to her. "Do not pull away from me."

She moved his hand away from hers and finished lacing her gown. "I can only imagine what you must think of my actions." She shook her head, wiping her tears with her fingers. "I am truly a woman without honor."

He gripped her by the shoulders. "No! I will not have you think that. If I told you all I feel for you, you would pity me."

He was confusing her with words that pushed her away, and yet gave her hope. "Why should I pity you?"

"What I have to look forward to is a loveless marriage, and every time I take her in my arms, I will be wishing it was you."

She shot to her feet and moved away from him. "Cruel words, Wolf Runner. You just sentenced us both to a life of misery."

He stood up beside her. "If I had you tonight, it would be much worse for me, for I would always know what was lacking in my life. It would be good between us—I know that."

Hesitantly she turned back to him. "Is it not better to have one night together, than to never have known the joining of our bodies?"

Wolf Runner swallowed deep and raised his head, looking at the ceiling, and she saw his throat contract.

Looking down at her, his hand shook as he touched her cheek. "Do not tempt me. You do not know how close I am to the edge. Help me to do what is right for you. What is right for us both."

Tears burned behind her eyes. Gently touching his face, she smiled. "How will I ever find a husband who can erase your memory?"

He took her hand and raised it to his lips, hating the thought of any other man touching her. He wanted to go to Blue Dawn and confess that he did not love her. But he could never shame her before the whole tribe. She would have already been working on her wedding dress, and her parents would already have given her their blessings.

"Cheyenne, I would have taken all of you tonight and let the rest of the world slip out of my mind. But if I guess right, you have never been intimate with a man."

Cheyenne's head fell forward on his shoulder, and she wanted to cry, but she dared not. "I have not been with a man, if that makes any difference. I never wanted to until . . . until . . ."

"It makes a difference." Wolf Runner turned away, moved to the fireplace, and braced his hand on the mantel, lowering his head. "This night I have done the most honorable thing I have ever done in my life—and the most difficult."

His trouble, he thought, was that he could not seem to keep his hands off her. He had always prided himself on his self-control—with her he had no control.

Suddenly Cheyenne was angry. "So do you think it's honorable to marry a woman you don't love? Is it honorable to turn away from what we have? I'm not saying you love me, but you wanted me, you know you did."

He bent to throw two more logs on the fire before he turned back to face her. "What do you want of me, Cheyenne? My restraint hangs by a thread." His eyes reflected his desperation. "More than anything I want you."

She realized what she was doing to him and she had to stop his torment—and her own. "Don't be concerned. I will not tempt you further," she said, sitting down on the fur and unlacing her boots. "There is no reason to speak of this anymore."

He stalked to the door, wrenched it open, and

slammed it behind him. Snow was swirling about him and the icy wind struck his face like shards of glass, and still he stood there, fighting the need to return to the cabin and take Cheyenne in his arms, to hold her to him, and to partake of her sweet body, to make love to her.

Walking over to the animals, Wolf Runner laid his hand on his horse's sleek neck, trying to clear his mind.

But all he could think of was Cheyenne.

He tensed when he heard the nearby cry of a wolf, and an answering cry in the distant woods. Wolf Runner bent down to Satanta, who nuzzled his hand. "You hear them call to you, yet you are loyal to your mate who waits for you back in the village. Give me the strength to have half your trustworthy heart. I wonder if a part of you wants to join the wild pack, or if you yearn for your mate."

Satanta looked up at Wolf Runner before settling himself near the horses, clearly unaffected by the call of the wild pack. Wolf Runner sighed. "Your noble heart is true to Madii—wolves mate for life, as must I."

"Do not let those wolves come close to the horses," Wolf Runner commanded Satanta.

Shivering from the cold, he returned to the cabin, glad he had finally gotten his wild passion under control. Once inside he saw that Cheyenne was curled up with her back to him and although he knew she was awake, she pretended to sleep.

He settled down by the fire and lay on the dirt floor, bracing his hands beneath his head. Against his will, he turned to look at Cheyenne. She was the perfect woman for him, and he thought he could make her happy too—but that could never be.

Again he wondered what his father had warned

him against—loving Cheyenne, or leaving her? Wind Warrior had also said Wolf Runner would suffer if he did not listen to his heart.

What did it mean?

His father often gave cryptic messages to members of the tribe, but it had been the first time he had ever told Wolf Runner something he did not understand.

He closed his eyes, already dreading the day he would look upon Cheyenne's face for the last time.

When the time came, could his footsteps take him away from her?

They must.

The wind howled through the cracks in the logs and the fire was dying down, so he added more logs.

"Wolf Runner," Cheyenne said, turning back to him, "there is no reason for you to lie on the hard ground. I will not repeat my actions. We are both adults."

He could endure the cold, but he could not resist a chance to lie beside her.

Wolf Runner placed another log on the fire and watched sparks fly. Taking a heavy breath, he lay down beside Cheyenne, turning his back to her and staying just far enough away so they would not touch.

Heartsick and weary, he closed his eyes, feeling her pull the robe over them both.

Gusts of wind rattled the door and the fire lent its warmth to the night. Cheyenne lay awake until she heard Wolf Runner's even breathing. He had fallen asleep so easily, but sleep eluded her.

It was much later when her eyelids became heavy and she drifted off to sleep.

She awoke sometime later feeling cold and noticed that the fire had died down. Wolf Runner had turned toward her, but she could tell by his easy breathing he still slept.

She knew she should get up and put more logs on the fire, but Wolf Runner was so near and Cheyenne wanted to drink in his essence while he was unaware of it.

In the glow of the embers she could see his dark hair fall across his forehead and down one shoulder. His long lashes lay against his tanned cheek. She wanted to touch him but she resisted the urge because she had given her word.

Cheyenne was taken totally by surprise when Wolf Runner's eyes slowly opened and they stared at each other for a long time. Wordlessly they hung on to the moment, not touching, just feeling the love that bound them together and the honor that kept them apart.

Chapter Twenty-five

Moments passed and neither spoke.

Then slowly Wolf Runner drew her to him, saying in the Blackfoot language so she would not understand, "If I had my way I would awaken each morning looking into your eyes. I want to hold you to me and feel your heart beat."

She was trembling, not from cold but from the tone of his voice. "I don't understand your words."

Wolf Runner closed his eyes, bringing her tighter against him while she touched his face. "It seems I cannot resist you, Cheyenne." Then he slipped back into Blackfoot language. "You are in my heart and in my blood. This I know for certain."

She laid her cheek against his, wishing she knew what he was saying to her, but it didn't matter; he was holding her, brushing his mouth against her ear and sending shivers of delight throughout her body.

"I have never felt this intense longing with a woman before, and I have not even experienced our coming together," he said in Blackfoot. "I never knew there was a deeper feeling than any I had ever known."

Her heart sang with joy and she wished she could hold on to this moment in time for the rest of her life. She would have to. This was all she would ever have of Wolf Runner.

"I remember the first day I saw you ride into town.

My heart sang with joy because I thought 'here is someone like me. He knows how it feels to be a part of two worlds and akin to neither.'"

Again he spoke in Blackfoot. "You are my world."

Bending forward, she lightly touched her lips to his and he stiffened, so she pulled away. Why was he always sending her mixed meanings? He drew her to him and then pushed her away.

Wolf Runner saw the uncertainty and the hurt in her eyes, and he could understand why she was confused. He wanted her, ached for her, and yet he fought with his honor to leave her untouched.

Wolf Runner nuzzled her neck—he could not help himself. Perhaps Cheyenne was right, and if they could be together, it would give him something to live on after they had parted.

"I'll put more wood on the fire," she said, pushing him away. When she started to sit up, his restraint broke and he grabbed her to him.

"I will keep you warm."

A sob slipped through her lips and she went to him. "Hold me. I need you to hold me."

His mouth came down on hers and he held her in a viselike grip, breathing in her sweetness. "I need you," he whispered in a tight voice. "I need you more than life."

Cheyenne felt him pull her gown upward and she lifted her hips so he could pull it up all the way. Her heart was beating so fast she could hardly catch her breath as his hand slid up her leg, paused, and pulled away.

"This must end before I do something we both regret."

"Wolf Runner," she said, looking deeply into his eyes. "I would not regret it."

"You are young. You do not know the consequences. I would lose my honor; you would lose your virginity." He started to pull away and she laid her hand on his arm.

"I give it to you freely." When he paused, her gaze settled on his. "This is what I want."

Taking her by surprise, he sat her up and unlaced her gown. He pulled it over her head and tossed it aside. "I cannot fight against your willingness and my desire," he whispered, wondering why he was shaking like a young boy with his first girl.

Although the fire was merely glowing embers he could see her body and he drew in his breath. Her eyes were wide with wonder as he moved his hand over one breast and then the other.

She caught her breath when he dipped his head and took a nipple in his mouth, sucking gently.

"Ohhh," she whispered. Her body slammed with want and need, and she felt like she was melting inside. "Oh, please."

All the tortured days and nights when he had wanted her, and now she was almost his. Wolf Runner raised his head and noticed her passion-glazed eyes were blurred by tears.

His warm, firm mouth moved over hers, and she moaned with pleasure and burning need.

Wolf Runner eased her down and hovered above her, his gaze feasting on her loveliness. She was perfect in every way—from her breasts, to her tiny waist, her soft curves. Bending his head, he plundered her lips, reluctant to pull away although he knew he should. He could not get enough of her, and he wanted more—he wanted everything she had to give him.

Slowly his hand began its descent, sweeping across her flat stomach. Going lower, he caressed Cheyenne while she squirmed, her body following his hand.

Cheyenne was surprised and grabbed at his hand when one finger slid into her softness. But her protest did not last long. She could not catch her breath—and she was sure she would never breathe again. But she did—she exhaled when he eased his finger farther into her and began a rhythm that made her body instinctively move in time with it.

She closed her eyes, lost in the beautiful feelings he had awakened. When he withdrew his hand, she started to protest until she saw he was removing his buckskin leggings.

Cheyenne moaned when she felt his naked flesh against hers. Surely this was what man and woman had been created for—she had been created for him.

"I must ask you one thing," she said in a voice so deep she did not recognize it as her own

He raised his gaze to hers, breathing hard, waiting for her question while all he wanted to do was kiss those tempting lips until she begged for mercy.

"You said you were honor bound to another woman. Would you lose your honor if you made love to me?"

Moving away from her, he let out a long breath, knowing he must speak the truth. "My commitment would be tarnished, my honor in tatters. But even knowing that, I want you."

Wolf Runner's words were like a stab to her heart—she was a temptation to him, and he would lose his honor if they continued.

Drawing on all her strength, Cheyenne moved away from him and sat up, grabbing her gown and holding it in front of her, suddenly feeling naked. "Forgive me for what I have done to you. If I cared about you less, I would urge you to make love to me. You place great value on your honor, and I will not be the one to deprive you of it."

At the moment Wolf Runner would have thrown his honor to the wind to have this one night with her.

He still watched her.

Pulling her gown over her head and feeling it settle about her ankles, she asked, "Is there no honorable way we can be together?"

"Only one, and you would not like it, Cheyenne. I hesitate to tell you because I promised I would take no other wife," he said in a pain-filled voice.

"Tell me and let me decide."

"You could have been my second wife. It is not an unknown custom among my people, but even that is denied me. I swore an oath to her that I would have no other wife but Blue Dawn."

Cheyenne's mouth flew open in horror. "It is just as well. I would never have consented to that anyway. Would your mother consent to be a second wife?"

Wolf Runner thought about it for a moment. "No. Most certainly not. My mother would never share my father with another woman. And he would want no one but her." He rolled to his feet, brushing his hair out of his face, drawing her gaze to his tall, sleek body. He pulled on his leggings and tossed two more logs on the fire, then slipped into his buckskin shirt and moccasins.

"It is but two hours until daylight. I will check on the horses. Gather the supplies so we can leave at first light."

When he went out the door, Cheyenne's head fell into her hands and her body shook with the sobs she was trying to suppress.

He had wanted her as much as she wanted him—but she had done the right thing.

Looking at the sky tinted red by the morning sun, Wolf Runner felt shame. He had stirred passion to life in an innocent young woman he should never have touched. He had pulled her close, then pushed her away. Indicated he wanted her, then confessed he could not have her.

If she was hurt and confused it was no wonder.

The last person he would ever want to hurt was Cheyenne. He would keep his distance, keep a tight rein on his feelings, and deliver her safely to her grandfather.

Pouring grain into a pan, he fed the horses, unmindful of the biting cold. He was not proud of his actions.

Chapter Twenty-six

The journey was becoming more difficult for Cheyenne—the long hours in the saddle had taken its toll on her. She was not only bone-weary but sadness also lay heavily on her shoulders.

For the most part Wolf Runner ignored her, slipping into brooding silence that cut her to the heart. He only spoke to her when it was absolutely necessary. And that was not very often.

They rode from dawn to dusk and sometimes even after dark, where the horses would have to pick their way across the prairie by moonlight.

Cheyenne knew why Wolf Runner was in such a hurry to be rid of her—he did not want to be tempted by her, and that suited her just fine.

Setting her jaw in a stubborn line, she urged her horse forward so she could ride even with him. What did it matter if Wolf Runner pushed them until humans and animals were so weary they could hardly go on? If he expected her to decry her plight, he would grow old waiting. If he could keep going, then so could she.

Even Satanta was feeling the effects of their fast pace. When they stopped to rest the horses, the wolf would flop down, panting.

Their pace slowed when they reached hill country that was thick with bushes and trees. The weather was bitter cold, and Cheyenne hunched over her saddle and pulled the blanket tightly about her. Her fingers were so numb with cold it was difficult to hold on to the reins.

Just after noon, heavy snow began to fall and before long the weary horses were forced to trudge through the high snowdrifts. Onward they pushed, ever forward.

Wolf Runner suddenly halted his horse and held up his hand for Cheyenne to stop. He whipped his head around, listening tensely, his hand on his rifle, apparently aware of something that Cheyenne could not hear.

"Dismount," he told her, sliding off his horse and nodding to her. "We are being watched. Whatever you do, show no fear."

She quickly dismounted, gazing through the heavy snowfall past a clump of pine trees, but she could see nothing.

"What is it?" she asked, turning one way and then the other, still seeing nothing threatening.

The fur on Satanta's neck bristled, and the wolf went into his attack stance when an Indian brave appeared just to their right.

The warrior's dark eyes flickered over Wolf Runner, and then settled on Cheyenne. Although his rifle rested across his arm and was not pointed at either of them, he was threatening nonetheless. He was young, perhaps Wolf Runner's age. He was tall, and Cheyenne would have thought him handsome if not for the scowl on his face.

Without warning, a second Indian appeared, and a third, and forth.

Cheyenne could do nothing but watch as the Indians closed in on them. Her gaze flew to Wolf Runner, who was watching one particular Indian with rapt attention.

"Are they Blackfoot or Cheyenne?" she asked quietly.

He did not answer, never taking his eyes off the Indian who wore yellow feathers in his hair and seemed to be the leader.

When Wolf Runner did speak, it was in a language she didn't understand, and she was frustrated, not knowing what was being said.

Wolf Runner, filled with anger, knew exactly who led these warriors—his greatest enemy. Staring into the Cheyenne renegade's eyes, Wolf Runner said, "Night Fighter, you will have heard of me—I am Wolf Runner, Blood Blackfoot and the son of Wind Warrior."

Night Fighter grinned, his hand stroking his rifle. "Yes, I got your message from the warrior you spared when you killed the rest of my war party. I knew the day would come when we would meet, but I did not think you would be so foolish as to seek me in my own village."

There was only coldness in Wolf Runner's heart. "Today I have another task, but I will see you again."

Night Fighter spoke heatedly, "You are an enemy to my people. Do you think I do not know you have hunted me and sworn to have my death?"

"I am not an enemy to the noble Cheyenne—only to the cowardly warriors such as yourself, who prey on helpless women."

"You are a dead man," Night Fighter hissed.

Wolf Runner stared at his foe. "The day will surely come when one of us will die, but this is not that day. This woman with me is the granddaughter of your chief, Bold Eagle. If I were not on a mission of honor to see her placed in his care, you would already be dead."

Night Fighter stared with hatred at the Blackfoot who was a legend among the Cheyenne people. He was filled with rage as he turned to the woman who stood beside Wolf Runner. "She looks white to me. I do not believe she is the granddaughter of my uncle. Why should I not kill you both now?"

"You could try, but you would be dead before your first blow fell," Wolf Runner said, unsheathing his knife before Night Fighter could raise his rifle. "If you harm the chief's granddaughter, you will answer to him."

Cheyenne tensed during the angry exchange between the two warriors. The stranger then turned his gaze on her, and Cheyenne felt a prickle of fear.

Wolf Runner showed no fear as he gripped his knife, so she didn't either. Cheyenne knew his aim was true; still they were outnumbered, and there was no advantage in that.

Satanta stood beside Wolf Runner as if waiting for the command to attack.

Cheyenne thought the two men would never come to an understanding.

Finally, the other Indian turned back to Cheyenne and looked at her long and hard. After a moment of reflection, he motioned for them to remount and follow him.

Cheyenne remounted, moving her horse close to Wolf Runner. "Who are they?" she asked.

"The Cheyenne I was speaking to is Night Fighter, the nephew of Bold Eagle—that would make him your relative. He is suspicious of us, but has agreed to lead us to your grandfather. Do not fear. You are in no danger."

"Then my grandfather is alive!"

"So it would seem."

Cheyenne glanced at Night Fighter, uncertainty swelling inside her. She could tell by how high he sat his horse that he was as tall as Wolf Runner and as proud. The robe he wore was of the finest fur, and he wore two yellow feathers in his dark hair. He was a handsome man, with a firm chin and a wide forehead. But the moment he turned those dark, seeking eyes on Cheyenne and discovered she had been watching him, she quickly lowered her gaze.

It was difficult for her to believe that after such a long, hard journey, they had finally reached her mother's people. So many emotions ran through her head; relief that the arduous journey was finally over, joy that she would soon meet her mother's father, but uppermost in her mind was the deep sadness she felt because she would soon be parted from Wolf Runner.

The Indians were silent as they rode. The one who was related to her led the group, while the others closed around Cheyenne and Wolf Runner. They carried rifles and kept casting suspicious glances at Wolf Runner.

This certainly was not the welcome she had envisioned.

They rode through the pine forest, where the deep snow muted the horses' hooves. Cheyenne ducked her head as she rode beneath a pine bough. Then, without warning, the path opened to a wide expanse and Cheyenne saw soft rolling hills and a number of tipis situated beside a wide river. She lost count after thirty-two.

That part of her that was Cheyenne told her she had come home. But that feeling did not last—it was replaced by uncertainty and fear of the unknown as women and children came out of the tipis draped in warm furs and looking curiously at her and Wolf Runner.

There was a frightening moment when Satanta came bounding out of the woods and one of the Indians raised his rifle and took aim. Wolf Runner defused the moment when he spoke rapidly to Night Fighter, who ordered the warrior to lower his rifle.

They continued toward the center of the village and Night Fighter motioned for them to dismount. While she and Wolf Runner waited, Night Fighter disappeared inside one of the lodges.

"Remember," Wolf Runner quickly cautioned Cheyenne, "do not show fear."

All she could do was nod because her throat was clogged with apprehension. What happened in the next few moments would affect the rest of her life.

Night Fighter reappeared a moment later and motioned for them to go inside.

Wolf Runner pointed to Satanta and spoke to him in Blackfoot, and the wolf dropped down on his haunches to wait. Out of the corner of her eye, Cheyenne saw several people drawing near, their curious gazes moving between Satanta and her and Wolf Runner.

When Night Fighter spoke to Wolf Runner, it was clear he was warning him about something, in heated words.

"He told me your grandfather is extremely ill," Wolf Runner explained to Cheyenne. "He said not to tire Bold Eagle."

Once they stepped inside the tipi, it took a moment for Cheyenne's eyes to adjust to the dim light that came from a small fire. Although it was cold outside, it was almost stuffy in the tipi. The first thing she noticed was a number of rifles propped against the tipi walls. She swallowed a lump of fear and revulsion when she realized she was staring at a string of scalps hanging from a lodge pole.

Her gaze finally settled on the Indian man who was watching her so intently from where he sat upon a reed mat. He was draped in a buffalo robe, but it was easy to see from his sunken eyes and the dullness reflected there that he was indeed ill, if not dying. His breathing was labored, and his eyes were pain-filled. Skin fell into deep wrinkled folds across his face and the hair that hung down his shoulders was completely white.

The old man finally turned his attention to Wolf Runner. The two exchanged words Cheyenne could not understand.

At last the chief returned his focus to Cheyenne and she was surprised when he spoke to her in hesitant English. "You look much like my daughter. It does my heart good to look upon your face, Granddaughter."

She felt overwhelming relief to find she was welcomed into her mother's tribe. "I did not know my mother. She died when I was a small child."

"I know this." Broken Lance continued to stare at her. "You also have the look of your white father about you," he said, patting a place beside him and inviting Cheyenne to join him there.

Cheyenne had longed for this moment, and now was disappointed. She was not sure what she had expected. To finally meet her grandfather had been her fond hope, but everything around was strange and frightening. If he were a white relative she would have given him a hug, but she thought it best not to make the first overture.

Settling next to him, she raised her gaze to Wolf Runner, who must have been told to sit because he went down on his knees, his gaze searching Cheyenne's as if gauging her reaction to the meeting with her grandfather.

"You do not speak the language of the Cheyenne, my granddaughter?"

"Sir, I do not. Where I lived in Santa Fe there was no one to teach me how to speak Cheyenne."

"You are welcome in this village. I hope you have come to dwell with us for a time."

Cheyenne raised her troubled gaze to Bold Eagle. "If you will allow it, I will remain with you."

He smiled a toothless grin and patted her hand. "It will be like having my daughter with me once more."

She wanted her grandfather to know how grateful she was to Wolf Runner for bringing her to the Cheyenne village. "I could not have come so far without the guidance of this grandson of the Blackfoot chief."

Bold Eagle nodded, looking at Wolf Runner. "Your name is known to me," he said, continuing to speak in English so Cheyenne could understand him. "Your grandfather, Broken Lance, is a great man. You are the son of the white woman who I have heard has music that soothes the soul."

Wolf Runner nodded. "I am Rain Song's son."

"Then you are the son of Wind Warrior, a great man. He sees that which others cannot."

Wolf Runner nodded his head. "I am glad you know of my father. I have heard him speak of you with respect."

The old man's eyes took on a cunning light. "Yet you attacked some of our warriors and slew them not so long ago."

Cheyenne's mouth opened in shocked surprise. Why had Wolf Runner never told her about that?

Wolf Runner met the old man's gaze. "I did," he admitted, his gaze never wavering. "It was done in retaliation against those who brutally attacked and killed our helpless women—on Blackfoot land."

There was a tense moment as each warrior took measure of the other.

At last Bold Eagle nodded, speaking so Cheyenne would not understand his words. "Your cause was just. I know of the incident."

Wolf Runner answered him in kind. "Then know this—your nephew was the leader. The matter is not over."

"You are a guest in my lodge," the old man said, his eyes growing sharp. "You are welcome, Blackfoot, but do not think you will have your revenge here."

"As a guest in your lodge, I will honor the code of friendship between our people."

Bold Eagle suddenly doubled over with a wracking cough, and it took him a moment to recover. Although Cheyenne's instinct was to help her grandfather in some way, the look Wolf Runner gave clearly warned her to take no notice.

At last the old chief was able to speak, and reverted to English. "Wolf Runner, I thank you for bringing my granddaughter to me. You are most welcome in our village. We hope you will dwell with us for a time."

Avoiding looking at Cheyenne, Wolf Runner replied, "I thank you, but I must leave for my home tomorrow."

"Then let it be known that you are welcome anytime you choose to come to our village. The Cheyenne and the Blackfoot have not always been friends, but we have no quarrel with your grandfather Broken

Lance's tribe. You are welcome to pass the night in my tipi."

"Your offer is generous, but I will camp outside the village. I have a wolf with me, and he seems to make some of your people uneasy."

"Then let it be so."

Cheyenne glanced up at Wolf Runner, knowing she would probably never see him again. "Please do not leave before I rise in the morning," she said, feeling lost at the thought of being parted from him. This was her grandfather, and he was obviously a kind man, but the Indian customs were still strange to her.

In a moment of panic, she was not certain she belonged there at all.

Would it ever seem like home to her?

Chapter Twenty-seven

Wolf Runner stood, his gaze on Cheyenne's pale face. He could read the terror in her eyes and knew what she was feeling. "I will not depart without first seeing you."

"You are leaving now?" she asked, seeing the glittering intensity reflected in his eyes.

"I must set up camp and tend the horses." Without ceremony, Wolf Runner nodded to Bold Eagle and left abruptly.

Cheyenne felt bereft. She struggled, not wanting to show her feelings, but evidently she did not quite succeed. Bold Eagle saw her forlorn expression and frowned.

"Do not think you are alone, Granddaughter. You will dwell in my tipi with my two wives and me. They will be happy to have an extra pair of hands to help with the work."

She was reminded that the Indian saw no wrong in taking more than one wife. "Is one of your women my grandmother?" she asked hopefully.

Bold Eagle shook his head sorrowfully. "Your grandmother has been dead for many winters. She was my first wife, and my favorite. Cloud Woman would have been happy to welcome home the daughter of her daughter if she were here."

It was difficult for Cheyenne to grieve over the

death of a woman she had no knowledge of, but she did feel sadness all the same. "I'm sorry I could not have known her."

At that moment her attention was drawn to the two women who entered the tipi, both smiling at Cheyenne. One was an elderly woman with soft black eyes; the other would have been somewhere in her forties, Cheyenne thought. Apparently they could not speak English, but they seemed genuinely glad to welcome her.

The youngest spooned stew into a wooden bowl and handed it to Cheyenne, smiling.

"Thank you," Cheyenne said to the woman, who only nodded to her and continued to smile.

Her grandfather answered, "Walking Woman is happy to feed you, Granddaughter. And my other wife, Soaring Bird, is happy as well."

Cheyenne took a bite and smiled at both women. "Will you tell them for me that this is delicious, Grandfather?"

The old man stared at her with his eyes glowing. "You are the only grandchild I have ever had; therefore, I have never been called 'grandfather' before. It warms my heart." Then he turned to the women and told them what Cheyenne had said about the stew, which seemed to make the women happy.

The old man turned back to Cheyenne. "What is the name your mother gave you?"

"I am called Cheyenne."

Bold Eagle gave her a toothless grin. "It is good. It is like my daughter to give you a name to tie you to her people."

Night Fighter walked beside Wolf Runner as he led the horses a little way from the village, where he intended to set up camp for the night. Wolf Runner did not trust the warrior and watched his every move.

"Do you want to settle this thing that is between us now?" Night Fighter asked.

"I will not take up a weapon against you while I am a guest of your uncle. I will meet you another time."

"What is to keep me from sneaking upon you tonight and driving my knife into your heart?" the Cheyenne warrior asked, his hand going to his knife.

Wolf Runner nodded to his wolf. "Be warned; Satanta will warn me if you come near. Before I could stop him, he would tear your throat out."

Night Fighter's eyes widened. "Then it is true you speak to the wolves."

Wolf Runner turned his back on Night Fighter. "I will no longer speak to you—I do not waste my time on those without honor."

The Cheyenne warrior stopped in his tracks, hatred radiating from his eyes. "Sleep well tonight, Blackfoot. And count the days you have left to walk this land." Pulling his robe tighter about him, he looked speculatively at the arrogant Blackfoot warrior, wondering if he might discover a weakness in his enemy he could use to his advantage.

"Let us speak of my cousin," Night Fighter said slyly. "She is young and fair—just the kind of maiden I like."

Wolf Runner whipped around, his sharp gaze cutting into Night Fighter. "You will not go near her."

A malevolent smile curved Night Fighter's lips as he thought of the power he now held over Wolf Runner. It had been too easy to uncover the Blackfoot's weakness—it was the woman. "You will not be here to know," he taunted.

Wolf Runner started toward him and then stopped,

realizing he could not break the slim peace that existed between the Cheyenne and the Blackfoot. If he attacked Night Fighter on Cheyenne land, he would be no better than his enemy. Conflicting emotions warred within him. "If you touch her, I will know, and you will die sooner than you expect."

"I like the look of her," Night Fighter continued, as if Wolf Runner had not even spoken. "I need another wife and she will need a husband—she cannot always live with my uncle and his wives. Age lies heavily on Bold Eagle's shoulder, and the death rattle has already settled in his chest. Our healer says he will not live out the winter. When he dies, my cousin will need to find a man, and that man will be me."

Wolf Runner was filled with rage at the thought of Night Fighter touching Cheyenne. It was the Cheyenne warrior's reputation for brutalizing women that had sent Wolf Runner after him in the first place. "You are not worthy of her."

Night Fighter's gaze became hard. "Have you lain with her?"

Wolf Runner grabbed Night Fighter by his robe and yanked him forward. "Look into my eyes and see your death. Cheyenne is an innocent. Remember that!"

Night Fighter drew in a sharp breath, and he felt fear such as he had never known. "You would not slay me on my own land. You have already said so."

Wolf Runner flung him away contemptuously, and when Night Fighter hit the ground hard, Satanta started toward him, growling low in his throat. Wolf Runner's command stopped the wolf, but the yellow eyes still watched Night Fighter's every move.

Night Fighter then knew he had every advantage

when Wolf Runner would not allow his wolf to attack. The fool really did see himself bound by honor as a guest to respect their land and people. Integrity had never been important to Night Fighter, and when he saw it in others, it aroused his cruelty. "Her purity makes me want her even more. I will speak to my uncle about her in the next few days."

"I will warn her against you."

Rising to his feet, Night Fighter stared back at Wolf Runner. "But you will not be here, and I will."

"Do not be so certain. You would be wise to look over your shoulder at all times."

Night Fighter stepped back a few paces because the hair on the back of the wolf's neck had stood up. "I think we will not meet again unless it is in a battle to the death."

"A battle I will win," Wolf Runner said in a deadly calm voice. He heard Night Fighter's laugh as the man turned and moved back toward the Cheyenne village.

Wolf Runner wanted nothing more than to drive a knife into the man's heart. Shaking with anger, he reached the place in the pine grove where he would spend the night. It was a place where Night Fighter could not sneak up on him without making noise.

Unsaddling Cheyenne's horse, he found her meager belongings and felt pain in his heart. What he wanted to do was to take her away with him when he left. He hobbled the horses and draped himself in his warm blankets, leaning his back against the thick trunk of a tall pine.

These were Cheyenne's own people—her family. He had started the journey with her to find Night Fighter, but now Cheyenne was more important to him than vengeance.

Why then did he feel he was betraying her in some way?

Where Cheyenne was concerned, honor kept getting in the way.

It would take all his fortitude to leave her tomorrow, but he must.

Chapter Twenty-eight

Cheyenne felt as though she were in an alien world. It wasn't that her grandfather and his two wives weren't kind to her—they could not have been more welcoming. This was not the life she had been brought up to experience, and she had not been prepared to live in a tipi with three strangers—although one of them was her grandfather.

Her grandfather's youngest wife, Walking Woman, had given Cheyenne a fine doeskin gown and knee-high moccasins. Her grandfather had explained to her that the garments had once belonged to her mother, and he had saved them, hoping Cheyenne would one day come for them.

The doeskin gown was soft and gave her a freedom of movement she had never experienced—it had wonderful beadwork on the arms and down the front. Her grandfather's eldest wife, Soaring Bird, braided Cheyenne's hair and wrapped the braids with leather strips, adding beads and small white feathers.

She wondered what Gram would say if she knew her granddaughter now lived among the Cheyenne tribe and looked just like one of them.

When evening fell and darkness descended, she was shown to a bed of furs at the back of the tipi where she would sleep. As she lay upon the soft robes, Walking Woman covered her with a warm blanket. Inside the tipi was almost stifling to Cheyenne because she had become accustomed to sleeping in the open air.

As her new family settled down to sleep, loneliness crept into Cheyenne's heart. At this moment, what was Wolf Runner doing? She had traveled with him for so long, she could imagine what his routine would be; after feeding and watering the animals, he would build a campfire. Since he had not hunted for fresh game, he would eat dried meat. Then he would bed down and sleep.

Cheyenne doubted she would sleep tonight. Her grandfather kept coughing, one of his wives groaned in her sleep, and the other one snored.

Everything was strange to her. Surely in time she would learn to accept her new life and feel at home with her mother's people.

Reminding herself that these people were family, she squeezed her eyes tightly together. She tried to reach back to her mother's girlhood and picture her here in this village, perhaps this very tipi. But since she did not know her mother's face, she could not imagine it.

Her thoughts turned back to the person she wanted most to forget, and never would.

Wolf Runner.

She missed him so badly she ached inside. Tomorrow he would return to his home and push her from his mind forever. He would take the woman who was promised to him and they would become a family. Pain shot through her and she doubled up with it— the woman would give birth to his children.

Cheyenne wanted Wolf Runner to be happy; she

only wished he could have found that happiness with her.

Since Gram's death, Cheyenne's life had taken an unexpected turn and nothing seemed quite real to her anymore. For weeks Wolf Runner had been her only reality. Right now she should be lying near him as they bedded down for the night.

Angrily she wiped unwelcome tears from her cheeks. Her life had been filled with people leaving her: first her mother, then her father and her gram. Tomorrow she would say good-bye to Wolf Runner and watch him ride out of her life forever.

Wolf Runner paced through the snow, his thoughts black and troubled. He could not take Cheyenne with him, nor could he leave her to the mercy of Night Fighter.

He paced and thought and finally became aware that Satanta paced with him. Going down on his knees, he looked into the wolf's eyes. The least he could do was send Satanta to her for tonight. She would be having a difficult time falling asleep and the wolf would soothe her.

"Satanta, go to Cheyenne."

The wolf looked at him until he spoke in Blackfoot. "Go to Cheyenne, Satanta."

A short time later Cheyenne jerked awake. Something warm and furry was nuzzling up to her! She smiled as Satanta licked her face and settled down to sleep beside her.

Her arms went around the wolf and Cheyenne wished she could keep him with her, that way she would have something of Wolf Runner to hold on to in the difficult days ahead.

Had Satanta sensed that she needed him, or had Wolf Runner sent him to comfort her?

She would never know for sure.

Cheyenne rested her head against the wolf's neck, burying her face against his soft, furry coat and falling into a dreamless sleep.

It was still dark when Cheyenne awoke and stirred. Reaching out for the wolf, she discovered Satanta had left her sometime during the night. Hearing two men conversing outside the tipi, she recognized the voices of Wolf Runner and her grandfather. Although she could not understand their words, she knew Wolf Runner was there to take his leave.

Her braids had come undone during the night and she hurriedly rebraided them. She scrambled off the fur skins and quickly ran her hand down her doeskin gown.

When she stepped out of the tipi, her grandfather moved away as if he knew she wanted to be alone with Wolf Runner at their time of parting.

"Were you leaving without telling me?" she asked, turning a hurt gaze up to Wolf Runner accusingly.

He shook his head, sensing how lost she felt here among people who dwelled in a world she did not yet understand. "I would not have gone away without first talking to you. I told you that yesterday." His gaze moved over her, and he smiled. "You are lovely in the doeskin gown, Cheyenne. You look exactly as I thought you would."

She did not hear his compliment and grabbed his arm in desperation. "My grandfather expects me to live with him and his two wives." She was trying not to cry. "I know I will grow accustomed to their ways, but at the moment it is difficult."

She looked so forlorn Wolf Runner wanted to snatch her up and ride away with her. Instead he said, "It will take time for you to feel like this is your home." He reached out to touch her and could not resist taking her hand.

Seeing his beautiful eyes smoldering with feelings, Cheyenne pulled away. She had not expected it, but she saw that he was having a difficult time leaving her. There was some small gratification in that, but it would not help the ache in her heart.

"Yes. I will soon feel at home here," she managed to say, although she did not believe it.

"Cheyenne, there is something I want to warn you about. Night Fighter is not to be trusted. Do not be alone with him."

"But he is family."

"Listen to me, for I speak the truth—he is dangerous to women. Will you promise me you will have a care around him?"

She nodded, thinking more of Wolf Runner's leaving than of Night Fighter.

Satanta came up beside Cheyenne and she bent down to him. "You wonderful wolf. I will miss you. You have been a true and loyal companion."

The animal looked straight into her eyes, and when she kissed his nose and stood, the wolf pressed against her. He was like no animal Cheyenne had ever known—there was protectiveness in him that she had never heard of in any others of his kind— from the beginning he seemed to sense what she was feeling.

"I gave your belongings to one of your grandfather's women, the younger one. She placed them in the tipi. I am also leaving your horse for you—I want you to have him."

She shook her head. "If you will remember, we were supposed to settle up at the end of the journey. If you will wait a moment, I will get the money and pay you for my share of expenses."

"Cheyenne, I have no need for money." He touched her cheek. "And for that matter, neither do you. Your money is no good here."

"But we made an agreement before we started out, and I don't want to be in debt to you."

"There is no debt owing."

Her head was too heavy to hold upright and she stared down at her beaded moccasins.

"Wolf Runner, do you think you will ever come back this way?"

"I do not believe I will."

"Then . . . accept my gratitude for everything you have done for me." Cheyenne was relieved that her voice sounded steady and did not quiver, as she did inside. But she did not know how long she could stand there without breaking down.

"You should leave now."

Glancing down at her for a long, silent moment Wolf Runner saw how helpless she looked—her cheeks were pale and her eyes were filled with unshed tears. He had looked after her for so long, it was difficult to leave her in the care of others.

"Be well, Cheyenne. And take care of yourself. Find happiness here among your mother's people."

"God go with you," she said. "And see you safely home."

Wolf Runner quickly turned and moved away, still fighting the urge to snatch her into his arms and carry her with him.

It had begun to sleet when he turned back to wait

for the wolf. Satanta had not moved from Cheyenne's side.

"Come, Satanta," he said in an authoritative voice, speaking in Blackfoot. "Come now!"

The wolf looked at him, then flopped down at Cheyenne's feet as if in defiance.

"I said to come here!" he repeated in English.

Satanta did not move; he just stared back at Wolf Runner with his yellow eyes.

Cheyenne was shocked. "Go, with him," she said, dropping to her knees and laying her hand on the wolf's head.

Still Satanta did not move from her side.

Wolf Runner came back to them and glared at the wolf. He told him in Blackfoot they were going home and he would see his mate.

Satanta seemed unconcerned.

"Cheyenne," Wolf Runner said, meeting her gaze, "I do not know how it happened, but Satanta is attached to you and he will not leave you. He is your wolf now."

Her mouth flew open in surprise and she looked from Satanta to Wolf Runner. "The gift is too great, I can't accept it." But she wanted to.

Smiling, Wolf Runner shook his head in disbelief. "A wolf will never leave its pack for any length of time. I thought for five years that Satanta belonged to me. But wolves choose who they belong to—he has chosen you. It will be a comfort to me knowing he will be looking after you."

Cheyenne could not watch as Wolf Runner turned to leave. She was certain Satanta would eventually follow him, but he did not. She glanced up and saw Wolf Runner disappear down the trail, and her hand landed on the wolf's head as she willed the animal to remain with her.

And he did.

She stood there empty inside, waiting.

Hoping Wolf Runner would come back for her and Satanta.

Then as the sun topped the pine trees, sorrow weighed down on her. She heard the faint sound of Wolf Runner riding away, and she listened as the sound disappeared into the distance.

Wolf Runner was gone from her life forever.

Her grandfather's younger wife came to her, motioning that Cheyenne should follow her into the tipi. Once inside, Walking Woman gestured to the clothing she had laid out on Cheyenne's pallet.

Smiling through her tears, Cheyenne picked up the fine doeskin gown with beautiful blue beading and gathered it to her. "Thank you," she said, smiling at her grandfather's woman. "This is lovely."

Walking Woman pointed to the moccasins and indicated they were for Cheyenne. "I now have two lovely gowns," she said, wishing the woman could understand her.

Later, when Cheyenne stepped out of the tipi, her grandfather was with a group of warriors. He looked pale and shaken, his shoulders hunched, but he grinned at Cheyenne.

When darkness fell, Bold Eagle had taken to his pallet, unable to rise. Both his wives fussed over him, trying to make him comfortable. Cheyenne's concern for him grew when she heard his labored breathing.

For long hours Cheyenne sat beside her grandfather, wishing she could help him breathe. But before morning he worsened. Had she come all the way across the country to find her grandfather, only to watch him die?

As the day progressed, her grandfather grew worse, and his chest rattled with each breath he took. Not thinking what her fate would be when her grandfather died, she was determined to stay with him to the end.

Riding down the trail that led through the pine forest, Wolf Runner felt as if he had left his heart behind. With each step his horse took, Wolf Runner battled the urge to turn back.

There was a place in his heart that was reserved for Cheyenne alone and Blue Dawn would never be able to touch it. He hoped Blue Dawn would never know she would be cheated of a husband's love.

He nudged his horse forward at a stiff gallop and the poor packhorse was having a hard time keeping up.

After a time Wolf Runner slowed his pace, thinking he was far enough from the Cheyenne village that he would not be tempted to return.

But he could not ride fast enough or far enough to leave behind the memory of amber eyes shining with tears.

Chapter Twenty-nine

Cheyenne gazed upon her grandfather's face, her heart heavy. His eyes were closed and it took every bit of his strength to draw each breath.

Just like Gram, she thought, holding his hand and trying to keep the tears at bay. She had only known her grandfather for two days, but already she had become attached to the dear old man.

Bold Eagle's two wives sat on the other side of her grandfather's pallet and many tribe members had gathered outside the tipi in what amounted to a death-watch.

From somewhere in the village, drums were beating softly, and it seemed to Cheyenne they were keeping tempo with her grandfather's heartbeat.

He suddenly opened his fever-bright eyes, his gaze fixed on Cheyenne's face. "My daughter," he said in a labored voice that seemed to steal what little breath he had left. "You have come home to me at last."

She did not understand his words.

He reached out a shaky hand to her and spoke in English. "You are not my daughter," he said, his watery eyes fixed on Cheyenne's face.

"Rest. Do not try to talk," she urged, feeling pain tear at her heart.

His grip tightened on her hand and Bold Eagle took a deep breath, let it out, and then he went limp, his hand falling away from Cheyenne's.

"No!" she cried. "Do not leave me!"

Walking Woman and Soaring Bird began rocking back and forth, chanting, their pain tearing at her heart. Lowering her head to rest against the old man's chest, Cheyenne cried bitter tears.

In the distance she heard the cry of the wolf and knew it was Satanta echoing her grief.

She did not realize Night Fighter had entered the tipi until he took her hand. "Come with me," he urged. "Allow the wives of our chief to prepare him for the ceremony."

Cheyenne felt numb as Night Fighter guided her outside, where others had begun their lamenting chants that filled the village with sorrow.

The morning sun had melted the snow, but dark clouds gathered in the north, and Cheyenne was certain it would snow before sundown. She raised her tear-bright gaze to the sky, not knowing how to show her grief in the Indian way.

Night Fighter tugged her hand, urging her away from the gathering. Forgetting Wolf Runner's warning about being alone with the warrior, she allowed him to lead her away from the village and down a path to the solitude of the woods.

Suddenly Satanta was beside her, matching her steps and placing his huge body between Cheyenne and Night Fighter.

"I didn't know my grandfather for very long, but he was easy to love," she whispered through trembling lips. Heartbreak and sorrow consumed her. She wished she'd had more time to get to know her grandfather.

There were so many things he could have taught her, so many things about her mother's people she did not know.

Leaning her head against the rough bark of a pine tree, she wept.

Night Fighter stood some distance away, warily eyeing the wolf that lay at Cheyenne's feet, thinking the wolf would have to die.

The chants from the village seemed to be rising in volume and Cheyenne remained there until silence fell like a whisper on the wind. Remembering at last that Night Fighter was near, she turned to face him.

"Is it over?"

"Not completely," he answered in English. His dark eyes swept her face. "The old man took his time in leaving this world."

Cheyenne was shocked by the coldness in his tone. "I don't know what you mean."

"It matters not. I wanted to tell you that the council is meeting to choose a new chief," he told her. "I believe it will be my father."

She could do no more than nod.

Night Fighter moved closer but stopped when Satanta raised his head and stared. "I wanted to explain some things to you that you may not know."

Sighing, she gave him her full attention. "There are many things I don't know."

"I want to speak to you of what happens to a woman when her husband dies, or, like you, your grand-father."

Cheyenne patiently waited for him to continue, not knowing why he was saying these things when her grandfather had just died.

Night Fighter could not hold back a smile. Cheyenne was ripe and ready for a man, and he intended

that that man would be him. "In our village you will
be respected as the granddaughter of our dead chief,
but if a woman has no man to look after her, she
will be abandoned by the rest of the tribe." He found
further satisfaction at the horror on her face. "It has
always been so and it is for the good of the tribe—
the weak cannot be tended by the strong."

"Are you saying I will be left to die?"

"Cheyenne, you cannot hunt for game, and no one
will be willing to share their food with you. You will
soon die from exposure and hunger."

Swallowing a lump of fear, she shook her head in
dazed shock. "Explain what you mean. What about
my grandfather's wives?"

"The younger, Walking Woman, will probably find
a warrior to take her into his tipi. I do not know what
will happen to the eldest wife, for she is so old no one
will want her as their woman."

Cheyenne met his gaze. "And you are telling me
that I have no one."

He waited for a moment, gathering his words.
"You have me."

Suddenly she remembered Wolf Runner warning
her about Night Fighter, and she glared at him. "I
will not live with you."

"You *will* be my woman. There is no other way for
you."

Most of Cheyenne's life she had lived by other people's rules and notions. Once more she was trapped
in a situation from which there didn't seem to be an
escape. "I don't know you—and I have no wish to be
your woman."

Night Fighter's eyes darkened when she turned
away to return to the village.

He grabbed Cheyenne's arm and spun her to face

him. "I offer you an honored place in my tipi and you scorn it."

Shaking in anger as much as in fear, she said, "I do. My grandfather just died. I can't think of anything else at the moment."

"It is him you want."

"Who?"

"The Blackfoot—Wolf Runner. You desire to be his woman and yet, he left you." Night Fighter's eyes held a dangerous glint and his grip on Cheyenne's arm tightened. "You must choose a man in our village, and I say that man will be me."

Satanta was stirring restlessly, and Cheyenne kept a calming hand on his head, not knowing if she could keep him from attacking Night Fighter. It had always been Wolf Runner who gave the wolf his orders. She didn't know how, so she tried to keep her voice calm.

"I will not speak of this now."

Night Fighter's anger flared. "You are a fool. Do you not understand Wolf Runner used you to find me? He wants nothing so much as to see me dead. Had he cared for you, he would have taken you with him."

"I don't believe you," she said, remembering Wolf Runner had offered to help her before he knew she was related to Night Fighter. "It's not true; he wouldn't do that."

Night Fighter clamped his hand down on her arm and jerked her to him. "Pity you cannot ask him. Then you would know I speak the truth."

She glanced quickly down and saw Satanta was baring his teeth. "Do not move, Satanta," she said.

"Take your hands off her," a deadly cold voice commanded.

Wolf Runner stood just behind them, his hand resting on his knife. He had come upon them so silently neither of them had heard him, but Satanta had, and was happily circling Wolf Runner.

Cheyenne shoved Night Fighter's hand away and faced Wolf Runner, uncertain why he was there. "You have returned."

Wolf Runner took her arm and moved her away from Night Fighter. "I had time to think, and I realized your grandfather had not long to live. What Night Fighter told you is the truth, you will be on your own if you do not want to marry him, or any other man who might offer for you."

Her heart fell. "I will not be anyone's woman."

Wolf Runner glanced at Night Fighter—his father had taught him to watch a man's eyes and read his intentions. He discerned that Night Fighter wanted to go for his knife, but the man hesitated. "Do not," Wolf Runner warned.

Blinking, Night Fighter's hand moved toward his knife, with hatred bursting in his heart. The man he despised above any other stood before him, touching the woman Night Fighter wanted for his own. "You have no claim on her—she is of my blood and belongs to me," he hissed.

"Then it is well I returned, for she does not want you." He gazed down at Cheyenne. "I will take you to my mother, where you will be protected."

Happiness burst in Cheyenne's heart. "I will need to get my belongings. It won't take long."

"Wait," Night Fighter said, speaking in his tongue so Cheyenne would not understand the words. "I say to you again that I have more claim on this woman than you, Blackfoot."

Wolf Runner answered him in kind, "Only if she

says you do. Since she has already refused you, she will go with me."

"I have seen the hunger in your eyes when you watch her." Then Night Fighter smiled. "She does not believe me when I told her you used her to find me. You and I know it to be the truth."

"I know where to find you, which I will do when I know Cheyenne is safely with my people."

"What is she to you?"

Wolf Runner paused in thought. "I vowed to see her safe. Her white grandmother charged me to take her to my mother, and that is what I will do." He watched the Cheyenne warrior grasp the handle of his knife and Wolf Runner's mood darkened. "I would not do that if I were you. You would be dead before you could use that knife."

Night Fighter had heard much of Wolf Runner's prowess as a warrior, and his bravery was legendary. With anger burning in his heart, he dropped his hand to his side. "This is not over between us."

Wolf Runner gripped Cheyenne's arm, not trusting Night Fighter. "I will accompany you."

When they reached the tipi of her grandfather, both of his wives were inside. Cheyenne touched the eldest on the arm. "Wolf Runner, please translate what I say."

He nodded.

"Tell Soaring Bird, I feel her grief. Thank her for all her kindnesses."

After Wolf Runner spoke to the eldest wife, Cheyenne approached Walking Woman. "Explain to her that I am going away with you. Thank her for her gentleness and her kindness to me."

Soaring Bird dipped her head in grief, but Walking Woman took Cheyenne's hand and spoke.

"She says," Wolf Runner explained, "that she wishes you happiness, and that your grandfather's last hours were made easier because you were with him."

Tearfully Cheyenne gathered her meager belongings and moved to the tipi opening. Meeting each woman's gaze, she nodded and stepped out into the sunshine to find Night Fighter waiting for them.

Cheyenne cringed at the hatred reflected in his eyes. When he moved toward her, Wolf Runner stepped between them. "Do not," he warned.

Satanta also edged himself between them and bared his teeth.

Stepping back, Night Fighter faced Wolf Runner. "I should have slain you the first day you came to our land. I will one day drive my knife into your heart."

"Do not make threats you cannot keep. I do not fear any man who intimidates a woman for his own needs."

"I do not care for your high opinion."

Wolf Runner had already gauged the Cheyenne warrior's character and determined he was a coward. "Watch him, Satanta."

When the wolf went into a crouch, Night Fighter took several quick paces back. "Take the woman and may you never know a moment's peace with her."

Cheyenne had no notion what the two men were saying to each other, but they were saying it angrily. She mounted her horse and waited for Wolf Runner, who backed toward his own horse, watching Night Fighter for any sign of treachery.

Wolf Runner mounted his horse, and they rode away, with Satanta and the packhorse following behind.

Cheyenne did not look back as they rode away from her grandfather's village. But she had left a piece of her heart with the dear old man whom she had known for such a short time, and his two wives, who had shown her such kindness. This was a day for mourning her grandfather's death, but also a day for rejoicing. For whatever the reason, Wolf Runner had returned for her.

She had been in the depths of despair, thinking he was gone from her life forever. When Cheyenne glanced at him she saw he was frowning. Yes, he had come back for her, but something was troubling him.

"I will not cause you any trouble," she said, wanting to reassure him that he should feel no obligation toward her.

He turned a dark gaze on her. "You have caused me trouble since the first day I saw you."

Chapter Thirty

Throughout the day Cheyenne and Wolf Runner spoke little. She had many questions she wanted to ask, but his brooding silence sealed her lips.

At sunset she helped him make camp, and after she had returned from gathering wood, she finally spoke. "Why did you come back for me?" she asked, going down on her knees and arranging the wood for the campfire, hoping he would say he had returned because he missed her.

He knelt beside her, striking his flint and lighting the campfire. "I knew when I left that your grandfather was ill and did not have long to live. I was nearby when I heard the drums that announced his death."

He decided not to tell her that he was already coming back for her when he heard the drums, and he would have taken her away with him even if her grandfather had not died.

"If you had not returned, would Night Fighter have forced me to be his woman?"

"Yes."

She smiled at him. "Once again it seems you've rescued me."

Even though he was taking Cheyenne to his village, where she would be safe, nothing could change between them, and he had to make her understand that now.

Studying her face, it took Wolf Runner a moment to speak. "Perhaps you will find a strong warrior among my people who will suit you."

Cheyenne dropped her head, studying the flickering flame that had just taken hold. Wolf Runner had not come for her because he wanted her with him. "I don't care to be anyone's woman." She frowned. "Is it also thought among the Blackfoot that a woman without family is a burden to others?"

"Only if they are alone and have no one to look after them. You will not need to worry about that. My mother and father will offer you their protection."

He reached out to her and then let his hand drop away. "To see you in a doeskin gown seems natural."

She forced a smile. "I find the clothing comfortable," she admitted, glancing down at her moccasins. "Knowing me, I will have a hole in the bottom of these before we reach your village."

Nodding, Wolf Runner watched the flames dance across her face and wanted to take her in his arms. "Yes."

Watching the night sky, Cheyenne stood. "Wolf Runner, for so long now I have not known where my life was going—I still don't."

He knew her well enough to discern she was feeling lost and unsure. "Look to my parents as your friends."

He had not said he would be her friend. Cheyenne bit her trembling lip. He would soon marry the woman he had left behind in his village, and she would have to watch them together.

"If you are ever troubled, I will be your friend," she told him in what she hoped was a strong voice. "I stand ready to help you in any way I can because you have done so much for me. It was not your duty to come back for me, but you did, and I am glad."

His throat had closed off. She did not even know she was tearing him apart inside.

"I look forward to meeting your mother since I have heard so much about her."

Wolf Runner turned to her. "I have thought almost from the time I met you that you and my mother are similar. I believe you will like each other."

Cheyenne spread the furs out next to a cliff wall, hoping it would protect them from the wind. "I worry about Grandfather's older wife."

"Do not. It is the way it has always been with older women alone." He finished tying a knot in a rope and looped it about her horse's hooves. "It may seem cruel to you, but it is necessary for the survival of a tribe."

Cheyenne curled up on the fur and covered herself with a blanket. The clouds had moved away and the night sky was clear and stars were scattered across a black backdrop like sparkling jewels. The moon seemed so near it gave the illusion you could reach up and pluck it out of the sky. "I still don't like it."

Once more her life was spinning out of control. *Oh, Gram,* she thought achingly, *where does the new direction take me?*

Will I ever find happiness? she wondered.

Satanta bounded out of the bushes and flopped down beside her. Resting her hand on the wolf's head, she fell asleep, knowing Wolf Runner was nearby.

But not knowing he watched her as she slept.

For over a week Wolf Runner led them toward the distant mountains. The closer they got to Blackfoot land, the quieter Wolf Runner became. Cheyenne did not feel like talking either. She was an encumbrance to him, and wished there was some way she could apologize for all she had put him through on the journey.

When she looked at him, she was reminded how wonderful his lips had felt against hers and how right it felt to be in his arms. She had never envied anyone in her life, but she had begun to envy the woman who would soon be his wife.

Once they had reached the foothills Cheyenne glanced up the great mountains. "I used to love imagining what it would be like to live in the mountains, so high above everything. These are much higher than the peaks in Santa Fe—do you climb there often?"

Wolf Runner turned to look at her. Cheyenne was exactly the woman for him. He wanted her as his woman so much he considered taking her to the mountains and making her his. Instead, he pointed to a distant peak. "My family has an encampment there, where I often spend summers. It is where my father took my mother after they were joined."

Swallowing a lump in her throat, Cheyenne looked into his eyes. "Is that where you will be taking your . . . woman?"

He turned his head. "Blue Dawn does not like the mountains."

The moon had risen above the pines as they enjoyed the two rabbits Wolf Runner had trapped and Cheyenne had roasted on a spit.

After she had eaten her fill, Cheyenne set aside dried berries and pemmican for breakfast the next morning, then repacked the rest of the supplies.

Cheyenne huddled beneath her blanket. The icy fingers of winter swept down the mountain, and she shivered until Satanta plopped his large body down next to her.

Wolf Runner lay so near she could have reached out and touched him, but she dared not bridge the gap, no matter how much she longed for his touch.

"For the last few evenings I have felt you are wrestling with a problem, Wolf Runner. Would it help you to talk about it?"

He turned his dark gaze on her, not at all surprised she had known he was troubled. "More than any woman I have ever known, you test me, Cheyenne."

She rose up on her elbow, shocked. "That has never been my intention. In fact, I've tried not to be any trouble to you. Once we reach your village, you can turn me over to your mother and never have to think about me again."

He watched the firelight play across her hair. "Never think of you again?" he said, giving her a searching look. "And how do you suppose we bring that about?"

"I don't know," she answered, confused. "I suppose as soon as you take a wife, you will move out of your mother's tipi and won't have to see me."

"Cheyenne, I have not lived with my parents since I was fourteen."

"Oh. A white boy of fourteen would never move out of his parents' house."

He sounded irritated. "I am not white, and my parents do not live in a house."

"Of course, it was just a figure of speech."

He sat up. "Cheyenne, I am sensitive to all you have suffered, losing your grandmother and then your grandfather in less than three months, but could you not look to the future with hope in your heart? I want that for you."

"Wolf Runner, I have always been happy, even as a child. But lately, life has been a bit hard. I will try to put all the sadness behind me. And I'm sure I'll eventually succeed. I will always miss Gram, but I hardly knew my grandfather before he died."

"What do you miss most about your gram?" he asked, trying to turn the conversation away from her unhappiness, which was what was really bothering him.

"A hundred little things—the smell of coffee in the morning, even though I don't like coffee. I miss her wise guidance and her loving nature." She sat up, tucking the blanket about her. "The one thing I discovered by living with the Cheyenne is that I am more white than I am Indian."

Wolf Runner lay back on his folded arms. "Yet you have been set upon a different path."

"And I don't know where it will take me." She fixed her gaze on the brightest star in the heavens and stared at it. "How did your mother adjust to the Indian way of life?"

"I never thought about it. She has always seemed Blackfoot to me. You will meet my grandparents, Chief Broken Lance and Tall Woman, who took my mother as their daughter when she was first brought to our village. They gave her a wonderful life, even if it was not the one she was born to live."

"They must be proud of you."

"They have a son, named Firethorn, who is my best friend."

"Your uncle is your best friend?"

"He is my uncle, but he is only two years older than I am."

"It sounds like you have a perfect family," Cheyenne observed.

He looked into her eyes, wishing she belonged to

him, and said before he could stop himself, "No, not quite perfect."

Cheyenne squeezed her eyes together tightly. Even the most innocent subjects led them back to their hopeless situation. Turning her back to him without a word, she lay down, feeling Satanta adjust to accommodate her.

What would I do without this loyal wolf to comfort me? she wondered.

Wolf Runner stared at Cheyenne for a long moment. In his heart he had to let her go, and he could do that now, knowing that his mother would take care of her.

The sacrifice he was making in giving her up was almost too great. He saw Cheyenne's shoulders shake and realized she was silently crying.

Without thought of the consequences, he went to her and gathered her in his arms, kissing her tears away. It was like a dam had broken and his feelings came tumbling out. "Do not cry, for your tears tear at my heart."

Her arms went around him and she looked up at him. "I can't help myself."

Wolf Runner brushed her hair out of her face, his lips hovering above her mouth. "And I cannot help myself."

Chapter Thirty-one

Wolf Runner kissed her with a passion that took her breath away, his arms tightening fiercely about her. She found herself quivering with a need she couldn't understand. She could feel the power in him, the need that tore at him, for it tore at her as well.

Pulling back, Wolf Runner studied her for a long moment. He bent his head and his ebony hair slid across his face, and he flipped it back with a trembling hand.

"Cheyenne," he began, his voice no more than a raspy whisper, "I want you. I look in your eyes for answers and I believe you want me as well." He raised her hand and placed it on his chest. "Feel how my heart beats for you."

She needed to clarify something that she had been avoiding, so she asked, "Please tell me the truth—did you only take me to my grandfather so you could kill Night Fighter?"

Wolf Runner did not speak for a moment. "I did use your journey to get to him," he answered truthfully, tangling his hand in her hair. He was glad she finally knew the truth. "But somewhere along the way, I began to want you."

"You mean you wanted my body?"

Her innocent question stopped his hand from sweeping across her breasts. "Yes." He closed his eyes for a brief moment before his heated gaze settled on hers. "That and other things I cannot have from you," he admitted as if the words were forced through his lips. The anguish he saw in her eyes was like a knife slammed into his heart.

There was no warmth in her voice when she said, "Take what you will of me. I give it freely."

Slowly lowering his head, Wolf Runner's mouth shaped to hers, but her lips did not soften beneath his. She tried not to think of his motive for helping her as a betrayal. But as Wolf Runner's hands moved beneath her gown, pulling it up and off, and his mouth moved down to her breasts, Cheyenne became incapable of any thought at all. She could only revel in pleasure, her breath coming in short gasps.

"Do you want this?" he breathed against her ear, then pulled back to gaze into her fever-bright eyes. "Tell me to stop, and I will."

Her plea was ripped from her throat. "Don't stop," she said, moving her head so she could press her lips to his. Some small part of her wanted to shove him away, but that part was quickly overruled as her body yearned for his touch.

Wolf Runner cursed himself for doing this to her, but he would no longer be denied the woman he loved, the one who stirred his blood as no other woman ever had.

He drew back and looked at her, with the campfire glittering across her beautiful body. His hands were gentle as they swept across her breasts, past her small waist, then moved caressingly over her hips, stopping on her flat stomach, and his voice came out raspy as he said, "We were made for each other. If your God had a plan, I believe it was to send me to Santa Fe to find you."

Cheyenne stared into flaming eyes. Reaching out to touch his dark hair, which had tumbled onto her chest, she closed her eyes, her mind taking her back to reality. "And I believe he sent you to merely use me."

When she opened her eyes again, he saw the anguish in their depths, and felt as if pieces of himself were being ripped away. "I cannot blame you for feeling that way. In the beginning it was true, but, Cheyenne, it is not true now."

She cried out as his head bent and his mouth took hers in a mind-stealing kiss. He touched his mouth to her brow, kissed her closed eyes, and rubbed his lips against hers. When his hand moved lower, Cheyenne moaned with pleasure. Yes, they were made for each other—and she would always be his. The other woman did not matter to her at the moment, only his words and his touch mattered.

There was no world outside the wonderful feeling that coursed through her body, awakening needs that would not be denied. Cheyenne did not know why she loved Wolf Runner; she only knew she did, deeply and lastingly.

Suddenly Satanta come running out of the woods, then stood beside them, his wolf eyes seeing into the darkness, his acute hearing catching a sound they had not heard.

Wolf Runner broke off his kiss and frowned, becoming alert. He pulled the blanket over Cheyenne and stood, his gaze sweeping the darkness. In a swift move he piled dirt on the fire, throwing the camp into darkness. "As quietly as possible, get dressed," he told Cheyenne. "Someone is approaching from the west."

Cheyenne quickly obeyed, although she heard no

sound until the rider emerged from the woods. She felt the tension drain out of Wolf Runner, so he must know and trust the Indian that approached.

"Have no fear, Cheyenne. It is Firethorn."

Firethorn slid off his horse and grinned at Wolf Runner. "You are growing careless, my friend. You were making so much noise I heard you from deep in the woods."

"You did not hear anything; you followed the campfire," Wolf Runner told him.

Firethorn's gaze moved to Cheyenne. "Who is this woman?"

"Someone who needs looking after. I will tell you about her later. Why are you here?"

"We got word this afternoon that you and this woman had passed onto Blackfoot land. We also got word that five Cheyenne warriors in full war paint were following you. They have been tracking you most of the day, but made camp less than a mile away. If I saw your campfire, so did they."

Wolf Runner had not known he was being followed, and he should have. His mind had been on Cheyenne, who was now staring at Firethorn with a puzzled expression.

Cheyenne watched the two warriors talk, not understanding their words. Her heart was still thundering inside her, and she could still feel Wolf Runner's kiss on her lips.

Wolf Runner buckled his knife about his waist. "I need to explain to her what has happened."

Firethorn studied his friend, his eyes narrowing. "What is this woman to you? I know what was happening between the two of you when I rode into camp. Why would you want to be with her when Blue Dawn waits for you?"

Wolf Runner spun around, facing his friend. "What I do is no concern of yours."

Firethorn's eyes narrowed. "What is she to you?"

Wolf Runner was angry. "The woman's name is Cheyenne. Right now, the most important thing to me is her safety."

Firethorn nodded. "You are right—it is not my concern, but those Cheyenne warriors who follow you are." He looked at the woman and saw confusion in her eyes. He traced the lines of her face and noticed she was a half-breed. "Tell me what you want me to do and I will do it."

"Take Cheyenne to my mother. I will backtrack and find out about those who follow us, although I suspect the leader is Night Fighter."

"Then I should go with you," Firethorn said. "Surely the woman will come to no harm if the wolf remains with her. There are too many for you to face alone."

Wolf Runner hoisted himself onto his horse and said to his friend in Blackfoot, "I go alone." Glancing at the clouds overhead he frowned. "A storm is coming and she will need you." He was quiet for a moment as he tried to decide how to answer his friend, who looked puzzled. "Know this, Cheyenne is the woman of my heart. Take care of her for me."

Firethorn's eyes widened. "I understand better than you think I do."

Cheyenne held out her hand to Wolf Runner. "What is happening? Are you leaving me?"

"Firethorn will take you to our village. You will come to no harm there."

Before Cheyenne could utter a word, Wolf Runner turned his mount and rode away, leaving her with the stranger.

"Do you speak English?" she quickly asked the warrior.

Firethorn shook his head and went about breaking camp.

"Satanta," she called to the wolf. "Go with Wolf Runner. Go."

The wolf looked at her for a moment before tearing off in the direction Wolf Runner had ridden.

"What am I to do?" she asked, turning to Firethorn.

Firethorn shrugged his shoulders and motioned for her to saddle her horse, which she did without hesitation.

Something had happened and Cheyenne did not know what it was, and this Blackfoot could not tell her. Wolf Runner was in danger—she felt it in her heart.

Cheyenne lowered her head as her horse trudged through a swirling, blinding snowstorm. Closing her eyes, Cheyenne warmed herself by remembering every word Wolf Runner had spoken to her. She was not sure he loved her as she loved him, but he wanted her, and that was enough for now. He said they had been created for each other, and she believed that.

Bone-weary, Cheyenne wished the warrior would stop so they could rest—he had been pushing them hard through half the night and most of the day— the horses were lathered and tired, but still he pushed them onward.

The sun had dropped behind the pine trees and it would soon be dark.

Why can we not stop to rest? she wondered, thinking she had never been so weary.

Something or someone dangerous had been following them, of that she was certain.

As the horses struggled up a snow-slick hill, Firethorn paused at the top and pointed below, saying something Cheyenne did not understand.

Blinking her eyes against the heavy snow, she could see nothing beyond her horse's head.

Suddenly Cheyenne could make out the flicker of a campfire, and as they rode farther, she saw many campfires and the outline of many tipis. It was a huge camp. Breathing a sigh of relief, she realized they had finally reached Wolf Runner's village.

As they started down the hill at a slow pace, the sure-footed horses picking their way across the slick ground, Cheyenne did not know whether to be happy or apprehensive.

When they entered the village, there were few people about. She imagined they had sought the warmth of their lodges to escape the snowstorm. But Wolf Runner was still out there, alone and in danger in the storm.

Firethorn led Cheyenne past many tipis, finally stopping before one. He slid off his horse and motioned for her to follow him inside.

Cheyenne entered after Firethorn and he began talking to a tall Indian who looked very much like Wolf Runner, so she knew she was in the presence of Wolf Runner's father.

The two men spoke in Blackfoot, and the older man glanced at Cheyenne and nodded. When Firethorn abruptly left, Cheyenne examined the Indian, waiting for him to acknowledge her. He was tall, like Wolf Runner, and handsome of face. His hair was dark with no sign of gray. Even with the robe draped about his shoulders, she could tell he was built like Wolf Runner with broad shoulders and muscled arms.

Wind Warrior studied Cheyenne for a long moment before he spoke to her in Blackfoot.

She shook her head. "I'm sorry, I do not understand you."

"I was saying," he said, switching to English, "that you are welcome in our lodge. We had heard our son was traveling with you. And you are Ivy Gatlin's granddaughter?"

She was surprised he knew of her and her grandmother. "Yes, I am. How did you know?"

Wind Warrior smiled. "There are few secrets once you cross into Blackfoot land."

Cheyenne looked at him skeptically.

"We got a telegram from Cullen, telling us your grandmother died and you had left Santa Fe. My wife was certain it was you who traveled with our son. We are saddened by the death of your grandmother."

Cheyenne could feel the power that surrounded this man. His eyes were probing, and she felt like he could read her every thought. Before she could answer him, the tipi flap was thrown aside and a woman entered.

Her hair, the color of summer wheat, was braided and woven with colorful beads. She wore a long buckskin gown and high moccasins, and Cheyenne stared into green eyes that were also studying her. Wolf Runner's mother—and the reason his dark eyes were flecked with green.

"You must be Ivy Gatlin's granddaughter," she said, coming forward and sliding her arm around Cheyenne's shoulder, drawing her closer to the warming fire. "You are most welcome in our home."

For reasons Cheyenne could not understand, tears gathered in her eyes and she leaned her head on Rain Song's comforting shoulder.

Wind Warrior left when Rain Song nodded at him. She took Cheyenne's hand. "Do not be distressed," Rain Song said. "You are among friends."

"Life has been so uncertain for so long," Cheyenne said, drying her eyes, and ashamed to have shown her emotions. "I didn't mean to cry."

Rain Song removed Cheyenne's damp robe, replacing it with a warm blanket. "You carry many burdens. Rest at the fire of a friend and have something warm to eat. Then you can sleep."

"Can you tell me about Wolf Runner—is he in danger?" Cheyenne searched Rain Song's eyes. "I had the feeling he was going into some kind of battle. Can you tell me about it?"

"Our son was being followed by several Cheyenne warriors. Firethorn thought they were a threat."

"Surely Wolf Runner will not take them on by himself," Cheyenne said, pressing her hand over her pounding heart.

"It is possible he will," Rain Song said. "But you should not be concerned. Even now Firethorn is gathering warriors to join my son."

"Wolf Runner has Satanta with him," Cheyenne said.

"Then that will be in his favor," Rain Song said, motioning for her to sit beside the fire.

The two women looked at each other, each trying to hide their worry from the other.

Rain Song scooped up a bowl of stew that was bubbling over the fire. "You must look after your health," she said, the mother in her coming out. "You are tiny—it looks to me as if you have not been eating properly. But then one cannot have a steady diet when traveling such a great distance."

"I have always been this size," Cheyenne said, taking a bite of stew, and thinking it was delicious, but she was so worried about Wolf Runner, she could hardly swallow it.

"My son has been trained to take care of himself," Rain Song told her. "He will not act hastily, or without thinking ahead."

Nodding, Cheyenne swallowed. "I know he is brave and strong. But I fear the man he faces is my cousin, Night Fighter, who will act without honor."

Rain Song studied the young woman. "You care for my son."

"Who would not? He has put himself in danger more than once to protect me." Cheyenne proceeded to tell Wolf Runner's mother about the events that had happened on the journey. She was not aware she was crying when she told his mother how Wolf Runner had returned for her after her grandfather died.

"Will you not rest?" Rain Song suggested. "You have come far. I will awaken you when there is any news of my son."

Cheyenne laid the bowl aside and wearily lay down, resting her head against the soft fur Rain Song had provided. "I am tired," she said, yawning.

And she slept.

Chapter Thirty-two

Wolf Runner slid behind a rock formation and then crawled forward on his belly. He could hear the Cheyenne warriors' voices, and they were arguing among themselves.

"It is not for us to capture the dead chief's granddaughter—she made the choice to leave our village," one of them said.

Night Fighter accused them all of cowardice. "Then return to the village and drink your mother's milk. None of you deserves to ride with me."

Wolf Runner recognized the warrior he had once fought with, the one who had wounded him. He was the one who was the most vocal against the raid.

"I say this to you all: have I not met Wolf Runner in combat and he survived, although the wound I inflicted on him would have killed a lesser man? And I say further, none here can defeat him."

"We are now on Blackfoot land, which could be viewed as an act of war. The council will not like our being here—our chief is dead, we have no chief and should return to the village until we have a new leader," said another.

"Cowards! You have me to lead you. And I believe when the council meets to choose a new chief, they will choose my father or perhaps even me. I have no one here to answer to."

Wolf Runner had been creeping closer and by now he had heard enough. Placing an arrow in his bow, he stepped out of the shadows, with Satanta at his side.

"Answer to me," Wolf Runner said, aiming his arrow straight at Night Fighter's heart. "Say what you will before you die. This is our land, and you were not invited."

A slow grin curved Night Fighter's lips. "I hoped I would find you. I have made a promise to myself that I will be the one to end the life of the Blackfoot's most valiant warrior." The way he said it was no compliment.

"I am but one of many," Wolf Runner said, his arrow never wavering, but his glance went to the others. "This is not your fight. But if any one of you dispute that, I will get to you in time." His gaze slid back to Night Fighter. "What thoughts go through a warrior's mind when he knows he is about to die?"

Night Fighter licked his dry lips. "Do you kill me without giving me a chance to defend myself?"

"Name your weapon," he said. "The rest of you throw down your weapons or Night Fighter dies now."

There were sounds of weapons hitting the ground, and Wolf Runner glanced down at Satanta. "Make sure the others do not join in the fight," he told the wolf. On cue, Satanta trotted toward the others, his wolf eyes moving over each warrior, quivering as if ready to attack at the slightest movement.

Night Fighter jerked out his knife. "I choose this weapon—I like to get near enough to my enemy to see his fear."

Before the Cheyenne warrior had a chance to react, Wolf Runner threw down his bow and withdrew his own knife. "Then let it be."

The other warriors' eyes widened at the bravery of the Blackfoot who showed no fear despite the fact that the odds were against him. In unison they backed up, eyeing the wolf, and watching two powerful warriors clash.

Muscles strained and bulged, and although it was cold, sweat dampened each fighter's face.

Night Fighter drew first blood—his knife slashed across Wolf Runner's face. Wolf Runner did not flinch, but went on the attack. With a quick movement, he slid his leg behind Night Fighter and drove him to the ground. Before anyone knew what had happened, Wolf Runner's knife found its mark deep in Night Fighter's chest. He watched his enemy twitch and then become still in death.

Wiping his knife on the dead man's shirt, he stood and faced the others. "Would any of you like to have a turn?" Wolf Runner asked.

"We do not wish to fight you," one of them said. "Your cause is just. We are on your land."

"Then take your fallen warrior and go. He does not deserve to lie on Blackfoot land." Wolf Runner slid his knife into his belt and picked up his bow and arrow. "This settles an old debt. Let no man from your tribe come to Blackfoot land with vengeance in his heart."

The others mumbled among themselves, as two of them lifted the fallen Night Fighter. Wolf Runner watched them until they rode out of sight and then he touched his face where Night Fighter had wounded him. It was little more than a scratch.

"Let us go home, Satanta," he said, walking up the hill and gathering his horse's reins. "It is over."

The night passed without Cheyenne waking.

Rain Song stirred restlessly, knowing her son was

facing danger. The part of her that was still white wanted to coddle and protect him, but in the Blackfoot culture, that was not allowed. Her husband did not lie beside her this night, and she knew he would be standing by the river, waiting for their son's return.

Just before sunup she heard riders and rushed outside to find Wolf Runner had come home.

Rain Song waited for him to dismount, then embraced him. "Thank God you are home safely. You have been gone so long I began to worry."

"I already told my father about the warriors who were following me. I came upon their camp and defeated their leader. I do not think we will be bothered by the Cheyenne again. Our women have been avenged."

Rain Song nodded, understanding her son had done what was necessary. "It is as it must be."

Wolf Runner smiled down at her. "It is good to see you, my mother." He glanced around. "Where are my brother and sister? Is it too early for them to greet me?"

"They have gone with a hunting party and should return in a few days' time. Sooner if they learn you have returned."

"How is Cheyenne?" Wolf Runner asked, glancing toward his father's tipi, where he was certain she slept.

"She was weary and fell asleep early and is still sleeping, as far as I know."

"Excuse me, Mother," he said, turning away and moving swiftly toward his father's lodge.

Wind Warrior appeared beside his wife. "His actions are unexpected. Why does he rush to the woman?"

Rain Song's brow knitted in worry. "I do not know.

Our son should have gone first to his intended bride, Blue Dawn."

Wind Warrior stared down at her. "This could mean trouble."

"It is strange," she said, looking toward the tipi where Cheyenne slept. "I never saw Blue Dawn as our son's wife."

"He has made his pledge to her," Wind Warrior reminded his wife.

"What if he does not love her? Would you have our son take a woman to be his if he does not love her?"

"I would have our son walk with honor."

Rain Song was quiet for a moment as she pondered the situation. "What would you have done if you had given your word to another and your heart was mine? Would you have turned away from me, husband?"

He touched her shoulder, his eyes flaming with emotion. "I would have taken you to wife and forgotten about honor." He gazed at his son, watching him enter the lodge. "But I did not have to make the choice our son will face. There was never any question that you would be mine."

"Wolf Runner will have choices to make," Rain Song said, staring at the clouds that were gathering overhead. "It could be that he does not care so much for Cheyenne, and is just worried about her because she had been in his care for so long."

"Let us hope that is so. But I do not think it is."

Wolf Runner stood over Cheyenne, watching her sleep. Now that he was home, he could no longer see her every day. He could not touch her, or listen to her laugh.

He had just turned to leave when she whispered his name, and he turned back to her.

"You are safe."

He stood stiffly before her. "I was never in any danger."

Cheyenne sat up, brushing stray hair out of her face. "Was it Night Fighter?"

"It was. But you must have no fear that he will ever bother you again."

"He is dead?"

Wolf Runner nodded.

"I'm not sorry. He was an evil man."

She could read many emotions in his eyes—he was remembering their last night together, and so was she. She stood slowly, wishing he would take her in his arms, but of course he never would again. He belonged to another woman.

Looking him over carefully, she saw no wounds, merely a long scratch on his cheek. "I'm glad you were not injured."

He moved to leave. "My mother will see to your comfort and teach you that which you need to know."

Reaching out to him, she touched his shoulder. "Wolf Runner, will you really take the other woman as your wife?"

Swallowing hard, he looked down at her. He wanted to hold her close. He wanted to take her to his mountain and shut the rest of the world out of their lives. But he could not have what he wanted. "I have not seen her yet. I must go to her now."

"Wolf Runner . . . I . . . wish you happiness."

His restraint broke and he gathered her in his arms, crushing her against his chest. "Never will a day go by that I will not think of you and wish you were mine. Know that I carry you in my heart, no matter who I am with."

He released Cheyenne and moved quickly out of

the tipi, standing in the snow, wishing he could return to her. He was sick at heart, and felt as if the world no longer had any meaning.

"My son," Rain Song said, coming up beside him. "Will you be able to give Cheyenne up?"

"Mother, it is the hardest thing I will ever have to do." He glanced down at her and saw the sadness in her green eyes. "Do not worry, and tell my father not to be concerned. I will do what duty demands of me."

Tears gathered in Rain Song's eyes. Yes, like his father, he would do what was expected of him, but he loved Ivy Gatlin's granddaughter, and his hurt was his mother's hurt.

Chapter Thirty-three

Cheyenne stepped out of the tipi into a chilling wind. Her gaze followed Satanta as he raced across the village, soon to be greeted by five other wolves that circled around him. The animals danced around one another, sniffing and licking, obviously happy to be reunited.

Melancholy struck Cheyenne. Wolf Runner would soon be reunited with the woman who was going to be his. Perhaps he already was. She hugged herself against the wind, now more unhappy than ever— Wolf Runner loved her, but there was no joy in that knowledge. She would have to watch him with the other woman, knowing the woman lay in his arms at night and received his kisses; it would be her body his hands caressed and her that he made love to.

Rain Song approached from another tipi and walked in Cheyenne's direction. After meeting the mother and father, she could see why Wolf Runner was bound by honor.

"You must be chilled to the bone," Rain Song told her, opening the tipi flap and sweeping her hand forward. "Sit by the fire while I make you something to eat."

Woodenly, Cheyenne obeyed, knowing she should not allow Wolf Runner's mother to wait upon her, but she was too weary to protest. Glancing at the beautiful white woman, she could not help but make an observation. "You are happy here in the Blackfoot village," she said. "Do you never miss the life you had before you were brought here?"

Rain Song handed Cheyenne a bowl and sat beside her. "This is where my husband and children are, and I have many friends here as well. My aunt and uncle often visit, and give me all the news of the white world." She shook her head. "Everything I want is here."

Cheyenne nodded. "I understand why you feel that way." She took a bite of something that tasted like mush and found it delicious because it was laced with honey, nuts, and berries. "What will become of me?"

"My husband and I have been talking about that. You will remain here with us until such time as you may want to accept one of our warriors as your husband. If you do not wish to marry, you will erect a tipi of your own and live in peace."

"That is allowed?"

"If my husband says it is, and he will, if that is what you decide."

Cheyenne hung her head. "You are kind, and I thank you for it."

Feeling the young woman's hurt, Rain Song knew what troubled her—the same thing that troubled her son. These two young people were meant to be together—but because of a pledge of honor, they would be made to suffer the rest of their lives, and that made Rain Song angry.

"Cheyenne, the Blackfoot have a saying that I will try to translate: if the wind blows in the wrong direction, you cannot reach out your hand and turn it in the direction you want it to go—rather go in the direction it blows."

Raising her head, Cheyenne nodded. "I understand, and I will do what is expected of me." Tears gathered in her eyes and spilled down her cheeks. "I hesitate to tell you I love your son, and I believe he loves me."

"I know he does, and it troubles me deeply." Rain Song was reflective before she spoke again. "This also troubles my husband."

"Pray do not trouble yourself about anything I've said." Cheyenne forced a smile. "I am happy to be here, and I thank you for taking me into your . . . tipi. I know now what is expected of me, and I will not disappoint you."

Rain Song knew her son would be happy with this sweet young woman, but she kept her thoughts to herself. "Let us put that aside for now. For the moment I can do something to help ease you into your new life. How would you like it if I begin teaching you our language?"

This time Cheyenne's smile was genuine. "I would like that. Wolf Runner taught me a few words, but I can't put sentences together."

"Then I will teach you to be fluent in our language. You will need to know what everyone is saying, and be able to speak to others so you can really feel at home."

Later, when the snowstorm had moved away, Rain Song took Cheyenne about the village and introduced her to other women, translating their words of welcome for Cheyenne.

"They think you are beautiful," Rain Song told her. "One of them said you would be pretty if your skin was not so white." Rain Song laughed with humor. "They once said the same thing about me. Now I don't think they see the color of my skin."

Cheyenne thought about what Rain Song had said. "It will be a blessing to be in a place where I am known for who I am and not how I look."

"Then this will be your home."

Firethorn met Blue Dawn as she came out of her father's tipi. He stopped before her, shaking his head. "I am sorry you have been so humiliated—it must be hard on you, with all the village knowing of your shame."

She stared at him in confusion. "What do you mean?"

"Well, Wolf Runner's actions. I was stunned that he brought another woman home with him, and to make it worse, she has Cheyenne blood in her."

"Wolf Runner is home?"

"I know, it is another shame you must bear that he went to the other woman last night and did not first come to you. I am sorry, you must be so humiliated."

Blue Dawn's face twisted with rage. "How could he do this to me?"

"There is more," Firethorn said with seeming reluctance. "He gave her a wolf—and not just any wolf. He gave her Satanta, the alpha of the pack."

"He gave her a wolf?" Her face was white with rage. "He should have given Satanta to me."

"I thought you did not like the wolves. I thought they frightened you."

"Even so, he should have asked me."

Firethorn tried not to smile—he had never liked Blue Dawn and had never thought she was right for his friend. "If only the word had not spread through the whole village, you might have borne the shame."

Her eyes widened with anger. "I knew he was not

to be trusted when he left. I made him promise he would have no woman but me."

Nodding, Firethorn said, "I believe he broke his promise, and everyone else must believe it as well. I only wonder which one of you will be his first wife, and which one will be second."

Blue Dawn stomped her foot. "I am glad I do not love him or my heart would be broken. I will not have him, and I will accuse him of being false in front of the whole village."

"That would make him understand your anger." Firethorn looked sorrowful. "Too bad."

Firethorn smiled when he turned away. There was no end of trouble he had stirred up today.

Chapter Thirty-four

Wolf Runner stood in the council lodge, where he spoke to the elders. "You charged me to punish Night Fighter, and the deed is done. I do not believe any of his followers will make mischief without his leadership."

"That is good," his grandfather, Chief Broken Lance, said, trying not to show his pride in his grandson. "The families of the dead women can find peace now that he is dead."

"What makes you think the other renegades will no longer attack our women?" Wind Warrior asked.

Wolf Runner glanced at his father. "They saw Night Fighter was a coward and deserted him in the end. The Cheyenne are a noble people, and it was only a few renegades who raided our land. If you cut the head off the snake, the body will die," he said.

"The council honors you this day, Wolf Runner, son of Wind Warrior," the elder, Cunning Fox, said. "You have set a fine example for our younger warriors to follow."

A short time later, Wolf Runner left the council lodge, and he found Blue Dawn waiting for him with a frown on her face.

"Why did you not come to me when you returned?" she demanded petulantly.

He stared into her eyes, wondering what had made

her angry. Her voice was accusing and shrill, and others paused to listen to her words since she spoke so loudly.

"There were matters I needed to attend to. I was on my way to see you now."

"Yet I heard you had time to visit the half-breed woman you brought into our village." Blue Dawn's voice rose in volume. "Do not deny it—everyone is talking about you and her."

Wolf Runner tried to push down his anger. "Let us speak of this in private. Others are listening."

Blue Dawn stepped closer to him. "Let everyone hear how you have disgraced me. Do you deny you went to the half-breed when you first returned?"

His chin settled in a hard line, and if she had known Wolf Runner better, Blue Dawn might have chosen to keep her thoughts to herself until they were in private as he had requested.

But she did not. "Do you deny it?"

"I do not," he said in a whisper. "Cheyenne had a very difficult time and I had to know she was not suffering."

"You did not care what I suffered, or the humiliation you brought down on my head." Blue Dawn's voice carried to those who had gathered behind her. "I even heard you gave her one of your wolves—you never gave me a wolf, although I wanted one."

"Satanta chose to be with Cheyenne—it was the wolf's decision, not a gift from me."

"You were with her for many days. This woman is an abomination because she has white blood in her veins and should be despised by all Blackfoot."

Blue Dawn heard a gasp from behind her and a mutter of voices. Cunning Fox, the head of the council, stepped up to her, anger showing in his dark eyes.

"You have insulted the man you chose to wed, for is he not half white—most of all, you have insulted his mother, who was born white, but is now fully one of us."

Blue Dawn's mouth opened, but no words would come out. Her own father stepped up to her and gripped her arm. "You have insulted a noble warrior and shamed me before the whole village. Mostly you have shamed yourself. Later, you will want to ask forgiveness of Wolf Runner and his mother, although I would not blame them if they refused to forgive you and Wolf Runner refuses to take you for his woman."

Blue Dawn realized what she had done, but it was too late. She had only one way to save face. "I do not want to be Wolf Runner's woman. I will never consent to live with him after what he has done."

Wolf Runner had been silent, but he now spoke: "I release you from your commitment. You are free to marry whoever you will."

"This is what you wanted all along," Blue Dawn stated heatedly

Her father's grip on her arm tightened, and he yanked her forward. "Forgive her, for I shall not. I take her now to her mother, who will pack her belongings and send her off to her aunt who dwells with the Assiniboin tribe. There it is hoped she may atone for what she has done to shame her family this day."

Blue Dawn was crying hysterically as her father led her away. The crowd broke up, muttering about Blue Dawn's shameful behavior.

Firethorn appeared beside Wolf Runner. "You owe me a favor—a big favor."

Wolf Runner was a bit stunned. "For what reason?"

"I will tell you another day. Now you can go to the woman you want and ask her to be yours."

But Wolf Runner stood like a statue, staring after Blue Dawn, thinking he had never really known her true character until today.

It had all happened so fast. Wolf Runner felt a rush of joy, then lowered his head in torment. After the way he had treated Cheyenne, why would she want to spend her life with him?

Firethorn looked serious. "If you do not want Cheyenne, perhaps I will offer for her."

Wolf Runner's heavy gaze landed on Firethorn. "You say this to me? You are not a true friend."

Firethorn began to laugh because he had never seen Wolf Runner jealous before. "I do not want your woman. I was merely helping you make up your mind. Your little Cheyenne maiden sees no one but you. When will you go to her?"

Wolf Runner headed toward his horse. "First I have much to consider. I have to be alone to think." He turned back to Firethorn. "At the moment, Cheyenne believes I betrayed her."

"Did you?"

"In a way. I think before we decide our future, we must first determine our present. I will go to the mountains to search my soul, while Cheyenne has a chance to learn more of our ways and decide whether she wants to stay here."

"How long will you be gone?"

"As long as it takes."

Chapter Thirty-five

There was a touch of spring in the crisp morning air. Already the grass had turned from straw color to green. Early wildflowers dipped their petals in the warm breeze that swept across the meadows.

Cheyenne held the hand of Running Wolf's sister, White Feather, as they walked down the path to the wooded area. She had come to think of the child as her own sister, and adored her.

When they came out of the woods, White Feather pointed to the river, where several women were dipping their water jugs. White Feather spoke some English, enough so the two of them could communicate.

Glancing up at the sky, Cheyenne's heart was heavy—Wolf Runner had been gone for two months. It was said that he sought solitude in the mountains. Each day Cheyenne watched and waited for him. She did not know what would happen between them when he did return.

"The ice has already melted in the river," White Feather observed. "Before long we shall be able to swim." She glanced up at Cheyenne. "Can you swim?"

"I never learned how."

The child looked shocked and then nodded with assurance. "I shall teach you, when my mother says it is safe to go into the water."

Cheyenne smiled down at the lovely girl whose

green-flecked eyes reminded her of the child's brother. Cheyenne had been practicing with White Feather to learn to speak Blackfoot. Thus far, her ability to hold a conversation with anyone was limited. "The weather has turned mild," she said, speaking slowly so she could concentrate on each word. "I like this time of season."

"You wait for my brother to return," White Feather said, pausing and looking up at Cheyenne. "Will my brother take you as his woman? Many say he will."

Cheyenne felt her heart ache. "I do not believe he will, White Feather. It is because of me that Blue Dawn left the village. It is a shame I must bear."

"I did not like Blue Dawn, and neither did my mother, although she did not say so."

Cheyenne quickly changed the subject. "Will you teach me new words so I can speak your language better?"

"Let me teach you," a deep, husky voice said from behind them.

Joy sung in Cheyenne's heart when she turned and saw Wolf Runner. "I did not know you had returned."

White Feather flung herself into her brother's arms, giggling.

He smiled at his sister, and then his gaze moved to Cheyenne. "I see you have been learning our language."

She shyly nodded. "There are still many words I do not know."

Wolf Runner set his sister on the ground. "I would have words alone with Cheyenne."

The child grinned up at him. "Ask her to be your woman—we do not want some other warrior taking her away from us."

His gaze moved to Cheyenne. "What if she will not have me?"

White Feather giggled. "She will. She watches every day for your return."

His voice deepened. "Does my sister speak the truth?"

Cheyenne stared into dark eyes that held a world of feeling. "In truth, I became so accustomed to you beside me, I missed your company," she said, switching to English.

"Then we must remedy that," he answered her in Blackfoot.

He gently shoved his sister toward his father's tipi, and she ran to tell her mother that Wolf Runner was home and he was asking Cheyenne to be his woman.

"It is a wonder you would even speak to me. I have wronged you in so many ways," Wolf Runner admitted in English so she would have no doubt of his meaning. He continued in a hoarse voice. "I do not know if you can ever forgive me for using you for my own purposes."

She moved closer to him, wishing she could touch him, but she dared not. "How can you believe such a thing? I owe you my life."

He touched her cheek and let his finger drift to her mouth. "Then will you agree to spend the rest of your life at my side?" He looked unsure. "I hope you will."

Then Cheyenne did something that took him by surprise and delighted him—she stepped onto his moccasined feet, rose up on her tiptoes, and stood almost eye to eye with him.

"Answer me one question—do you ask me this because you feel obligated to take care of me?"

His laughter was warm. "I ask you because every day I have been without you has been dreary and all

I did was think about you. I ask you because you make me smile and warm my days."

She lowered herself and stepped down. "Wolf Runner—"

He turned her toward the river. "Let us seek solitude—many are watching us and what I have to say to you must be said in private."

He led her along the river and down a path that led to the woods. When they were away from the village he turned her into his arms. "I need you, Cheyenne. Say you will be my woman and walk the path of life with me, for if you do not, I will have no other."

Tears gathered in her eyes and clogged her throat. "I must think," she said, leaning forward and placing her head on his chest. "There are things that stand between us."

He brought her to him and tightened his arms about her, holding her close to his body. "I will say this to you: it was wrong to use you as a means to find Night Fighter." He tilted her chin up and forced her to meet his gaze. "I ask for your forgiveness."

She thought for a moment and then slowly nodded. "I forgive you."

Relief flooded his mind. "Then know this: if you do not accept me for your husband, I will never have a happy day."

Cheyenne saw the truth shining in his eyes. Touching her cheek to his, she whispered, "I want your happiness above all else."

There was doubt and uncertainty in his eyes. "Are you saying you will be my woman?"

Her face brightened with a smile. "I've been your woman for a long time; you just didn't know it."

"Then let us be joined as quickly as possible." He nudged her ear and whispered, "I want you; my body craves you." His hand slid up her back and made a circular motion. "I went to the mountains to clear my mind and to think. I knew I had wronged you, and I did not know if you would have me. But now I have come for my woman."

Smiling up at him, Cheyenne said, "Will you take me to the mountains with you?"

"I will." He took her hand and led her back toward the village. "Then let us tell my parents."

They were both surprised when most of the village had emptied out of their tipis and were waiting for them, smiling and nodding in approval.

"Apparently my sister has spread the word that her brother cannot live without his woman."

Heat and excitement burst in Cheyenne's heart. How could she live with such joy? Wolf Runner did love her, and she would spend the rest of her life at his side.

Satanta came bounding toward them, the rest of the wolf pack following behind. Wolf Runner and Cheyenne suddenly found themselves surrounded by the affectionate creatures.

Cheyenne bent down and put her arms around Satanta and looked up at Wolf Runner, whose eyes were shining with warmth. "If you have a rival for my affections, it would be this wolf," she told him.

"I will brook no rival," he said, laughing and raising her to her feet. Lowering his head Wolf Runner kissed Cheyenne with warmth and feeling.

When she could finally catch her breath, she said truthfully, "How could anyone ever rival you in my heart?"

A look so tender poured into his eyes that it took Cheyenne by surprise. Taking her hand, he led her toward his mother and father.

Chapter Thirty-six

They had left the horses to find their way home, and had been steadily climbing for hours. The farther up the mountain they climbed, the lighter Cheyenne's heart became. That morning she had become Wolf Runner's woman, and now she belonged to him. He was taking her to the place where his father had taken his mother after they had become one.

"What is this wondrous place you want to show me, husband?"

He paused and lifted her pack from her back. "We will not arrive there for three days. But it is well worth the climb."

She moved against him, her hands resting against the strong contour of his upper arm, where she felt his strong muscle. "I don't care where you are taking me, as long as we are together."

He kissed the top of her head. "Are you not weary?"

She gave him a smile. "After the paces you put me through on our journey to this land, you should not question my stamina."

"My dearest heart, you never complained then, although I knew there were times when you were weary."

"I knew you expected me to fall short of your expectations; therefore, I was not about to complain."

"I loved you even then," he whispered against her

throat, then cupped her face in his strong hands. "I think I must have loved you from that first day in Albuquerque when you were so obstinate."

"I was afraid of you at first—then I was annoyed, and then the love came. When we were on the journey to my grandfather's village, there was no logical reason you should love me after all the trouble I caused you."

Wolf Runner's mouth curved in a sensuous smile. "Then I loved you for all the illogical reasons."

"Love is illogical," Cheyenne said, frowning as she tried to define the feelings that ruled her thinking.

"Tonight I will have you in my bed." His tone deepened. "It has been difficult for me to keep my hands off you these last three weeks. Though knowing my mother was watching my every move helped." He looked into her eyes and saw an answering fire in the amber depths. "Do you know what it feels like to ache inside?"

"Yes," she freely admitted.

"Then you know what I feel."

At that very moment Cheyenne ached for him. She sighed and laid her face against his chest, where she heard his heart hammering. She was astounded and grateful that this wonderful man loved her. "It was hard for me as well. I want you to teach me what it means to be your woman."

Wolf Runner grabbed her to him and lowered his head, his mouth sinking into hers.

She quivered and yearned while he quaked with desire.

When he raised his head, she asked, "Must we wait until tonight?"

Her innocent question set his body on fire. He would like nothing better than to lay her on the ground and give her what she asked for. But this was her wedding night and he would have her remember his restraint, not his animal urges.

Reluctantly, he handed Cheyenne her pack. "Firethorn set up a camp for us farther on up the mountain. It is a small cave. I think you will like it." He looked pensive. "But perhaps you had enough camping out on the journey here. I did not think of that."

She giggled. "Nonsense. I am strong and I love the outdoors. When I was young I was always wondering what was over the next hill and then the next. Now I know. You have shown me."

Wolf Runner could hardly swallow for the lump in his throat. His woman would match him step for step, and even go him one better.

Cheyenne's heart softened when she looked into his glowing eyes and she wondered what he was thinking.

Taking her hand, he helped her over a wide boulder and paused to kiss her before setting her on her feet. He took her hand and assisted her up the steep trail, where he slid his arms around her waist, holding her against his body.

Touching her hair, he breathed against her ear. "If I continue like this, we will never reach camp."

As they reached their destination, the sun was just going down and painted the sky in brilliant crimson.

Placing her pack on the ground, Cheyenne smiled, looking at the trail that led to a cave. "This is wonderful."

Without pausing to think, Wolf Runner lifted her in his arms and carried her into the cave. Going down with her onto the soft fur Firethorn had left for them, he stared into her eyes. "How long I have suffered for being denied that which I wanted most in the world." He swallowed deep. "Tonight, I will have you."

She touched his face, then laced her fingers through his ebony hair, a tangle of emotions throbbing inside her. "You have that right."

Wolf Runner buried his lips against hers, holding her so tightly she could scarcely breathe.

When he raised his head she saw smoldering flames in the shimmering depths. Her body trembled and so did his—she was glad she could move this strong, honorable warrior.

While kissing her, Wolf Runner methodically began removing Cheyenne's clothing. At first he was gentle, but when she touched his bare chest, he grabbed her in his arms and ground his mouth against hers. Impatiently he disposed of her moccasins, wanting her completely naked. His own clothing quickly followed and naked flesh met naked flesh.

With his heart drumming in his ears, Wolf Runner gently brought his mouth to each tempting breast, suckling, nipping, and teasing until both nipples stood in erect peeks.

Cheyenne's eyes were fever bright with passion, and he felt satisfaction that his woman wanted him as much as he wanted her. His heated gaze moved down her body, appreciating how perfect she was.

She felt shy at first, but could not long resist the temptation to look at him. His naked body was magnificent. Her eyes widened when she saw how large he had swelled.

Frowning, Cheyenne pulled back, knowing some of what was going to happen. She could not imagine how something that large could fit inside her.

As if Wolf Runner read her mind, he assured her, "There will be some pain, but it will not last. As my woman, you are built to receive me, just as I am made to join with you."

Bringing her gently into his arms, his hand swept over her body, moving ever lower until he touched her between the legs. Like the petal of a flower opening to the sun, she spread her legs to him and he caressed her until she thought she would scream from want. Cheyenne gasped with pleasure when his finger slid inside her.

He paused, nuzzling her ear. "I am impatient to bury myself in you, but do not fear, I will not rush you."

She felt as if her body had come alive as he buried his finger farther inside her. She groaned, thinking nothing could have prepared her for the wonderful feeling that washed over her, and it could not get any better.

But she was mistaken.

Wolf Runner smiled against her lips as her innocent body flowered under his touch. He moved between her legs, kissing her all the while.

Cheyenne's eyes widened when she felt his swollen manhood against her. She closed her eyes as he slid into her and clawed at his back when he broke through her virginal barrier.

He waited until she accepted him, and then thrust deeper inside her.

Feeling her bow with pain and then cling to him in passion, he slowly withdrew and slid forward, setting a slow rhythm, when what he really wanted to do was drive deep. He had ached for her so long, he kept a tight rein on his thrusts, fighting against the need to bury even deeper inside her.

Cheyenne moaned and tossed her head as her body willingly met each of his thrusts. When he pulled back, she held her breath, waiting for the next onslaught as desire and need coursed through her body. She heard the beating of his heart and her body sung to his tune.

She cried out his name as his mouth settled on hers and her heart felt completely exposed. She loved him and he loved her; at last they were joined.

Cheyenne thought he was finished because he had paused, but she caught her breath when he surged forward again, filling her with pleasure, hot and wild.

Her body was his to do with as he chose. She felt tears dampen her eyes and knew she was crying from the beauty of their joining. Her hands slid down his back, pressing him toward her.

"My woman," he whispered in a deep voice. "You are my heart."

Afterward, they lay in each other's arms until dark shadows encroached across the cave. "You filled me with joy," he said, his lips on her brow.

"I have never been so happy. Will it last—will it always be this way between us?"

Laughter lurked in his green-flecked eyes because she delighted him. "It will only get better." He rose up and started to leave. "What kind of husband would I be if I let my woman freeze from lack of a heat? I must build you a campfire."

She pulled him back. "I am not cold."

His hand sprayed out across her stomach and moved lower. "Are you sore?"

She shook her head, looking up at him. "Not at all." She kissed his lips and they both drifted back upon the fur.

"I will warm you," he said, taking her once more.

The next morning, as they continued their journey up the mountain, neither could keep from touching the other. Wolf Runner's eyes followed her with a new feeling of possession, hers followed his with a new understanding that the more she knew the man she loved, the deeper that love became.

They stopped to rest, and Wolf Runner watched her lean against a boulder. "I love this mountain," she said, staring at a pine forest in the distant valley.

"I hoped you would."

She took a drink from the water skin he handed her. "Where did you say the wolves are?" she asked mischievously.

"My brother, Little Hawk, has promised to keep them in the village."

Cheyenne laughed as she gazed back down the trail. "No one can keep Satanta where he does not want to be."

As if talking about them caused them to appear, the pack came loping up the path. Satanta approached Cheyenne and looked at her as if scolding her for not bringing him with her.

Her laughter filled the air, and filled Wolf Runner's heart.

Wolf Runner had been teaching Cheyenne how to tell what time of day it was by studying the shadows that reflected across the ground. At the moment she was standing in her own shadow. "It is the noon hour," she said, glancing at her husband.

He laughed. "It is. I suppose you need feeding."

"Of course. I can always eat."

He tilted her chin up to him and his gaze swept over the face of the woman who had brought joy into his life. "I am amazed at how much you can eat and still remain so small."

"If I grow fat, I suppose you will no longer want me," she said, raising her eyebrow and giving him a laughing glance. "You do not want a fat wife, do you?"

Wolf Runner pulled her to him, bracing her backside against him, noticing how perfectly she fit against his body. While his hands swept to her stomach, he whispered, "I want you fat with my sons and daughters growing inside you." He touched his mouth to her throat, smiling with satisfaction when she shivered. "I never thought much about children until I gave you my heart, but now I look forward to looking into the eyes of our child."

"Am I with child already?" she asked innocently.

Turning her to face him, he rested his cheek against hers. "This I do not know. It is too soon to tell." He grinned, clasping her to him. "But I have been inside you enough to sire many children."

She curved to his body, content and happy. Moving a little away from him, she gazed down into a wide valley with a river running through it—the noon sun hit the valley, turning everything scarlet, and she held her breath.

Glancing at Wolf Runner, she found him watching her with softness in his eyes. She ran to him and swooped into his arms.

Laughing, he held her to him. "I wonder how I lived before I met you?"

"The same way I did," she said, pressing her head against his chest and listening to the thudding of his heart. "I always yearned for something, but I never knew what it was."

"I thought I was content with my life." Fire leaped in Wolf Runner's eyes. "I now know a deeper contentment than I thought possible."

"When I think back on our first meeting, it was mere chance that brought us together." She shook her head. "No, that cannot be right," Cheyenne said, changing her mind. "It was my grandmother who brought us together."

Wolf Runner's mouth was only a hairsbreadth away from hers. "And I will be grateful to her every day for putting you in my path."

They stood clasped in each other's arms while the sounds of nature filled the air. The cry of a hawk echoed across the valley, and an eagle rode the wind currents.

"How long will we remain in the mountain encampment," Cheyenne wanted to know.

"I want you all to myself, so we will remain here until the leaves start to take on the color of autumn." He touched his mouth to hers. "It can be bitterly cold here in the winter season."

Her heart swelled with happiness. "I would not mind the winter if you were with me."

He knew in that moment his woman shared his love of the mountains—their spirits were as joined as their hearts were and warmth surged through him like hot honey. He raised his head to the sky, his arms tightening about her, feeling as if their minds were so alike. He had found the one woman who thought as he did.

"The weather is too bitter for you to stay here through the winter. I have spent but one winter here myself. It would be too much of a hardship for you to endure."

"It was sometimes cold on our journey here," she reasoned, smiling. "And now I can sleep in your arms to stay warm."

Wolf Runner's eyes seemed to blaze. "I now have

the right to take you in my arms and keep you warm and safe."

They stood there, unaware of anything but each other. Both went to their knees. His kiss almost stole her breath, and when he gently touched her breasts, she sighed and then groaned.

The golden days of spring spread over the lower elevations, but there in the mountain encampment, the crisp clear air still held a chill, not that the lovers noticed.

Cheyenne and Wolf Runner were unaware of the passing of time. Each day was filled with new and exciting discoveries in each other's arms.

They laughed, they teased each other, and they grew more deeply in love.

For Cheyenne, her nightmare existence was over. Safe in the arms of the man she loved, Cheyenne knew she was home at last. There would be no more fear or uncertainty about where she belonged—she belonged with the legendary Blackfoot warrior with the green-flecked eyes.

Epilogue

The sun had barely risen atop the pine trees as Cheyenne stood near the river watching the water from the spring runoff flow swiftly by. There was peace and tranquility beside the Milk River.

A week ago Cullen had arrived in the village, stirring up excitement. He had brought Cheyenne a letter from Maria, which she had read over and over. In the letter, Maria explained that she had married Francisco, and they were expecting their first child.

Cheyenne missed her friend, but it was a comfort to know Maria had found happiness with her Francisco.

Cullen had also told her how Señor Mendoza had delivered a breakfront to the ranch, along with several crates that had been stored in the attic. He laughed as he told Cheyenne how Hattie had polished the piece of furniture and had the ranch hands place it in the dining room, where her grandmother's green-and-white dishes were displayed.

It had taken several letters, and Cullen's aid, to convince the Mendoza family that she was happy in her new life, and that she had found contentment in the Blackfoot village.

Cheyenne had gone from having no family at all to being a part of a large and loving family.

She glanced down at her infant daughter and her heart swelled with a mother's love—Prairie Flower had her father's features. Tiny fingers clasped around hers, and the child gave her a toothless grin.

Wolf Runner adored his daughter, and was laughed at by Firethorn because he made such a fuss over her. When Prairie Flower smiled at him, he could hardly contain his elation.

A shadow fell across Cheyenne's face and she felt Wolf Runner's hands slide around her to rest on her still-flat stomach, where his unborn baby lay. This time she hoped the child would be a boy, although Wolf Runner said it did not matter to him.

"Are you happy here, Cheyenne?"

"Entirely," she told him.

"Do you greet the morning?" he asked in a whisper, laying his chin on the top of her head.

"I do each morning."

"You are the joy of my life."

She grinned up into his dark, green-flecked eyes, her own eyes filled with mischief. "Husband, there was a time when you thought of me as nothing more than a nuisance."

His large hand moved over her stomach, and he arched his eyebrow, joining in her teasing. "That's because you were a nuisance."

Cheyenne shook with laughter. "And I thought you were arrogant . . . because you were."

Wolf Runner walked around Cheyenne and lifted his daughter in his arms. Prairie Flower giggled at her father and he cuddled her close.

"Our daughter looks like you," he observed.

"Not everyone would agree with you. Your father thinks Prairie Flower looks like you."

Wolf Runner looked pleased as he nestled the tiny

child in his sheltering arms. "She will be beautiful like you when she grows up."

There was a mountain of love reflected in his wonderful eyes when he looked at Cheyenne, and it took her several tries before she could speak.

"If I find favor in your eyes, I am glad."

Handing Cheyenne the child, Wolf Runner slid his arm about her waist. "My mother spoils her first grandchild."

Cheyenne's laughter was like music to his ears.

"And you do not?"

His dark eyes swept across the river and he raised his proud head. "No one will ever make Prairie Flower suffer the way you had to."

She thought about that. "No. Here in the land of her father, she is accepted as a Blackfoot from a fine and noble family." Cheyenne touched his arm. "But let us not dwell on the past—you have made up for all the unhappiness I felt then."

"And you gave me a life I never imagined. We are so alike, you and I. It is as if we were cut from the same cloth and fit together perfectly."

A birdcall stirred in the stillness. The village was coming to life, and the people were beginning to emerge from their tipis, ready to begin their daily chores.

Cheyenne breathed in the fresh air, thinking how wonderful life was here in the Blackfoot village.

"Do you mind so much that I cannot accompany you to the mountains this spring with the new baby coming?"

Wolf Runner shook his head. "I will not go into the mountains this year."

"You love it there."

"I love you more. I will not leave you until our

child is born. We will all go next spring when the baby is old enough to take to the mountains."

It was a poignant moment, and Cheyenne could not speak.

Wolf Runner's eyes rested on her mouth. "I like waking up with you beside me."

She laughed. "Me, the baby, and Satanta," she reminded him. "Soon there will be our new baby. Are you sure you will not grow weary of us and seek solitude in the mountains?"

"Not without you," he said, touching her hair and allowing his hand to drift through the silken strands. "I want only to be where you are."